Praise for *Driving Lessons*

"There's a forensic sort of elegance, precision, to these narratives, descriptive of an inelegant and mystifying and generally threatening world, that holds your attention as to a crime scene. So meticulous an obscurity that you cannot look away—exactly because you can't quite see, or can't yet see, some ominous thing. Some larger issue out there looming. And because your not-quite-seeing is, itself, so beautifully drawn, just as the author's pencil drawings, illustrations of what seem like critical mysteries, things and moments periodically presented like exhibits toward some strange and terrible verdict.

No one writes like this. There's no one I know captures the emotional precision of such accidental passages in accidental lives—all at the edge of some precisely indeterminate destruction."

—David Searcy, author of
The Tiny Bee That Hovers at the Center of the World

"Tim Coursey's stories are like dioramas, tiny rooms that open up into universes of ideas, but his are carved from complexity, beauty, and precision, with a voice that is both familiar and uncopiable. A master of dialogue and observation, he is a literary cabinetmaker, planing words, scene, and character into beautiful equilibrium."

—Kerri Arsenault, author of *Mill Town*

D1260386

Driving Lessons

a novel

Tim Coursey

DEEP VELLUM PUBLISHING

DALLAS, TEXAS

Deep Vellum Publishing
3000 Commerce St., Dallas, Texas 75226
deepvellum.org · @deepvellum

Deep Vellum is a 501c3 nonprofit literary arts organization
founded in 2013 with the mission to bring
the world into conversation through literature.

Copyright © 2022 by Tim Coursey

First Edition, 2022

Support for this publication has been provided in part by a grant from the Lesley
Family Foundation.

LIBRARY OF CONGRESS CATALOGING-IN-PUBLICATION DATA

Names: Coursey, Tim, author, illustrator.
Title: Driving lessons : a novel / Tim Coursey.
Description: First edition. | Dallas, Texas : Deep Vellum Publishing, 2022.
Identifiers: LCCN 2022001180 | ISBN 9781646051748 (trade paperback) |
ISBN
 9781646051755 (ebook)
Subjects: LCGFT: Novels.
Classification: LCC PS3603.O88648 D75 2022 | DDC 813/.6—dc23/
eng/20220114
LC record available at https://lccn.loc.gov/2022001180

ISBN (TPB) 978-1-64605-174-8 | ISBN (Ebook) 978-1-64605-175-5

This book is a work of fiction. Names, characters, businesses, organizations,
places, and events are either the product of the author's imagination or are used
fictitiously. Any resemblance to events, locales, or actual persons, living or dead,
is entirely coincidental.

Cover art: This project was presented at the SMU POLLOCK GALLERY in
collaboration with RISO BAR. Photo by Kevin Todora.

Interior layout and typesetting by KGT

PRINTED IN THE UNITED STATES OF AMERICA

For Melanie Jane

CONTENTS

Idyll • in the verge

Household goods that had been fitted into the VW bus like the pieces of a tavern puzzle were now in the house and mostly in service—three hours, moved in. Now a war-surplus parachute artfully swagged from the ceiling of one of the three rooms like a fairy-tale Bedouin tent, tent floor a Goodwill cotton oriental rug—big faded pastel rug with bright serapes over its bald spots; in the doorway a bead curtain nuisance; the door itself, doorknob removed, laid horizontal on fruit crates with a fringed paisley shawl tablecloth—all in all a crummy Xanadu anyplace but America, and wholly unintentionally, a good fit for dry plateaus cut with steep valleys and marked out by strings of mountains. To almost anyone, a quintessentially American room, though chilly in here, pretty cold, not too far above freezing.

Backing out through the rattling wooden beads and waiting while the other finished fastening a strap of her bib overalls, and handing her one of a pair of thick air mattresses, he followed her into another room, into their cache of warmth and warm incandescent electric light, shut the door behind him.

Careful to keep the inflated bed away from the stove, she felt around under Victorian fringe, turned off the lamp. A dozen tiny blue flames seen through the sides and flat top of an ornate little butane heater, hearth and home, barely lit the room, and the last of twilight became visible in the high horizontal window. They'd moved to a remote place, no ground light to speak of reflected off the overcast; sparse snow on the ground would've marginally brightened things had there been anything to light it, but outdoors was becoming fundamental night—identify your hand in front of your face, a roofline against the sky, a neighbor's lit window a hundred yards away mostly occluded by some intervening structure. The last visible thing in this room's one window at the moment, on an invisible distant ridge, a relay tower's vertical line of intermittently glowing red specks within their auras in the otherwise unseeable cloud.

"We ought to get a black light."

"Think I have ringworm?"

"Shelda and Perry had one in that servants' quarters. Cool." The boy had a slight stammer, or hesitancy or difficulty beginning without a pause first. People tended to talk over the unaccustomed pause.

"Servants' quarters where?"

"Uh well it was behind the Abadie house. The first one. Smoke a J?"

"You go ahead."

"Me neither."

"Sh! Listen," the girl touched his forearm. Silence nearly pure on the windless night—quiet, steady exhalation of the burner. A muffled tic from the house itself. Quick bursts of yipping and gibbering from outside, one here one there, in different places not that far away.

"Never heard them talk like that, um, not often a howl or a little laugh kind of thing but usually not anything at all really, pretty solitary too really, just . . . little dog tracks in the snow right out there is all you know. Coyotes."

"Maybe they're saying hi."

"Huh. Yeah. Fuckin' wow . . . don't know why but I just flashed on . . . just kind of trippy for a second."

"Shelda lit up in there."

He laughed, "Would you . . . Don't mind-read would you."

The boy was aware of the girl's patience, that she sometimes came back to insights she'd made and gently, obliquely would have him say more; his perpetual wonderment was that she'd care what went on in his head. Taking a liking to him after finding he could actually talk—he'd recited "Jabberwocky" once, lively and for no particular reason, and without his stammer at that—the girl had paired up with him. And early on had risked a shared eight-hour chemically induced hallucinatory experience, with pure and righteous doses by Owsley Stanley's own hand that she'd been saving for such a potential. A rare, positive outcome with that; in the boy's case, the one good among several god-awful. Each of the new friends was left unshakably knowing they'd always known the other, such abiding benevolent hogwash. Un-awkward and convivial as a result, infatuation wasn't entirely randy, not exclusively—best buddies while getting to know each other. Moony in love as well, obviously. Each wondered how it would turn around, too good to be true.

"A house called Abadie?"

"Two. Houses on Abadie Street."

"Okay?"

"I stayed at two but there were ... whole neighborhood was infested with us, it was big rickety two-story wooden houses. This one, the people were sort of a crash pad cooperative, 'know?"

"No."

The boy said, "This one house, and it wasn't a co-op, that just sounded cool to call it that, but some of us did build some extra rooms in there, a little communal lentils and rice, somebody moves out, you cut through a wall and stick a door in it, divide the room. There's this great wrecking yard, you can get old doors with transoms, nobody wanted the stuff forever, then the hippies come and clean 'em out in a year, and we ran extension cords and red rubber gas hose all over, draped them all over up on nails, looked like a Tarzan movie, all the vines ... Fig tree outside my window and there's a long cord plugged into my room—male plug on the other end too—hung it on the fig tree and out to the servants' quarters because the power company took their meter away, uninhabitable. Your apartment in San Francisco was beautiful, it was ... you know, everything supposed to be that way and you like it when it's just intentional. No paint on the windowpanes! I mean, Jesus."

"Two roommates, and my parents had to help with the rent," she said, "I love hearing this, feel like a voyeur, keep talking Abadie Street, lover."

"Okay, uh, the extra little bedrooms, rent averaged zipola and water and electric and gas got paid out of some office on the umpteenth floor of the Mercantile, and everything stayed on. Mil was at that house, he was the top dog. Nobody decided, he just was. I got a ladder from Midnight Ladder and fixed the attic fan, couldn't give the ladder back because in the meantime they'd put a guy with a flashlight there at the job site."

"Who's he? Mil. You never said."

"Uh well ... something about the army but it maybe wasn't the normal army, and that's all you would get, and he did time for smack, but that's all you'd get on that too, but you know how certain guys want to look like they have a mysterious past, but Mil said flat-out he didn't feel like being entertainment. Whatever, man. Itinerant store-window dresser. His old lady was out-to-here pregnant, never came out of their room except to hog the bathroom, there was one up and one down, I rigged showers in the bathtubs. Put a door on the upstairs parlor and that was their room with a stereo and a window fan and a toaster kept blowing fuses, the whole house had two circuits and she lived on peanut butter toast, you could hear her screaming in there when her fuse blew and that same damn Buffalo Springfield album shut the fuck up . . . I didn't grow up with cockroaches but got used to it, three kinds, walking cigars and regular ones and little black ones. I put in twenty-amp fuses instead of the fifteens, 1900 house, fifteen-amp could burn the place down let alone twenty, little bitty verdigris bare wires, the kind with the friction tape hanging off, you could see them in the attic when I went up to fix the fan, but it was gas leaks were going to off everybody."

One of the lovers propped the air beds against the wall at the end of a rococo swooning couch—the other room trying for the exotic, this room's stage set represented quaintness—and having shaken out a feather quilt, the other shucked her coveralls again, held arms over head as her friend pulled an extra sweater over her. Wrapped in the quilt and sharing a big tasseled cushion on the floor, each other's shape a dear fit, the pair leaned back against the asymmetrical little couch to stare at their prim blue campfire. In the way that people given the chance have always stared at their fire.

After a while, he said, "Not sleepy are you?"

"Nope."

"Want to screw?"

"Just this minute did that for pete sakes, what I'd really like is for you to keep talking to me, it feels good."

"You talk to me even when we're at it, I mean, could be about the weather or the drive up here, you talk while I'm at you. Kind of a turn-on."

"Good, likewise, but now tell us a story, man, you're on a roll, this is new. Please?"

Shrugged, "Okay uh . . . Just as well you'd never see Mil's wife, nearly anything would set her off. Rip you a new one if you said 'nice day' because it's August and she's out to here. There was that fig tree out my window that smelled good, attic fan sucking air through the transom. House full of sweaty women, not a bad thing."

"Sweaty women, sure. Right, sounds like heaven. Was this a long time before I saw you out there last year? In SF."

"I was already in the servants' quarters. Shelda and Perry moved to the Bay and I got the servants' quarters. I gave up the student deferment 'cause it wasn't fair and I am a fuckin' moron. Mil . . . never, ever, got uptight, 'know? Didn't get high either. Wish there was any more of the Cheerios and raisins and stuff you fixed for the road. Been living on that for two days."

After a minute she said, "Can of sauerkraut up there. Can't believe we left the food box on the counter. There's Bisquick and some things in that metal cabinet, powdered milk. Wish we had an onion. Something. No salt, even. What I want is doughnuts."

"Cheeseburgers, doughnuts."

"Wish we had popcorn, that would be so perfect," she

said, "There's oatmeal. Unembellished oatmeal. Or canni-balism. Girl Scout bread and kraut doesn't sound . . . in fact warm biscuit bread might be really nice. That's half a brick of something up there, I bet that's what that is, white mar-garine. Or lard."

"They left a bottle of Worcestershire, if there's some-thing in it. That stuff never goes bad, does it? Oh man, that scrap yard, or surplus or whatever it is, lucked into that. Guy said buck and a quarter an hour chipping off mortar and stuff. Yeah doughnuts. Ten bucks a day. Make a list. Need to find the post office tomorrow, notify USGS where I'm at."

"I wonder why they haven't assigned you," she said, "Maybe the mail just hasn't caught up."

"Yeah. One did, I think it's from Abbie, got forwarded. She's trying to talk in code, I think she's talking about Pog got busted so they need to get rich quick. Never mind, you don't know them I guess but she's trying to talk code but it's pretty stupid, wants to know can we manicure a kilo if she drives it, or somebody drives it. I already tell you this? Or can't be just one kilo, I don't know how many. Camper top."

She said, "Chances are pretty good you get your teeth broken out in prison. Nice polite teeth."

"USGS, hard to imagine they're in, you know, they're desperate for grunt'n'carry no-degree people in geodetic, uh, geodesy, amazed they took me," he said.

"Physical geography major? Can't be that plentiful, c'mon, I'm not even sure what that is."

"How many geography undergrads does it take to use a theodolite? Three—one to carry it and two to turn him and read his azimuth angle. Sure as shit not going to call 'em up to remind them—'Hey hurry up, post me post me'—because I'm pretty happy right here. It was that girl at your apartment told you about it?"

She said, "One roommate awol and we had another month paid up so what the hell, I let her in."

"Tall, kind of amber."

"Alma. With the little kid. She was in a traveling show and show folks called her up sometimes, word about this place came from them is all I know. Owner lives right there in the Bay Area . . . I saw Alma asleep once. Her eyes were open a little bit and her eyes were rolled up, I thought she was dead. And when I was about to touch her she jerked and gave me this look. Like pity or sympathy or something, it was weird. Anyway, there's sixty-odd left after we gassed up. Pick up some groceries at—what was it—Aguado's tomorrow, looked promising, they might actually be the post office in there too. It'll be two weeks anyway 'til I get a paycheck. Assuming assuming assuming." Yawned, "We had a nice, nice groove going didn't we," she said, settled closer.

"Tut tut," said the other.

"Wait, like oh tut tut think nothing of it, 'twas no trouble at all, miss? Huh? Want to try that again, suave?"

"Great idea. See what I can do."

"No you jerk, try again with tut tut," she said.

"Oh. Okay uh . . . Honey, you're beautiful when you rut like that?"

"Better," she said, hard palm slap to his forehead, a satisfactory pop.

The boy said, "Still think you got a job? DMV job pays pretty good, being tool crib lady seems like more fun, unless they start hitting on you for real. I mean, you just told me a minute ago, but we were starting to get serious and all your stuff got so interested all of a sudden and you quit talking and uh what you said didn't stick, and then, *then* you kind of—what *is* that, estrus or something you guys sometimes do, the shape thing, my god, woman. Prehensile! Mercy!"

"Thank you, that's so sweet and embarrassing. Shh-shh! Don't get excited . . . shh, easy, ol' paint, easy now big fella. Okay, but promise you won't forget how to talk again? Get a towel."

After a while, the girl said, "The new job, I hope it's that other one, seven to three assistant manager Tuesday-Thursday-Saturday. I go in Monday for the interview but it's a done deal supposedly, start right after Christmas. Oh for pete sakes, hey! Down boy! That is just not an urgent matter is it, you trying to show off? Listen! We got to talk during those moments when you're polysyllabic—but so, would you sort out a couple of things for me? I'm real curious. Like real curious. So you knew Mil from before you . . . you know, each independently flipped out and met up again in Dallas, okay, brings up other stuff I'd love to hear, but check that one off . . . Oh yeah, about Alma! She knew Mil too, I didn't tell you that. From the traveling show, small world.

"So anyway were you and Perry and Shelda all best buddies together? Ladder thieves. And attic fans, I don't even know what an attic fan is, but anyway. And you and Shelda, she's your sister or something seriously taboo, man? Huh? You two ain't over it are you, I catch you both with the eyes thing. Neil, Perry, who are they to you? I mean really, *Neil* for god sakes? Sasquatch? Perry! God! Toxic waste assuming he's dead, or even if he isn't."

"Hold up a sec, how do you keep all those proper nouns straight? Takes me a second just to hear . . . Gail."

"Boorham. And your birthday, Boorham, is October thirteenth. I'm . . . it's so weird that I don't know your story. Is all. Lover."

"Well uh. You are a wise girl. Category. It's like you'd just know and tell *me* what the fuck the story is, 'know?" A coyote in the middle distance sang a brief minor-key phrase. "I'm the last one to get what matters and not, whole different story depending on which way I uh . . . go with it."

"Wise girl, right. In your mind, man! Little hard to live up to? C'mon just start talking, you're a Texan, come on, tell stories, it's a good night for a story, self-contradictory's fine," said the girl. "Tell us one about—get ready, here's another noun—Vicky. Crashing at my apartment to get away from her criminally insane husband. That whole scene, you talked her into leaving, what'd you do that for, you don't have a duplicitous bone in your body so what was that whole thing all about? She was safe at my place." An interrogative-sounding two-note sung from just outside caused the boy to press the girl hard against him for a moment, a manly gesture with some self-mockery in it.

"You think we're safe in this place?" he said.

"Don't say stuff like that though," Gail said, glanced up at the window, shivered. In the darkness, not even the hazy red specks of the relay tower, only the dirty storm window's faint blue glow reflected from the room's tiny fire.

•

Though he'd much rather have listened to her talk, the boy did as his darling asked—did his best to select scraps of recall that might form a context for her to put him in.

Vicky ran a microtome, the slide makers' trade, one of a small colony of English tech girls at a big research hospital where volunteer subjects, after a questionnaire and a brief physical and briefer interview, signed the release and at the end of a day of having experiments run on them were paid cash, a ten, a twenty. About that time, some research with human subjects began to be administratively disallowed out of caution or on ethical or litigious grounds—researchers intended no harm but what works precedes what's known, and by definition there was a lot they didn't know. Vicky's medical scientists were as yet fairly unencumbered—it was enough to go with the consensus of peers as to what's allowable to do to a human volunteer.

Neil volunteered as often as anything was available, got paid for lying around all day. No objection to repeated exposure to X-ray, to unknown injections or, his specialty, to swallowing a condom full of mercury. Mad-scientist dirty joke, the condom, sometimes attached to a surgical tube to be fished out from a certain depth, and sometimes simply to be shat out, dragged some small, sometimes radioactive apparatus down into his guts, or all the way through him from one end of the alimentary canal to the other.

That way introduced to biomedical research, Neil thought being a doctor would be really cool, had acquired a great pile of textbooks. Age twenty-four, Boise High dropout, happened to be discharged from the army in Boorham's town. Vicky had gone to parochial boarding school in Coventry, England, then spent some time in Bonn, and winding up for some reason in Dallas, Texas, married at age twenty the professional guinea pig and completely unenrolled premed. Big strong guy, rangy, charismatic, manly jaw, hair so coarse and dense it couldn't be combed, capable of growing a full beard at short notice, whose jumbo male parts sometimes hung pants-less at home. Lout. Not medical school material, except when they collected his data. She and her American medical student lived in a partitioned-off room that had once been the "library"—alcoves of bookcases built around a pair of windows; just space for a mattress, woodgrain vinyl–covered chest of drawers, small oak desk and swivel chair discarded by Vicky's workplace.

Inner-city streetcar neighborhood of indeterminately styled 1890s–1900s houses hadn't been occupied by prosperous young families in thirty years, though the families' rooms had since had respectable renters. And to judge by mail still delivered to the houses, those shabbily respectable people had fled only a year or two before. Seventy years old and already beyond their unambitious lifespan, hastily built two-story frame, six bed two bath plus powder room. Stuck on top of this particular house, a mother-in-law room accessible by vertiginous outdoor stairs, the treads so tilted away from the building and the railing so untrustworthy that hand loops had been nailed to the siding. Narrow lots, tiny front and back yards, and often a servants' quarters surviving next to the alley; here and there a house on a double lot with a looted and tilting carriage house. Outbuildings on those streets were built right on the ground as if temporary and, with ceaseless processing by termites and wood ants, over a few decades disintegrated. Some structures dispersed into the mud of seeping drains; further refined then, in other worlds of magnification, a decomposing servants' quarters gradually, patiently, became earth even as people came and went in it, carpentry transubstantiated to nutrient-rich soil. Beneath the various smells that people brought to a place, a fundamental note not of decay but of fallow soil, dirt, the earth.

Offended by the offensive ways, the proud squalor of

the disaffected bohemians they were supplanting, gays and lesbians were slow to gentrify those blocks. Anonymous owners bided their time, secured zoning changes for the future, had no intention of dropping by to have a look, sent a man around to collect a little rent; the amounts collected from a house from month to month surely must've varied, but apparently within acceptable limits. The vague old lady who'd lived in this house time out of mind was given other boarders' weekly remittances to hold for Tweedledee, the rent man. In the right circumstances, you'd take him for a ghost of the original man of the house—brown fedora, pleated brown pants cinched under his ribs, short wide tie, dapper little mustache.

In the big front room of this particular house, a small group who'd taken "peace pill"—phencyclidine—tore wallpaper and scrim off walls and as best they could from eleven-foot ceilings, vandalism a common side effect of a drug noted mainly for crippling paranoia that didn't go away. Artists and artisans, the majority of the tenants, recognized potential and began pulling tacks from the exposed wood walls, but soon bored, passed a joint and lost interest altogether. A speed freak among them, though, who'd borrowed from her job a pair of sharp, flush-cutting diagonal nippers, pulled out myriad scrim tacks that night, went to her job at the picture frame shop, came back to pull out tacks all night. Got to hand it to her. Eyes burning, fingers bloody and swollen, neck in a lot of pain from hours standing on a ladder looking at the ceiling, she crashed for only a day and a half before rejoining the aesthetes scraping off remaining desiccated crud, varnishing the resulting bare, time-ambered uneven boards—hard and tightly grained old-growth southern yellow pine stippled with tiny blackened tack holes—looked great with the contrasting beat-up paint on baseboards and doorframes, became the envy of the colony and a kind of tourist attraction.

Sometimes, renters and visitors gathered in the newly shabby-chic rooms to sit on and among salvaged couches and furniture stolen from midnight porches—the furnishings that'd once belonged to the rented place having mostly disappeared—those people and others sitting on the bottom stairs and on the floor among parts of a disassembled BSA, passed a pipeful of weed. Making labyrinthine circuits around the darkened front room and foyer, the Sioux-style calumet was refilled as required and handed back beeline to where it'd run out. Beyond their mainly being some sort of white person, and their not being averse to sharing spit with semi-strangers, any selected set of one person's variables was shared by few others, the room a Venn diagram like a chrysanthemum.

Thickly built poker-faced man who rarely responded when spoken to, who wore first-rate tattoos of the SS eagle over a paragraph that insisted something in Anzeigenschrift black letter, who rode his hog up the front steps onto the porch every evening and spent the evening with other men whose boots implied threat, endlessly dicking around with an old Matchless on the groaning screen porch above; idiot art student, apparently researching oblivion, making it back to the jug in his room from time to time with a slumming Marxist intellectual on his fifth teacup of burgundy; priapic theology dropout painstakingly ignored by the classically trained female folk-rock multi-instrumentalist, she an outed Republican seduced in tenth grade by Ayn Rand as so many smart girls were.

Chatty, Spanish-accent Choco who held his job at the tractor trailer wash despite a cervical collar; fish'n'chips lady, jaw still swollen from grinding her teeth for several hours during her introduction to psychoactive chemicals a few nights before—the following morning barely snatched back from falling into the deep fryer and so saved from crippling burns by her boss, who'd taken second-degree burns doing that; ambivalent slob polymath flicking cigarette ash into an upright typewriter; a deaf girl you got to know anyway, even without a sign of ASL; thirteen-year-old runaway girl.

Childish graybeard hitting on the fish'n'chips lady; pudgy, acned twenty-year-old called Batman, tonight without his fifteen-year-old sidekick Robin; fashionable radicals who spoke of People's this and that (real ones a few houses down, huddled around the kitchen table like proper commies, played at plotting and daydreamed arson and ambush); boarding-school rich kid from Pakistan, dark brown seventeen-year-old, spoiled rotten, chain-smoking Benson & Hedges and stubbing the butts on the floor, whose line of anti–Imperialist West patter was far superior to the radicals'; self-taught Satanist couple in the corner huffing Robitussin; buckskin-fringed despite the heat, an annoying espouser of any contrarian viewpoint—and according to the multi-instrumentalist, a serial date rapist back in high school—in endless argument with a rabidly centrist freelance machinist with one-off parts in satellites, whose disassembled BSA it was in the middle of the foyer.

Mil, with his set of particularly hazy identifiers, stayed away from things like this.

Crew-cut gun-freak IBM engineer who from time to time, as he'd done this evening, donated a lid of chaff-like marijuana (unit of dry measure equivalent to a quart jar); sari-affecting white libertarian lesbian who worked as secretary and sometimes extra hand in a mom-and-pop foundry in Denton, Texas, passed the pipe—a fine red pipestone job with eagle feathers, though no one there was Native—to a Black Trinidadian known as Pig, able somehow to reconcile his fundamentally anti-authority Anabaptist primitive Christian lay preaching with a career in criminology.

The mutual friend of the last two had fled as the pipe was brought out for the first time. On bond awaiting trial on a dope charge that might arbitrarily be dismissed or get him fifteen years, he was a shorn, shaved, deodorized, and polo-shirted Québécois, honor bound to stand trial so's not to forfeit the bond guaranteed by the home folks. His girlfriend had vanished sometime before being charged, possibly to do with her having almost no English. Hitchhiking from Montreal toward Mexico City, he and girlfriend stayed overnight the night a particular house was busted; the boys and girls there had taken the precaution of stacking on a second toilet tank for a quick second flush should cops raid, but in principled, idealistic, pathetic denial, doors were never locked, people freely wandered in and out like the police did that time, cuffing kids on their mattresses. At area hardware stores afterward there was a run on the brackets used for door-barring with two-by-fours.

Out of place and no longer comfortable to be with because of his convincing disguise—his madras Bermudas and penny loafers—the Canadian had come to visit the couple in the servants' quarters out back in order to buy a standardized 150-microgram gelatin flake of pharmaceutical-grade LSD, but Shelda and Perry were doing the last of it right then. The couple's trashy everyday stock came from other dealers' remnants and seconds. The couple crushed pills with a brass mortar and pestle, dumped in the contents of stray capsules, randomly stirred the anonymous compounds to load into caps for resale as "synthetic" or under some made-up street name. Worked bare-handed and therefore got completely ripped in the course of a day's work. Shelda and Perry, in a cycle of immersive hallucination for a week, and two or three days of semiconscious sleep, and a few days of feeding, were celebrated as able to function just fine throughout—as casually observed anyway.

In the rooms with the stripped and varnished walls and ceilings, Sun Ra jazz stopped abruptly as someone put on an LP more to her taste; 13th Floor Elevators flowed from open windows as the biker, a Hells Angels Berdoo reject who had no use for those assembled in the big room, clomped through diagonally, intercepted the pipe, took a deep drag, and left to give the indicted Canadian a lift, the two an odd sight. In the crowded front room after the massive, older-model stock panhead had thudded down the front steps and rumbled away, the relict crazy lady that had come with the house farted, giggled, got to her feet fanning her face, and though in declining health, shuffled toward the kitchen to scrub the sink for the second time that day.

•

The boy said, "This woman I sort of knew showed up in the house one time. Thought she was there proselytizing because, 'know, a box-pleated skirt like she must've had it since high school, got her hair ratted bubble-head style and the sleeveless blouse with the ruffles, shaved her pits, she had on makeup, she had the stockings, she had the shiny pumps, but what she was doing was going around some of the houses she knew, trying to recruit people to put on the costume, the uniform like she was wearing because she had a child custody hearing, wanted to fill the courtroom with good vibes." The boy cleared his throat, "Break your fucking heart, man. Actually got takers. Said I'd go, and she came back, cut my hair. I took her up on it but I forgot and missed the hearing. Fuck! What a fucking goddamn moron!" After a minute he said, "But anyway she lost the kids, and I want to listen to you tell *me* stuff because you are not a raging downer. Your turn."

"Nope."

"What nope?"

Shrugged against his ribs, yawned, "Not a downer and not my turn," adjusted the quilt.

The boy yawned, waited for more from her. Shrugged, "Okay. One time this complete jerk thought it would be funny to drop the fish'n'chips guy, dosed his beer after work. John the fish'n'chips guy. He wanted to be everybody's new best friend, but he wasn't trying too hard or anything like that, he was just a completely nice straight arrow. So Asshole's deed is a betrayal of, you know . . . just about anything. Small little bar was in the next block from the fish'n'chips shop and the barkeep that night was a man I'm proud to have known, stayed up all night with the guy . . . I mean, innocent like some innocent animal somebody tormented and it had no earthly idea why and the animal's trying to fight it off. I was underage but I was there, but I was a coward and didn't go talk to him, I just gawked. Deep-fryer burns must've hurt. He fixated on the bandages like they were causing whatever this was. His . . . outlook or however you say that, it was so badly, you know, mauled. Practical joke. Got rid of his shop and went back to

Peoria or wherever it was. I'm just guessing all that, because he never went back to the shop again, far as I know, and anyway it closed.

"Same asshole that dropped the fish guy sold ketamine to the soldier. This vet moved into the second Abadie house—it was the house that had got busted so bad and nobody wanted to live there, only Mil and his wife, and then me and then pretty soon the soldier, wherever the hell he came from. Nobody holding, although I and the soldier might smoke one elsewhere. Mil and his old lady moved over there looking for a lot less company and he took me along too. Like you bring the dog, fine, why not.

"Heard about the ketamine later, and I don't know if it's related, but the soldier went off without his stuff, so God knows. Likely nothing good but God knows, could be anything. Mil called the county jail and the county hospital and the VA and after a couple more days I went through the guy's room—everything still in his duffel, T-shirts and toothbrush and what all, but a bronze star in its box along with this other medal that says 'Lover.' No Saigon souvenirs, no pictures, no address book. Marianne Faithfull and the Animals and Bob Dylan and nothing to play them on. Half a carton of Pall Malls, half a box of .45 auto bullets. Ha! The usual, you might say. Bag got stolen along with my toolbox and my crap radio because some dudes figured out you could walk right through those houses in the daytime if no one was in evidence. Mil wasn't very big, and like I say, he always had this, you know, his composure, and you wouldn't expect to see him bat an intruder off the back steps with a two-by-four door bar. Dude bounced up off the ground, then he tripped over the crap radio and got up and tried to run and fell on his face again and kind of weaved down the alley. You almost wished him well. Other guy was already long gone."

Gail asked, "Would you be able to make a chart of who's okay to steal from whom?"

"Um, maybe. You mean like classical logic? Doubt it, too messy, I'm not that smart, but I'd do anything for your love, swim the deepest ocean."

"That is such a relief. The ocean deal has been nagging at me all blessed day."

"Listen, I, uh, something a minute ago if I can think what it was . . . yeah, Mil. Baggy fatigue pants always. But he's in his jockey shorts when he chased those guys out, though. Scars on his thigh kind of like you'd do a tattoo but it's thin raised scars—little, you know, gingerbread men like a chain of paper dolls, I'm thinking what the fuck? Some kind of prison art? Little chain of figures going around his thigh. And in my head right now they had these terrified expressions but that can't be real. And right in front below that, there's a round circle the size of your palm, what I still think looked like the full moon, sort of like, you know, the features on the moon, drawn with scar. No fucking way surgery, and if it was burns, what could look like all that. No point in asking and none of my business, but I mean, Jesus."

•

Even more than usual, wastrels and rebels were current fashion. Shelda and Perry went looking for greater dissolution, quickly assumed minor royalty status on the houseboats of Sausalito along with their dog, an all-black sweet-natured unaltered free-range German shepherd named Satan, on his own a local celebrity. Vicky and Neil moved into the gradually dissolving Abadie Street servants' quarters, Vicky already done with trying to romanticize sordid. Wanted ordinary, or normal at least; to get husband Neil away from the erratic people and pervasive dope and investigatable political activity and intentionally bad behavior and completely needless potential of prison time so he could concentrate on the American Doctor fantasy. Waking up married to the idiot, Vicky did what she could. Found a microscopy tech job and a bungalow in semirural western Washington State. Mil and his angry wife had already moved to the coast, for its government-assisted obstetric care. And the boy's token moved to the romantically dank servants' quarters in its turn.

It was where he'd gone to ground after an implausible, fraught-melodrama trip up US 101. He had holed up in hopes that his personality, provisionally established but not well set, might adapt itself to the confounding experience. The Pacific coast episode ended with his running away with Vicky, that episode not soon settled, complicated by the boy's having subsequently lost track of her, and by the expectation of her profoundly warped husband coming to see him.

Face disfigured now, not the boy's mere mental kind of trauma, within another day Mil climbed out of a late 1940s panel truck followed by a dog. Glad for a lot of reasons, the boy was pleased that the truck and the friend and the dog turned out to be actual. Alert, aloof, the black-and-tan mutt was called Lincoln.

•

"Okay well my mom and her mom were sisters, her dad and my dad are brothers. What do you guess, along about half-sister?"

She said, "I don't know, all those grandparents. Seems like sort of half-sister maybe, however it works out, but somehow doesn't sound, you know, too icky. But so you guys are stuck with that."

"Ha! Permanent, huh," he said.

"'Nuff said."

"No shit," he said.

"Right." She waited.

He said, "But uh, you want to know is it okay to ask, like, were we screwing like nutria at some point. Yes you can ask, nobody else can ask because it pisses me off, conditioned thing."

"I don't know what a nutria is. Are. They are. But you and she is interesting, you gotta say."

"Uh-huh . . . You remember high school, gossip gossip gossip gossip. Sneer city and you're everybody's business. Jesus. Then, uh, the lunch counter sit-ins with Black kids downtown and everybody started making up this wild stuff about her, started asking me ugly stuff, everybody scared not to cold-shoulder her and the hell with them! Her friends! She was varsity everything and the damned fucking coaches benched her! Hell with 'em I mean fuck 'em! Every one of those bastards! Still pissed, hell with 'em!"

The girl waited.

After a couple of minutes he said, "So she didn't have all her usual, you know, you're good at sports and you have friends and all that, and didn't have all that normal stuff all of a sudden, and started hanging out at my house, her aunt and uncle's house. Age fifteen and sixteen when everything matters. Draw you a map?"

"You guys, wow," said the girl, "You guys are mated for life."

"Well. I wouldn't say . . . Learned 'Jabberwocky' together." Quiet for a while, until he said, "Something happened to her. I mean she's still the same but, uh. I don't get it, what she's like."

"Yeah. You don't think it was Perry getting killed? Assuming he's dead."

"Maybe." He shrugged, "Maybe. Don't really think that's it."

•

There was no telephone at either flophouse, but most people wrote letters out of town as a matter of course, even across town for some in demographics where phones were scarce. Those willing to pay for long distance depended on the kindness of a reluctant clerk at the corner Rexall, who might not break a five to a pile of coins for a non-customer to plug into a pay phone. Neil had a shortcut, conveniently made calls from the West Coast charged to a third party's number without authorization. Interstate fraud, but a message to the boy would probably be relayed through someone who'd picked up the phone in the physical sciences department.

Right after exams and right before Christmas break and right after the campus clinician called up Selective Service to postpone his preinduction physical, and right after being laid off from the foundry, the boy got word saying come to Sausalito right away, Neil and Vicky will show you around town then drive to Seattle, got some big bucks lined up, quick cash, a working vacation, come on out. Obviously idle and aimless bullshit and anyway what's he doing down there at the Bay instead of Washington State, but sure, why not.

Idiotic stratagem for a reasonably robust young adult male, the boy had been fasting for the next draft physical, so to graduate pathologically underweight before inevitable conscription. So, light-headed and stupider than usual; so, a one-way ticket on TWA closed his passbook savings account. A reservist heading to muster proffered cigarettes and talked from the next seat about big plans once he got 'Nam behind him. Three and a half hours in the night air an indistinct coalescence within the general miasma of surreality.

No one showed to pick him up of course. Dithering, drawing down his pocket reserves on an airport-priced Bay Area tourist map, he asked around without much luck (curtness or snide condescension to his class of newcomer in that time in that region a point of pride with a lot of natives) and gradually bracketed in on the right intercity bus. Sighting the water and then clusters of houseboats, the boy made his way to the driver, who had nothing to offer. Off the bus and asking directions at a chandler's shop, carried his bag a half mile back to the correct pier, where the addresses on the mailboxes were not numbers but fanciful names, many in the long row of boxes marked with multiple names—*Snow's Drift* had become *Yowza* and then HMS *Redundant*—former names left there ostensibly out of courtesy to do with forwarding mail, but mostly it looked cool.

Fried on acid such that it was surprising he'd sounded sentient less than three days earlier, Neil was aboard with his brother, Perry, who was handling his drugs as well as ever. Clinically insane due to them and things attendant to them though, neither was interested that the boy had come, that he'd traveled there carrying his welder's kit, ready to get to work to pay for return plane fare. In possession of his wits, he would've acknowledged a dumb move and walked out on the pathetic drama, begged the home folks for a bus ticket. Even a seventeen-hundred-mile hitchhike home wouldn't've seemed farfetched to a boy with all his marbles.

•

To his truelove, "Half the stuff I remember is made up, you're telling a dream and you notice the way you're saying it tries to make it make sense." The stammer had come forward again, required sidestepping more often, "And that was a year ago and your own head changes all this stuff for you like you're just some lackey feeb gofer and not . . . so I know exactly jack shit for certain about where I been. Babbling. You talk now."

"Screw reportage, this is the rabbit hole," shrugged with the shoulder snuggling him, "Or just shut up whenever, but I'm not done listening," slipped her hands between her thighs. The stove breathed quietly, making a little warmth and a little light in the room at the verge of a federal wilderness in profound darkness. Friday, December twenty-second, winter solstice 1967.

"This is good," he said, absently adjusting her breast scrunched against him, absently kissing her mouth, looking nowhere, half-closed eyes reflecting their small fire. "But uh, so you saying if I quit talking, we pop out of a rabbit hole? See, then we have to deal with them coyotes."

"Don't try to creep me out please," she said.

"Wanna tell ghost stories?"

"So you got there and Neil and Perry are wrecked. Where was Shelda? And I thought we were talking about Vicky."

"Okay well, so. I wandered around 'til it got dark, looking at all the kinds of floating, you know, things people were living in. Neil and Perry, zero interest in entertaining company, so I eventually unrolled the bag and went to sleep. God I was hungry. Woke up around first light when Shelda and Neil's chick came in."

"Edie is not, I mean way emphatically not, Neil's chick," the girl said.

"Guess I knew that. Okay, Neil was, oh say, aware of his actual surroundings at this point, sort of, and I asked him 'where's Vicky' and he said 'city.' She was at your place. And I asked 'who's that' and he said 'that's my chick.' Nice person, Midwest accent, let me borrow her boat, big ol' beat-up wooden rowboat named *Candyass*, real clean, you could tell it was her baby. Oh wow. She had a uh, her dog had wheels on it, swear to God. Edie kind of saved my sorry ass that night, it was the same day . . . man that was just one day."

·

The boy rowed among the houseboats and dead cabin cruisers people lived in, and shanty scows with proper stove pipes; waved back at a couple sitting under the rainfly of a tent pitched on the bamboo deck of an oil drum raft. They sat in dinette chairs roasting enormous carrots on a hibachi, greeted him good morning. He rowed among mats of garbage, occasional floating turds flushed into the harbor from houseboat potties or simply shat over the side. Sluggish outgoing tide in the shallow harbor did only a fair job of cleaning up after people living on the water, but individual chunks of the considerable effluent from Sausalito itself were at least not identifiable to the eye. A twenty-yard bolus of gel, translucent gruel barely stirred by his oars, re-coalesced behind *Candyass*, placidly rose and fell in his wake.

Tied up at the houseboat, shaking from the mild exertion, he hiked to the chandler's, came back with a new rowlock for the one he'd dropped in the harbor, "most people just leave it," Neil's chick had said. He'd returned to a feast, almost entirely meat, sat down apart from the table, faint, nauseous. The Chick told him that if he were vegetarian, at least there were potatoes—thanks no, but he appreciated it; offered French toast, oh thanks, no, looks good though. Asked was he fasting, he'd guessed so.

An old man at the table, whose nose and eyes were visible in a mass of yellowed white hair, had berated the eaters in a put-on of an old crank—hey what are we doing today, unloading boxcars, carrying I-beams, tossing hay bales, Jesus X Christ that's enough hog protein to etc. Then wanted them to buy his newsletters. Walking around town by himself that afternoon, the boy ran into him again, in front of a coffeehouse carrying a clarinet case. The old guy stopped him,

"Word, man."

The boy looked at him.

"You need a word, so spake the sheila of your new acquaintance, we once would have said. She is concerned and solicitous of you."

The boy said something like "Huh?"

And the old man said, "She thinks you woke up on the wrong side of the mirror, muchacho, dig?"

The boy replied something like "Uh yeah. I uh, dig, but ..."

The old man sighed, "If there's anything you want to know about these strange strands you find yourself upon, blinking like a baby possum dumped out of its turnip wagon into the bright ground fog of day, I'll tell you if I'm able."

"So then, oh well thanks. So, like, do you know about the FuMan? So hard to believe, is that the way stuff is?"

"Apt! Apt," the other had said, "I do know a little. What else?"

The boy said he couldn't think of anything else to ask at the moment.

"FuMan's particulars lack consensus," the old man said, "In simple, the person is a performer, does exist, despite the very hip comic book moniker. If that's all you need. Also FuDog, known as. Er? Enough?" Batted at his beard like a dog scratches with its hind foot.

The boy passively waited for more.

The old man drummed fingers on his clarinet case, said, "FuMan in context? Thus. Among your hordes of recent arrivals, witless invention proliferates like a plague of lobe-fin catfish, each a nonchalant *liar* lying with every draft of the open air over the gills, crawling ashore wave on wave to walk among us—strolling slippery lobefin-in-hand with doddering old Verity. In other words so much make-believe asserts actuality that each passing wave of it builds upon its own substance, as film of not quite ephemeral handprints accumulates on a crud-encrusted stair rail in other words. Our FuMan is a marginally successful huckster mistakenly invested with dark powers, arcane understandings, in the malinformed hive mind of the street, an investment he greedily arrogates, but hey that's just my take. No, that hambone has no power you don't hand over. That said . . . You fingered a Thing, kid, peered over the hoardings—that is, that the agreed-upon known-to-be unravels. I agree with you, it unravels here, don't it. Tendrils of its formerly coherently incontrovertibly agreed-upon cloud find the ground fog alluring, seductive, tendrils of the known-to-be pump their substance into it. Look again, the known is drained empty, there's only fecund fog. Or if you like, egregious little cloudlet sheep stray in numbers from the evidentiary common, with so few tropospheric Jack Russells to round 'em up, you know? Muchacho? Look at it through a straw hat, the pinholes put everything in focus, but to what end." The old man moved toward the coffeehouse.

"Uh, could you wait a second, would you mind? What's the graffiti, the little round black stencil?" Boorham asked. Where the other's mouth would be, orangish whiskers moved. He may have been chewing his lip.

"It is the queasy common boundary of old Verity and young Witless Invention, possum savant. Dunno. Ya got me, kid."

•

Gail went up on one elbow. "That little black symbol, you used to see it all the time around the Bay for a while, still do some. Boorham, I swear I saw that in Kansas three years ago. In the middle of nowhere. Creeped me out when it started showing up in San Francisco."

"Why? What's it mean?"

"No idea. Just bad associations."

"Why?"

"Don't know, it's just one of those things."

The boy learned for the first time there were things she wouldn't tell him.

•

Not really a boat at all, a narrow two-story house teetering on a twelve-by-thirty-foot platform cobbled onto the pontoons of a little prewar navy push-tugboat. Permanently listing three degrees—design considerations weren't beholden to balanced loading—the houseboat this evening was sunk nearly to the plywood deck with partying art colonists, of whom many joined Perry in the frenetic, stomping dance of local acidheads, the deck and porch-like upper deck, even the topmost shed roof, quaking and thundering and threatening to capsize them, heads hung, arms limp, stomping as if terrified marionettes desperate to escape through the floor, any rhythms random coincidence and nothing to do with the band. Loud, loud band, amplified harmonica like sounds from a satanic heavy manufacturing plant.

Shelda nor Neil's chick anywhere around, Neil inside in the deafening, hyper, strobe-lit lower room in a chair, pants off, eyes expressionless, jaw slack, not drooling yet. The boy began to feel his light-headedness merge with the sound, as if it were part of what he heard. Hm, that's odd. Began to notice kaleidoscopic patterns in the strobe-lit partygoers, and that the dancers left tracks in the air. Oh shit.

Hoping it was just LSD, hoping that it wasn't a lot, certainty flooded in that he was broadcasting a spiritual alarm, attracting malicious attention; and all the while telling himself hey, just go with it, don't fight it, don't fear it, just let it be, he made his way to the dock to look for shelter. A hidey-hole as an ill or injured animal would seek. Wanted quiet and craved darkness, as auditory distortion enhanced by imagination pounded and wailed, immersive, nuts, shuddering along with the multiple afterimages now merging with the jiggling wallpaper patterns that had begun to envelop him. Really, one of him thought, this is just so damn dumb. It was getting hard to see, and the developing churn of undifferentiated realities pressed him to hole up as well. The boy squared his shoulders and marched resolutely down the dock headed away from the brighter-lit pier. Saw the water down there, thought to jump in—maybe a plunge into the harbor would clear his head. Heard his name called from the water below. My name? Oh c'mon now. Neil's chick horse-whistled, yelled louder, getting his name slightly wrong.

The first bare shade of daylight through the crack between the doors coincided with a mild euphoria settling over him. Intensity of the trip diminished, vision clearing some, visuals gently collapsing on themselves like deteriorating red and green soap foam, the boy became aware he was shivering, and that his unresponsive legs and feet were swollen from standing all night. Wrapped in a paint-spattered canvas drop cloth, he burst through the shutters of a shallow equipment locker that had been hooked shut from the outside, and immediately fell sprawling. Too stiff and too smashed to trust walking, he got out of the drop cloth, crawled to the edge of the deck, got to his knees and managed to pee over the side without falling in, and made it down the gangplank backward on all fours. Sat on the dock shivering and rubbing his legs and gathering the resolve to assay standing, and laughing with real mirth at his pitiful self.

•

Spooned together on an air mattress now, wrapped in quilts and staring at the essential firelight of the little heater, the girl listened, sorting and editing the scrapings as they fell out of the other's mind. Being entertained by them and by her silent part in the storytelling.

•

On the bridge on the way over, Neil had told him that Perry was dead. "What? He was across the table from you a couple of hours ago, fuck are you talking about, man?"

A hitchhiker, someone Neil knew slightly, had spoken up from the back seat, "Oh Boorham. You haven't learned anything by now? Linear time, my friend? The ancients didn't have the concept. It's a fairly recent concept, something invented in the so-called Enlightenment to re-enslave the minds that had just freed themselves from the death grip of the Church of Rome. The Linear Time Fallacy, my friend . . . a fiction, a cunning fabrication—it worked so well at mind control that it was adopted by the Shadow Elite that have existed since the time of the Crusades, burrowed beneath the so-called Organizing Principles of every Society above the level of Band, Tribe, and Chiefdom! Now you think it's a natural law of the universe!"

Neil had glanced at the boy, "He's giving it to you straight, you need to listen to this."

The hitchhiker had said, "It's all the same, see. Everything,

everything, it's all the same. Time too. Past, present, future, those words didn't used to mean what they mean to you now."

Boorham had said, "So what happened to Perry between then and now?"

"Oh Boorham, you're just not . . ." the hitchhiker had trailed off, shaking his head sadly.

"He's my brother. I'd know," Neil had said, and then, "That old man that came in with my chick, he'll turn you against me if he can, but you're loyal to me and I love you. He's turning everybody against me. His name's Albert, everybody calls him Doots. Haven't done the numerology on it yet but you bet your ass it's going to turn out demonic."

"Why's he your enemy?" the boy had asked.

"God sets a feast before you as your enemy looks on," Neil had answered, "God's looking out for you, you can shoot the Devil the shaft," and suddenly pointed, "There! There's some!"

"Some what?" the boy had said.

From the back seat, "Graffiti. The little round black ones, called a Crown or a Wreath, FuMan leaves them to summon his children to their work."

"FuMan," Neil had said.

"Uh, what?" the boy had said.

"It's a selection process, a winnowing. The Goat of Amalthea, she suckles only those with the Spark of the Divine in them, her milk is poison to the unfit, to those of us who are a little less. Most are left behind, many of those sicken and die. But when enough of the Chosen are found, they'll take on our slave masters, the nameless über-cabal, the puppeteers who've ruled unseen, controlled our minds for generations. The Chosen have the power to cut those strings, to set us free!"

"Oh. Cool," the boy had said.

•

Prone to demonstrations of its neglect, its overheating and its oil pressure gauge that might peg at either end, their ride needed an attendant driver, and of the three he was the only one who'd do. But the boy ordinarily drove only because if he didn't drive and he dozed, Neil would lose himself and them down some imaginary shortcut, or Vicky, who hadn't said a word since San Francisco, would put them on the shoulder, hood up and radiator blowing off, having lit out backtracking toward the Bay, unable to take her foot off the gas. At forty or forty-five the sad pink Nash wagon would keep going—twenty-four hours to Seattle at that rate, had there been no sleet or endless construction zones, no cool-down stops, side trips, backtracks.

Clinical academicians often label their observations with names that sound self-satirical—Hallucinogen Persisting Perception Disorder is the bio-perceptual hangover that hadn't faded in the two nearly sleepless days since his drug-hammered night in the storage locker, and pervasive déjà vu was hard for him to take. Now convinced too that someone had arranged for all this.

At some point along the Oregon coast the boy nodded off. Woke finding that he wasn't at the wheel. Miles off US 101, almost as if he'd known where he'd been going, Neil stopped in the drive of a solitary, vandalized abandoned house. House that the boy, of course, was certain he'd seen before. In an attack of déjà visité, he knew in advance the exact maze-like floor plan of the house, and just as bad, in an unwelcome fit of precognition knew he'd be back to it, or to some place just like it. Vicky pulled down her jeans, squatted to pee beside the car, likely afraid of being left. It had in fact crossed the boy's mind to leave Neil there.

Ceiling dripping in places, stink of animals nesting there, moldy floors covered with muddy shoe prints and inexplicable lengths of colored ribbon still attached to their spools, a derelict house whose yellow porch light was none-theless burning. Neil apparently slept with his eyes partly open, and Vicky sniffled intermittently, probably crying, or wheezed rhythmically, probably asleep; the boy drifted, frequently snapping rigidly back to sharp awareness. Dark when they got there, dark when they left.

Hoarding Vicky's small reserve of cash, the boy paid for gas with Neil's Texaco card from God knows where; masking tape on the back held enough of the card's crumbling essentials in position, and as the attendant worked the knuckle-buster card imprinter in the office, a cashiered-out noncom ranted about America's descent into chaos, found some sympathy in an audience of a few men crowded into the place, found a convenient hollow-eyed long-haired boy to personify his grievance. The ex-careerist followed him back to the car, the man's shouted imprecations becoming hysterical barking; as the Nash began to pull away, Neil got out, picked up poor Sarge by the throat and the crotch, threw him with great authority straight to the concrete.

Encountering old Albert peddling his Bay Area newsletters three hundred miles north of the Bay, sleet sticking to his whitish mass of hair and beard, the old man had seemed not to recognize the boy he'd spoken with that morning, and berated him for not buying a paper, "What in blazes are you doing here then! What are you doing in Oregon, you don't have a dime to your name!" The old man was having fun with him.

Conspiring against Neil with the demonic old man and with the lords of the world mind-control cabal—in a reasonable but insistent voice, Neil argued the evidence, for an hour at a time.

In a stretch of road under reconstruction, Nash parked between the cones in the cold drizzle, a gray VW van swung in and stopped. Neil and the boy under the pink car's hood made way for Perry, who after a while assessed the current problem, and then went away. "Fuel filter's clogged. Poke a hole through it with a coat hanger or whatever you got." Neil apparently thought nothing remarkable about encountering his brother on the coast highway five hundred miles north of San Francisco. In the front seat, open-end wrench in hand and looking in the glove box for a wire or something to poke a hole with, the boy thought he heard Vicky speak,

"Why were you so adamant I come with you to Snohomish?"

He said, "Your life was in danger where you were."

He thought he heard her say, "My life! Jimmy, I thought you were nice, I thought you were the sane one."

"I'm Boorham, Vicky."

"What? What are you talking about!" Vicky said to him from the back seat, speaking for the first time since she'd come along with him.

Near their destination north of Seattle, Boorham drifted into awareness as he himself parked beside Perry's gray bus at a burger stand. All he remembered about it. The eerie Persisting Perception Disorder, the after-trip, had not diminished.

Neil left the bungalow before daybreak, took the old Nash wagon.

"He was brutal," Vicky said to Boorham, who didn't understand, but then did, asked if she was alright. Now clearly in some pain, she just looked at him. After a while she said, "He found my checkbook. Bank isn't open 'til Tuesday, as many hot checks as are left on the pad."

"Oh. Oh man," Boorham said. She said that a friend from work was picking her up. He pressed his luck wondering if a ride into Seattle might be possible.

"I'll ask," she said. She bought their bus tickets to Dallas from another pad of worthless checks.

•

"One time that thirteen-year-old was out trying to flag down cars, trying to turn tricks, she's little, looked like eleven or twelve. Middle of the afternoon. Must've known she's bound to wind up dead whether or not awful shit happened to her first, so at least daylight. Tiny little thing. Uh, so. Fish'n'chips lady went out to talk to her, same time as a squad car came up. Lady told the cop the kid was just trying to drum up business for the shop, misunderstanding, she'd fix it; well why's she home from school; oh the teachers are having meetings all day, conference day.

"And uh I imagine the cop was still in the car and didn't know the girl smelled like a wet puppy, and the cop woulda looked her over, woulda looked at her hair and given the lady a look like he had serious doubt about the whole thing, 'know? But anyway he drove away. Fish'n'chips lady was a runaway herself all when she was growing up, they always found her and dragged her back, and it's like the kid is a chance to get it right, get run away. I really liked that lady, she said funny stuff, like ha-ha funny. But uh. She said the abuse she had was 'baroque,' but she didn't act messed up, I didn't think.

"John the fish guy wanted to turn the kid in, got

persuaded to feed her instead. Lady took her home to Abadie Street that night and washed her, found the bruises of course, plus there were some duct-tape burns where they'd had her tied up, incorrigible thirteen-year-old. So the lady gave her a vitamin, looked in her mouth and all her teeth were still there, bought her a toothbrush and clean shorts and stuff and a clean tank top, parked her in a booth. Wrote poems in a spiral notebook, the kid did, and she was so, you know, patient and quiet. Didn't really like fish but I guess coped for those couple of days and ate hush puppies while the lady tried to work something out—that house was, I mean it was like utterly, top to bottom dangerously wrong. God, for some of the grownups it was dangerous, much less for that little girl. No shortage of creeps.

"She's from up in Oklahoma, family's something like, oh, a gas well driller struck it rich, or anyway just runs this one town up there, goes hunting with the congressman. No one up there's ready to piss off the bad dad, shelter his daughter. So the fish lady was talking to uh, to local churches and whatnot, and nobody would have anything to do with it of course. So here's Mil. You guessed it, right? He's on his way out west scouting places to move to with the pregnant wife. There's some utopian farmer families, it would've been right out here someplace I'm pretty sure, and they do like they used to do, take in stray kids like back in the old days and raise 'em like their own kids working on the farm. You want to hope there's a whole little village, barn raisings, a school bell, a church bell, washing the firetruck, we need to go see if we can find it. If we ever run into Mil again. Everybody just doing their deal . . . said they look like they're in a Western, women in high collars and bonnets, maybe I don't like that part but . . . You want to hope it's not some uptight obedience thing, not . . . uh, anyway you want to hope it's beautiful so maybe that kid is okay. You know?"

.

There'd been long, comfortable pauses all evening. This time she said,

"Bet you don't say another word for a week."

"Hm."

"Kind of excited about tomorrow. Going exploring," she said.

"Want me to make that Bisquick thing? I know how to. Oh wow if that's margarine I could make us some kind of fry bread. Better yet if it's lard."

"Tomorrow."

"Smoke a J?"

"No," she said.

"Me neither. But you're not sad."

"Feels nice right now."

After some time he said, "Gail? You know?"

"I'm not sure," she said.

Best of friends drifted in and out of reverie and sleep, in their happy little cabin by the great dark forest, oblivious of the coyotes, who'd shut up anyway.

Business Card • a silo, an Alma

Loading unsalable beets into a pair of his father's coveralls, Felix put the ticking-cloth dummy through a rusty portable shredder. His elderly parents had died within a month of each other, and a two-acre retail patch was all that he kept in production these days, having sold one field and kept another "idle but ready" so to bring in a small subsidy check, a little automatic income for however long that might go on. Felix was an extra hand, a farmworker perennially temporary due to his reputation for wasting time on the job, a fairly unusual trait in the neighborhood. When he'd unjammed the shredder often enough to make a satisfactory mess of the beets and the old coveralls, whistling through his teeth he shoveled the chunky blood-red debris into a gunnysack, tossed it into a high-sided wagon, towed the wagon to a neighbor's field. Hitched it behind an old Allis two-row cornstalk chopper.

On the tractor in front, a little girl set the gas lever at

a particular notch, the magneto at a shade past some imaginary mark, the choke the same way, barely out; retarded the spark a hair by tapping the lever gently. Climbed down and cranked upward once with the left hand, thumb on top rather than wrapped around, mindful of crippling injury should the engine backfire. Gave it another half-crank, then reached back up and reset things a nudge, cranked, and the three-banger obediently lit and popped along quietly. For all the manly hauling on the crank, Edith didn't weigh a hundred pounds. The tractor's steel seat wasn't adjustable, but she'd learned as a much smaller child to drive standing up.

Rain of chopped cornstalks had reduced to an infrequent patter in the open-topped silo; hanging on the ladder inside the chute, she hefted a wood door out of the vertical ribbon of them, stooped into the silo bringing along a heavy silage fork. In a wide-brim hillbilly hat dedicated to the purpose, braids down her shirt, chore coat buttoned to the top, Edith was down there raking and stepping the air pockets out of new layers of sticky cellulose, curling her toes to keep too-large rubber boots on. Shrieked when a brief shower of sloppy red stuff and pieces of somebody's overalls pelted on and around her. Edith's mama, Alma, partway down the outside ladder when she heard her kid's scream, charged up to the loading platform, looked down into the silo. Turning around, "Felix!" over the roar of the blower, "You are a goddamn loaf of shit! Pranks on a twelve-year-old, you halfwit!"

Grandpa Linnaeus's state-of-the-art 1919 steel-banded

concrete stave silo with its gleaming silver dome had been his proud ebenezer marking conquest, the march of progress. Forty years later it was roofless, still fermented the silage just fine. Little Edie marched around inside it, waiting for the next wagonload. Under the square bales in the hayloft lay parts of horse-drawn field machines, thrown up there against future need. Grandpa Lin never had a chance fully to trust the mechanized equipment he'd brought in, because he'd been killed when the silo was new, by a man who worked for him.

"Lin," the man had said, "You know what? This resort ain't never going to be and I do not like breaking my back digging a cellar when there's crops in the field—why in holy God's name did you hock the farm for this mare's nest! Where's my wages you owe me? Chicago people ain't coming here! You ain't no tycoon, you just a teat-puller like the rest of us and that's all you got!"

Prohibition had recently gone into effect, and local bootleggers were doing well; others too were going into the smuggling business with Canadian partners, and there was enough business for all.

In lilting, accented English, Linnaeus said, "Go on home, Frankie, come back tomorrow you ain't snockered."

The man threw down his shovel hard enough to bounce, "Yeah we see about that, sorry little rook," beginning to work himself up again about what'd set him off to begin with—a dispute about whether rowboats should be

In Which Irusta-dis found a Burning Whalecrack

scraped, caulked, and painted when you take them out of the water in the fall or before you put them back in in the spring. After a half hour the man returned, gave the smaller Lin a hard two-palmed poke in the back. Lin stumbled, dropped his heavy four-foot wood-and-brass carpenter's level; the man snatched it up for a good solid two-handed whack across the shoulders, missed and broke Grandpa Linnaeus's neck instead.

•

A decade after the beets prank, Edith came back to catch her breath, get out of the enveloping, insulate world she'd been living in, retreat to the rural Midwest. To see home, a place and a folk that would be difficult to figure out for anyone not of it and of them. To see home, but mostly Edith wanted to make up with Mama. And too, visiting there she wouldn't be so closely observed by whoever the hell it was had begun keeping tabs on her in her adopted world. Over a few Heilemans, she got her taciturn mom going, often not an easy thing to do,

"I am not in the dark about what happens out there. Nothing wholesome about those houseboats, Edie, use your eyes, use your brains, you know you're better than that." Moderately beery, Alma unloaded the predictable grievance, then surprised her child with praise,

"Run a dairy operation top to bottom and do every

honest thing known to man! You can type and you're a whiz at math and plus, you're pretty!"

A broad and kind of flat-shaped person, frequent smile, expression unshy and evaluating, Edith wore granny glasses, parted her frizzy yellow hair into a pair of loose bunches most of the time. Intentionally emphasized the wholesome. Mama'd omitted specifics—the strength and willingness to chop out frozen silage in miserable weather, get dirty and sore fixing and modifying big machines, wrangle the hired guys, competently handle veterinary tasks. Needed the help of a couple of large men to keep the animal sprawled, but she was adept at stuffing a cow's enormous prolapsed uterus shoulder-deep back inside, with further reinsertion through the cervix, marshmallow through keyhole by feel, never showing the animal any uncertainty. For that and other procedures, neighbors stocked antimicrobial in gallons and often called on her rather than rely on themselves or the vet.

"Edie! Those houseboat people are all as depraved as they are useless!"

"I'm a businesswoman, Mama. Licensed, bonded, and insured to provide local color or something. Thanks Mom. Love you. You're still not going to talk about my father, right? Hey did you guys really remember to get married when you went down to meet the ship? Must've been busy with other things, screwing like bunnies down there?"

"Edie! Girl, you do not talk to me like that!" Immediately

softened, swallowed a small laugh, "Thin ice. Sleeping dogs lie and . . . I had another one," said Mama.

"All's well that ends well, shoe fits?" said Edith.

"No, uh, oh! Glass houses, kiddo. But Jesus the gossip you had to put up with when you were little." Alma thought a moment, "And you don't even have a motor on it. And the boat might have a license but you have no such thing."

"Mother, tell me about going out dancing to Whoopee Wilfahrt and his polka orchestra at the Grange Hall."

"Very well then daughter, fun of me all you like you jerk."

All Edith knew about her father was that he came back from the Pacific after the Second World War, left again with her mother pregnant, eventually sent one check for six hundred New Zealand pounds.

"Mama, ah, I don't know why it isn't just a regular story."

"Baby I wish I did have a colorful hidden past for you. Didn't have time. If I have a story, nobody let me in on it. Unbeknownst to me. Ha! Your long-lost father least of all. It's all just . . . oh, all just around here."

Wishing her mother would go ahead and say the things she was obviously recalling, Edith knew to stay silent, on the small chance that that would happen—once in a while it did. No luck this time.

Since his teens, the county judge had worn a leg brace to keep his foot from dangling, an injury the result of wrecking his motorcycle on his postal route. Tapped his cane politely on the door of a log house, the smallest cabin at the resort, an old one hauled in on skids from the woods and set onto a cinder-block-lined cellar built to receive it. He waited, saw the place was in need of jacking up to have a layer of blocks added under it. Basement walls tended to sink into the centuries of pine mulch soil, bedrock fifty or a hundred feet down. Alma came to the door,

"What can I do for you, Richard?"

"Alma, I came out to tell you that you cannot stay here over the winter."

"CCC won't turn loose of my brother 'til March or April, they put him in charge of that highway."

"I know that, Alma, I know you battened down the place for the season, I know your husband came back and then left again, I know you put in cordwood and stocked the pantry and you're all set to caretake 'til your brother gets here or kingdom come. But you have to pack your clothes. I'll wait. I'll give you a lift into town, or out to the farm."

"Richard, that is crazy. I'm staying put."

"Alma, Felix Beck had a load on up at Schatzi's last night, talking about you being here by yourself."

"Oh for heaven sakes, I've been fending off old Felix since I was ten and I am not in the least concerned."

"That's as may be, but it crossed his teeny-tiny mind, and it will have crossed many others as well. Sheriff cannot stand guard, Alma, go pack up and that's that."

Fulminating, she tossed her suitcases and shotgun into

the back seat of the county Packard, sat in the passenger seat leaning against the door, arms folded, snorting, scowling, occasionally baring her teeth. Already knocked up of course, and abandoned, now Mama Alma had even less say in what she could and couldn't do.

A few days before, Felix had shown up as she was trying to get the truck started. Alma was helping out at the farm that late fall day, where they'd put the sides on the stake-bed and loaded on sacks of brewer's yeast and dry molasses, shoveled it brimful of corncobs and oats to take in for grinding. At the feed mill, cables hooked to the front of the truck winched it nearly vertical to dump its load, after which it wouldn't start, had to be pushed out onto the apron. Happened every time.

"What's the good word," said Alma, from under the hood.

Felix said, "I was out the lake to see if you needed help with the boats. Your husband took the car."

"Okay. So?"

Felix said, "He had his things, his duffel bags. The colored man was there, and the little colored girl."

"Say where he was going?"

"Yeah sure as heck did, said he was gone. The colored people went with him. Want me to come stay out there with you, Alma?"

·

Edith said, "Your dad Lin died before you were born and your mother ran off when you were like three?"

"You know all that. And I was two. And she didn't run off."

"I really don't know, Mama. I don't have that."

Alma said, "You've got the big picture." Edith continued to hope her mom would turn loose some stories, however abbreviated. Seeing her daughter beginning to stand,

"No more for me thanks baby," and poured the last three ounces into a little glass with an art nouveau Indian maiden on it. Edith waited. Alma started off reciting her big sister's words and words of others with the lore; remembered things then as if she'd been around to see them,

"Your gramma Josefina gave the resort property back to the bank, stuck them with it, owed so much they didn't even want to loan for seed 'til, jeez the whole county jumped on them. My father'd got killed, my mother was having me, your uncles were way too little even with the, jeez, the whole everybody helping out."

"You were 'on the county'?"

"Yes we were, me oh my and tsk," Mama said, "Seriously it just kills Sister to this day. So your gramma got a job with the post office." Considered, decided on an aspect to emphasize, "Sister was eleven or twelve, your gramma Josefina left her to run the household, cook, keep twenty-six cows, and all the whole rest of it! Sister and her little brothers and a lot of help from the neighbors, Lindgrens ran our farm as well as their own for years, and believe you me it was a stretch for them. God bless 'em, came back and helped again during the war, my brothers away." Mama was bragging on her culture, had a point of pride to make, scolded Edith with comparison.

Edith prompted, "Your mother worked at the post office when you were a baby?"

"She drove! She was quite the deal. Rural Free Delivery—it was new, you didn't have to go into town for the mail, they brought it out to the farm, so the post office was hiring. Progressive. Grange had clout. Postman I remember most was a kid on a motorcycle, that was Richard Pavlicek, he was county judge for a while, died not that long ago now, little sister Julie in the sidecar bringing up the sorted mail out of a big sack just about covered her up, she's down there under it handing up Montgomery Ward catalogs and electric bills and letters from Sweden, and she's stuffing the outgoing mail over her shoulder into another sack and trying to keep it all out of the spokes. Or snow and ice they drove an outlandish thing the post office cobbled together, oversize back wheels, little girl stood on the back platform trying not to fall off and sorting for the mailboxes. Wish I had a picture, that truck looked like somebody'd made a drag racer out of that Columbia mail wagon."

"Bet it went through clutches a lot," said Edith.

"Ja! I bet. Jobs program right there," said Alma, "Chains on, sounded like it was ten of them idling up the road, but . . .

Well but here's the thing—God help you if you got hurt or got sick or something, and with everybody, it was always either boom or bust, but you had a remedy, you could save, save, save and it would tide you over, get you ahead of the game," another comparison with Edith's supposed way of living.

"Only route they had for Gramma that winter, 1921-something . . . I doubt she ever got to vote once in her life . . . anyway it was the Apostle Islands up there and the Red Cliff Reservation. Tribe government's in Red Cliff, or they call it some Chippewa name too, and she had the reservation post office and the little township post offices, but some outlying farms and camps too, and Sand Island. Farms and stores and a school out there then. Assigned Gramma a great big war-surplus Liberty B that'd need a platoon to pass those roads, my lord. She got the postmaster to hire a one-horse pony trap, little open platform, not much of anything but four big giant wheels, or they could rig it with ski runners. Pretty snazzy really. I need to put that box of pictures and stuff into some kind of order or nobody's going to remember her . . . Edie, do you remember that picture? The pony trap was just big enough to carry that pile of mailbags and your grandmother. She got some looks don't you know it."

"There was buried treasure or something, right? And ghosts and all that shit, right?"

"Vulgar, Edie. But yep all of that. Across from Red Cliff there was some coot still tending apple orchards on Basswood, he was left over from the quarry days. Brownstone buildings—it's just as if all of a sudden somebody rung a bell and brownstone went out of style, top-dollar buildings still on the drawing boards. Even under construction. Thirty, forty years of high style and then dumb as dirt one sunny day, and so there's quarry villages, ten-ton cut blocks ready to go, it's all out there to this day. Upshot is, everybody left and this old coot's still out there tending the company truck patch.

"Lake steamers'd buy fish barrels the old guy made, sell him supplies, steel strap and flour mostly I would imagine. Coffee, whiskey. Lamp oil. Never set foot off, guess he planted parsnips and shot birds or I don't know, would've smoked some whitefish, canned some apples, lived like that. Story had it he was paid in gold for fifty years of barrels, stockings full of gold coins and untold banknotes. Nobody found it, or wouldn't admit to it, or it's pure tavern malarkey, how much money can you get for a fish barrel. And oh sure ghosts hither and yon, abandoned real estate all over the place out there, to this day people play cards and gas about . . . that. My own mama was a ghost story all while I was growing up and I didn't like that one little bit. Anyhow the old man's smoke was gone one day and your gramma was the last to see him. All winter long the sheriff up there kept hauling her in giving her the third degree. Didn't have much else to do, and she was a good-looking widow."

•

Woolgathering, gazing into space, inattention to the job at hand, wasn't something to be caught at among Edith's mama's people. On the other hand, it's not a bad thing if someone poked fun that they could see the wheels turning in there— meaning it was obvious your focus was on the mind's eye— because you were still almost certainly attending to business and had a handle on things. A task that looked dreary, repetitive, rote to an outsider wasn't so to these folks. Much that was routine on those farms was dangerous as well, or costly should attention drift too far; a divided mind was just fine, woolgathering wasn't. Get it done, no screwups, no injuries.

Make an expensive but honest mistake with the grain auger, everyone's just glad you didn't get pulled into the thing; observed slack and dreamy though, presence of mind out the window, there is a little shame in that.

Alma missed her mother, at an age when almost everything that gets the attention gets the whole attention. Hard to say what goes on in a toddler's awareness, but any daydreams in there would've taken her whole attention, and been about her mother. A little later on, girl-child Alma was pretty often called back to presence with a touch or a soft word or two, and occasionally with a jerk of the arm and a sharp "Alma!" from a teacher. Daydreaming was the kid's secret vice as she got a little older and cultivated subterfuge, her cherished brain fog present but kept turned down most of the time, only allowed to take her over when the coast was clear. Alma's child Edith never had an inkling of the invisible life her no-nonsense mom indulged.

By her teens in the middle of the economically devastated 1930s, Alma had constructed her mother completely, an intricate and lyrical piece of work, a woman with faults and virtues, built over the latticework of others' memory and supposition; the girl loved her mom, the recreated person Josefina.

A summer day, having walked into a neighbor's hay barn, Alma glimpsed the neighbor lady bent over hip-high field bales and being bounced against them by the International Harvester man, his trousers around his ankles. Ducking out quick and not wanting to deal with such fraught stuff at all, fourteen-year-old Alma imagined instead Josefina's postal route, a favorite place to go daydreaming. Dove right in, saw and heard the story as she made it up.

After three weeks on, Josefina would have five days off—just needed to complete this run before taking the train home to see her kids, check on the farm. She'd driven her route all the way across the peninsula, traded bags with the Sand Island postal clerk who'd come across the ice to meet her, and Josefina figured there'd be enough daylight to get rid of this letter to "Albert, Basswood Island, Ashland County, Wisconsin." The return address was New York City. Pulling up at Red Cliff, she asked the postmaster for directions to "Albert, Basswood Island," and he said,

"Missus, Albert ain't expecting anything more than another termination notice. Leave it for another run, you done your route and you can get the heck home—or give me the letter, I'll walk it out to him in a couple days. And missus, you might ought to go on back pretty soon, some weather coming in for sure."

Josefina considered. Coal and wood smoke from a few hundred cast-iron stoves stung the eyes, tasted bad.

"Missus, look at that sky. Not even done getting lower. We had mares' tails this morning and this come in from the wrong direction this afternoon—still as death right now, smoke don't rise. Lake froze in an onshore gale, so rough it's a real hard walk. Give me the letter, missus, blizzard bury you over before you know it."

Josefina said, "Thank you sir, I do appreciate your kind concern, but I believe it will be alright. If you could stable my horse for the rest of the afternoon, though, just in case?" The middle-aged reservation postmaster may have been thinking "jackass Swede," but only sighed his even-tempered exasperation,

"Take your oilcloth and your tarp both. You will want to stand on top of the ice swells to look around but don't do it, lightning strike you dead. When the storm hits and you can't see your backtracks no more, kick out snow as far down as you can, wrap up, don't you wait to hunker down and curl up low, and keep an air hole open in the snow. You going to get real cold. If it lets up tomorrow and you see the cliffs, come on in, but don't you try to get back in the blizzard. You just hope it lets up tomorrow, we can't come looking for you 'til it lets up." Raised a forefinger to his eyebrow, dismissing her, "Ma'am."

A day later, the postmaster said, "Pulling my leg now, missus."

"What? No sir. How do you mean?" Josefina said. She'd thawed on her walk back, but hadn't begun to recover from shivering violently through the evening, night, and morning, the duration of the storm. Further exhausted by snowshoeing two or three miles on fresh snow over rough ice and then uphill into town, she'd eaten pea soup and wild rice, a little smoked whitefish, and the Chippewa fry bread so like the pannebröd of her childhood. The afternoon was blinding white.

"*Sounds like a ghost story you heard someplace,*" he said. *She shook her head. He said, "Okay, it's just his nose and eyes you can see for all the white hair, right, that's Albert.*"

"*Yes sir, very accomplished on the pump organ.*"

The man nodded, "Two sisters and another man and a child?"

"*Yes,*" she said, "*The ladies were quite musical as well.*" *Snow-blind, she couldn't see his ever-composed face, or that he found something funny.*

He said, "Ergot poisoning out there a long time ago. People kind of went crazy. Sounds like Albert, he'd keep company with ghosts." Standing, "See you next time now missus."

Turning to go, she bumped into a chair, then another. Asked, "Sir, is there some way Albert could've known my name?"

The postmaster, mildly surprised, thought for a couple of seconds, "I don't know of any. Can't help you there. Here's my arm missus, take you to your rig."

•

At the kitchen table, same one in the same spot since her grandparents had put it there,

"What did happen to Gramma?"

Yawning, Mama answered, "Edie you heard it two dozen times."

"Most unsatisfactory family lore I ever can imagine. Needs a lot of embellishment for a campfire tale," said Edith, "C'mon Mom tell us a story."

"'Night sweetie, tomorrow is another day."

"Mama? Don't know when I'll be back."

After a minute Alma said, "She kind of went crazy I think. Selfish is the only way Sister could understand it but I know that's not right. Post office laid her off in the spring, gave her route back to the man that quit for the winter. I know what she was like, I know those people. Bear the burdens 'til the second coming of Christ, she was doing her duty. Stuffing got kicked out of her, husband killed and all of it. Must've thought poorly of herself like we'll do, homesick to death, by the letters she kept. I can imagine her losing her marbles and not missing 'em one little bit but still doing her duty first second and third. Your grandma spent time away when we needed her and money we didn't have getting up there to poke around those islands. I do not know why. Doing what she was supposed to do, whatever that was in her mind. She'd come back emaciated. Dark as an Indian. Running over to her when she came in, that's all I can remember about her, remember how it . . . felt. See myself doing it, but I think it's a real memory. And she wouldn't ever tell anybody where she'd been and I do think it's because she had no idea. One time she didn't come back. 'Night sweetie, tomorrow is another day.'"

•

On the mud porch, about to go shovel shit in the milking parlor, Edith stopped short and stepped back into the kitchen doorway; before, she'd have gone out to investigate the car now driving up, decided not to this time.

Helping out as a matter of course, her barn chores this morning included shoveling out the gutters into an enormous wheelbarrow hung from an overhead rail, to be taken out to the manure spreaders; the rig might decide to tip and dump itself without warning, require more shoveling were she not adept at wrestling the thing. Hosing down, cleaning the raw-milk-filled tubing and pumps and pipes and tanks, moving the herd out and the rest of it, she and her mother would be in and around the barn for a good part of the day before bringing the cows back in. Then evening milking and a lot of other duties attendant on the farm's livelihood, a delicate, highly perishable, and easily contaminated food produced intimately among enormous hay-digesting creatures walking around hoof-deep in each other's waste.

In the last few months, Mama'd had to do some fieldwork as well as the barn for days at a time by herself—help was scarce at homecoming then Christmas then prom, complicated by the assimilation of the local high schools into a newly consolidated two-county district. She was keeping a smaller herd that fall, winding down the operation, no calves in the calf pens—still, there was enough condensation that morning from the breath of seventeen three-quarter-ton mammals to trickle down the cinder-block walls in a brown sweat. Carrying around two sets of pulse-milkers in the dim, chilly, humid barn, scrupulously cleaning udders and teatcup liners as she went, Alma adjusted hissing, rhythmically chugging, obsolete equipment, gave each teat a preliminary squirt to check for problems, ran the bone of contentment down the knobby, ribbed hides. An ancient practice in small dairies, gently tapping or stroking the cows with a reassuring stick to move them along their routine. The bone served that purpose here—it was a miraculously surviving artifact of her father's cellar-digging in the extraordinarily deep soil, excavated along with two arrow points and a knapped flint core, a native-copper fishhook, a cache of drilled iridescent discs of shell traded from a thousand miles away. And an elaborate pictogram barely discernible on still-supple hide as thin as parchment, well preserved with something waxy, as was the bone of contentment that had been wrapped in it.

.

Baby moon hubcaps and some kind of official license plates, a new beige Ford Custom had driven into the yard, three men in suits climbed out, and Edith thought it better she stay inside for the time being.

Mama peered around the back of a cow at the men.

"Wisconsin Food Code, ma'am, give us a minute?" Done on that animal, she stood,

"Three of you? You guys look ridiculous, since when you guys wear sunglasses inside a barn?" One, taking off his sunglasses, said,

"Ma'am you took a forty-day extension back on August twenty-fourth. Mind if we see your paperwork?"

"Let me see *your* paperwork," she said. The man reached into his suit jacket—what the hell is this, even the sheriff didn't ordinarily go armed. Light was poor, the miniature nickeled badge bore an unfamiliar emblem, the ID card was difficult to decipher through a transparent gray departmental seal in the lamination. "Who are you?"

"D of A helps out on request. Overflow. Routine," the man flipped closed his badge wallet.

"Wait here," she said. "You wait here," she repeated over

her shoulder as they followed her to the house. Watched her get out of galoshes on the mud porch and go inside. A few minutes later Mama came out with a handful of envelopes; a minute after that, two of the men came from around opposite sides of the house, went to the car, the conspicuously innocuous car. Handing the papers back, the first man said,

"Okay, looks in order, ma'am."

"Wait a second, give me your card," Mama said.

Alma went inside scowling, ignored Edith's questions, stalked to the phone. Shooed away the teenage neighbor on the party line, called the county dairy inspection office, then the state agricultural extension, who hadn't heard of the branch named on the card, or of the feds doing anything of the sort.

"Call the number," Edith said.

"I am not paying for a trunk call just to get some run-around," said her mother.

Edith took the receiver, dialed zero, "Long distance please."

"What city please?"

"Station to station, please, Stoughton, Wisconsin, TR3-6523."

"Area code 608, connecting."

Faint machine-gun stutter from the rural punch-card switching equipment, then nothing, no ring or busy signal, just the hollow sound of a completed connection with no one speaking.

"Ma'am the call did go through," said the operator.

Each wondering what had warranted such open intimidation, Edith and her mother went out to the barn, concerned that a cow may have suffered injury from the unattended machine attached to her.

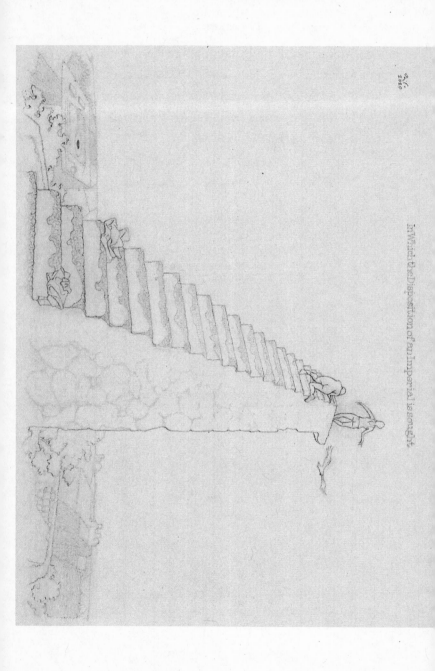

In Which the Disposition of an Imperial is sought.

story three

Shelda • a fable involving a well

Echoing, distorted drumming noise from way down in the hole, rhythmic pulses from fire hoses sloshing downslope, men shouted to each other over the noise of an enormous diesel generator and over the short grunts and extended revs of a four-axle truck crane, boom angled out over the stories-deep shaft, reeling something up. A big upside-down sedan from the 1960s trailing watery silt dangled, swaying over to the pile of tires and other debris that had been dumped in over the decades. Repositioning the grapple, the crane operator dragged the car right side up onto the prairie, a couple of sharp groans coming from the wreck. A crewman looked over his shoulder at old Boorham, the superintendent on this job. Who shouted, "Oh hell yeah. Bound to be the Brinks Robbery, Jimmy Hoffa." Motioned prying open the trunk.

With a stink like something sold to gardeners, the contents of the trunk were hard to decipher at first, jostled and covered as they were with the mud of flesh and clothing, but yeah, that had been a big guy, judging by that shoe. Boorham pulled out the satphone the company had issued him— didn't store numbers or other avoidable vulnerabilities— began keying. Told the guys to put a tire on the trunk lid.

The phone made dramatic noises and haptic buzzes in his hand, white-on-red *tornadoes on the ground take shelter now* blinked one second off, one second on, began scrolling *seventy miles either side of a line Salina-McPherson moving eastward 20 mph*. He looked at the sky; yeah right. Spoke to his boss in Wichita.

Two strong huffs of wind, sky still looked okay. Hail hit him like hurled sacks of ice, made it hard to help up the crane operator, who'd been knocked sprawling off the bottom step as she climbed down; ice shattering on his hard hat, followed the rest running for the tunnel leading down to the mossy launch crew bunker. They stood, wet and beat-up, against the walls of the echoing corridor as the noon sky went dark. Strong gust, pause. Wind shuddered loudly across the entrance, drawing out a breeze from behind them.

"Anybody got a flashlight, my phone's got no light," Boorham asked, doing a head count; no reason anyone should. Two lights came on. "Okay, this could be a shitload worse. EF5, we just walk down the hall, head downstairs. Save your battery."

Someone answered, "EF5, bruv, they're running three-fifty mile an hour, mile fucking wide per each. Hunt in packs."

"Hey, maybe it's just paid downtime 'til we get new gear," Boorham said, "Just wish to God." Sudden vacuum hurt their ears, physically made the eight of them exhale. Wind blew out of the lightless corridor behind.

Someone else said, "Best case, we end up on cots in a lunchroom someplace."

"Yeah. Hope they come out for us sooner rather than later," said Boorham.

Noise suddenly abating, one after another of them trailed up to the entrance. Saw a vast white column as wide as it was high. At the base, a dark approaching avalanche of atomized prairie, the column merging at the indefinite top with the green-black overcast, where streamers of cloud were drawn to the thing, whipped into it. Descending gracefully in the intervening distance, a berserkly churning cloud briefly obscured the more distant monster before walls of horizontal rain abruptly blocked the entire spectacle and the crew retreated, hands over their ears, into their deafening cave.

•

In the yore that Boorham thought of as home, there remained people who hadn't outlived it. Women, or girls, of great importance to him, the more important for their having never left his home, who'd never lived anywhere else, never become others.

All the usual after-school things with friends, girls' varsity sports, and a two- or three-day-a-week job as gofer in an architect's office kept Shelda out until evening daily, and she took as many overnights as could be gotten away with—nothing really wrong with home, she just didn't like to be there. Started showing up at her aunt and uncle's place, her mom's kin, sometimes slept on the foldout. They were fond of the girl, the aunt's namesake; those equable, dutiful people were glad to have her in the house, just a matter of keeping tabs on her and their adolescent son, Boorham.

Shelda's mother'd had a wartime job with the Air Corps repainting standard instrument dials with glow-in-the-dark radium numerals, and bone cancer had gotten her a couple of years before. The mother's people calmly accepted the girl among their own, as a matter of course passing along a formidable range of kitchen and garage skills. Proper fried chicken, proper carburetor rebuild.

Not unusual in Texas, they were descendants of Ozark aristocracy, inheritors of Scots-Irish virtue, resolute and loyal and proudly self-reliant. Through a pronounced cultural quirk of holding multiple mutually exclusive views, they were hospitable, insular, tolerant, and suspicious. Welcomed "progress," kept the grievances of their grandparents alive. Weren't out of place in insecurely cosmopolitan Texas in that they read about the world in two daily newspapers and the *Saturday Evening Post, Life* magazine, and *National Geographic*, while making their home in a very Southern city, in its bones chary of intrusion. Collected oddities were on every shelf and sideboard, a book of *New Yorker* cartoons on the coffee table in the living room.

Knowing better, Shelda's people almost reluctantly reinforced her difficulty in reassessing a position once taken—"Don't back down, Shel"—a real disability sometimes. The girl readily learned from mistakes, but it had to be her own call to make. Her mom's kinfolk reinforced in her as well the immemorial pride of being proud, the mulish stubbornness Shelda'd received with her mother's milk. Very bright, headstrong kid drove her dad and her young stepmother crazy; kind of a relief that she wasn't around much.

Had she not been so recognizable on TV, her father wouldn't have objected to her going to the desegregation sitins. The classier department stores had years ago replaced brown, "Colored Only" water fountains with standard ones, and attitudes weren't so uniform or dogmatic anymore, though the old signs were still up on most of the walls they'd ever been on, brown or black porcelain fixtures still in place in their own cramped areas needing no printed signs. Signs labeled separate and unequal places, sometimes even what lines you could wait in at municipal, county, state buildings, officially enforced there and privately elsewhere. Shelda as a little white kid might wander to the back window of a bus to join little Black kids looking at the street's phenomenal rushing away, and have a colored lady gently direct her forward again. Those polite Negroes she marched with were unlikely to go running around setting fires like they did up in New York and out in Los Angeles, but Shelda was a favorite of the local news cameramen—mingled races and organized civil disobedience, a new form of teenage scandalous behavior, embarrassed her father and got her a reputation at high school. Rumors of other wild-child stuff were invented, and her friends began to keep a distance.

Boorham was a grade behind her, remained predictably steadfast, pretty much a big male version of her, maybe not quite as bright; stayed away from the picketing though, had teammates to deal with. Sociable kid with diminishing opportunities to socialize as the school year went on, Shelda had the idea to make a jewelry chain out of heavy copper wire—in the era, labor-intensive adornment made of humble materials was fashionable. It was Boorham's idea to wrap the wire around a piece of rod to form a coil. She refined things by sawing off links rather than clipping with pliers, so leaving a tight joint. After it got to be a foot long, they worked at opposite ends of the chain, sitting hip to hip, first cousins unknowingly engaged as their ancient ancestors would approve. They handed off tools, scraped burrs, bent the links closed, rarely handled each other, aware that that'd be ungovernable once underway. Repeatedly at first made an irremediable glop out of hours of work, teaching each other to silver braze so precisely. It got steamy in the garage workshop over the course of a few winter evenings, enthralling, a robust mix of fumes and pheromones. Boorham, a very long time later, figured he'd imprinted on his cousin, like a hatchling imprints on an irreplaceable other—he liked women a lot, a fundamental and not entirely sexual thing. Despite and because of close proximity, and with intermittent parental interruptions, they eventually came up with over a yard of chain, 170-odd stout little links, neatly joined into a loop that hung well past Shelda's navel. Something to be proud of. Proper swain, Boorham relinquished his share in it.

Abruptly leaving toward the end of that school year, against intense objections of family she went with a group out of state to register voters. With good instincts for whom to stay away from, robbed but never otherwise molested, Shelda still did have a creditable résumé: concussion, sprains, third-degree abrasion from being "dispersed" tumbling up the asphalt on one occasion. Slight, fair, freckled child, the bruises were glorious. The counties were proud entities, a highly efficient stage of social organization, more chiefdom than state. They preferred not to ask the state for tear gas or a lot of troopers, relied for social order on simple tradition reinforced as needs be by indigenous assets like the Klan. Troopers came anyway, and it was the state that eventually turned her loose with a fine, into her folks' custody. Idealistic, Shelda may have been the least so of the half-dozen mostly Black, middle-class, underage volunteers she went there with. It'd been an opportunity to leave home for some unchildish reason, a matter of self-respect. The experience was deeply memorable, not transformative. Civil rights wasn't her calling.

In what would've been her senior year, Shelda wrangled a spot in a program up in Kansas at a progressive little college, where her course of study involved a slew of disciplines: archaeology, sociology, history, geology, statistical analysis, and others. In that end of academia, the works, emphasis depending on the instructor. In a couple of classes with her, an achiever named Gail hoped to have some college credits when she graduated high school.

The spring semester was over and Gail was staying put, enrolled in summer classes. Shelda's dad was leaving increasingly angry messages with the college, demanding she come home. Mil was at the basement window, there under the front steps, looking out at her—she put a finger to her lips and he made a similar gesture—Mil was quick. He lived in the basement apartment with his haggard wife and two infants, was supposed to collect the other tenants' rent, had let Shelda slide for half a month now. She was hiding under there because a man in a suit and another one in a polo shirt were ringing the doorbell; she assumed they were there to take her back to Texas. Mil went out and dismissed them. Under the porch, she scrubbed her chain between her palms.

Gail said, "No phone listed in their name up in Russell, but they'll be fine with it. Mow the place. Swim in the reservoir. Get your shit together."

"Oh man, you came through!" said Shelda, "Already

gave my sheets and stuff to Mil," picking up an Army-Navy store canvas pack, "Outstanding! What's the address?"

"No idea. Going with," said Gail.

Their first ride got them halfway there in an hour and a half, let them out at the northbound gas station. Being choosy about their rides hadn't been a problem; ninety-five pounds apiece, those kids got lots of offers. In a newish Chrysler Imperial, pressed shirts on hangers behind his left shoulder, Caesar haircut, maybe late thirties, a good bet for a ride—they took in the daddy-man car, the Franklin Junior High Lady Falcons sticker, trotted up to talk to him. After they spoke briefly, the driver heaved an apparently very heavy two-foot-long cylinder off the seat and onto the floorboard, leaned over, and pushed open the passenger door. Gail got in; Shelda, having hesitated until the other two turned to look at her, slowly climbed in the back.

•

Now and again Shelda had some version of the same dream. In a concrete maze of broad tunnels and house-sized rooms barely lit by occasional slits to the outside, a girl's wildly echoed shouting, protesting something being done to her, became frantic. No direction to the unintelligible screaming, just everywhere. Sudden terror of the dark, of not knowing the way out. It was a barely embellished memory, in fact, of a nighttime experience in the abandoned shore batteries at Galveston.

Lying in the weeds near the tunnel entrance of an underground bunker, Gail dreamed of anthropology lab: a druid-age bog mummy with the usual garrote around his neck, raising one eyelid on a moist white eyeball. Grayscale dream, but a jewel-like amber, green, and blue iris slid across the partly open eye, pupil stopping to look at her. In the dream, she tried to shout; the effort and sound woke her. Sat up. Immediately regretted vocalizing into the moonless, nearly complete darkness.

Whispered, "We killed somebody?"

"You didn't kill anybody," Shelda hugged her, cupped the bruised back of Gail's head, nuzzled her cheek.

"Should've just let him," Gail said.

Shelda murmured, "Huh-uh! Baby, not in a million years, don't you even."

In a little, with a squeeze and a pat, both lay back down.

After some length of time, Gail said, "Bet that's east."

Waking, Shelda said, "Or . . . yeah, ain't going to be a city. Rise and shine. Watch your step. Jesus I'm thirsty."

Shelda pointed a flashlight down the giant well. Gail crawled alongside, took a quick look down, backed away. Many stories below, the surface of the water was unbroken. Nothing to be done about the short skid marks on the concrete beside her, but there were a lot of other forklift and heavy equipment tracks around.

•

Closing the trunk, panting from exertion, one or the other of them said, "Okay, then we take the car most of the way out to the highway. Walk out and hitch. No. Shit that's stupid. Car's a cop magnet. This is horrible."

The other said, "People at the gas station saw us going up to him."

Neither woman had bothered to say that they would be jailed for murder. Runaway chicks lured the respectable guy, it turned fatal, they freaked out and ran. Some such construct. His bereaved family. Nope.

"He doesn't make his appointment or get home or whatever, the cops do 197. Serious, serious hairy eyeball."

"Okay, we take the car up to US 40. Back roads. Not really that far north. Maybe. I think. Forty goes all the way to San Francisco."

"Gail? The car. The trunk."

"Shelda, God damn it! I can't stop shaking! I don't know! Why'd he do that! Oh God. I smell his cologne on my hands!"

"Sorry, sorry," said Shelda. Then, "I want to go on up to Russell."

After a while one of them said, "Where do you hide a Continental on the prairie anyway?"

"Imperial," the other said.

A couple of hours later, lucky enough to've encountered no one as they drove up the narrow hogback lane, "Pretty sure I know where we are. USGS map called it Rec Site Ruin, always wondered what the fuck's that," said Gail.

Scouting places that might possibly conceal an enormous car, they'd bounced down an overgrown, buckling, unmarked concrete boulevard wider than the two-lane they'd turned onto it from. First caught sight of a fallen down truss-work structure that must've been a small Ferris wheel, then saw a number of solid ramps and towers rising out of a blotchy pond, saltwater grasses in patches at the margins. Seagulls in the middle of Kansas. A weasel sitting up on its haunches looking back at them. The durable ruin, constructed of big chunks of stone rubble and concrete, the lower parts fractured, pieces falling away from heavily corroded rebar, was as much damaged by decades of vandalism as by deterioration. Rec Site Ruin covered less than two acres, encircled by a wavy, collapsing wall that still had remnants of little train rails on it and a couple of sizable rock buildings built into it that extended outside, galvanized roofs partly intact. Stunted volunteer trees did badly in the salty soil, graffiti everywhere, rust everywhere.

"Roadside attraction? Out here."

"The fuck road anyway," Gail said, pointing, "That one has a door big enough."

"I don't really see how we can drive it over there," answered Shelda after a minute.

"Building's packed with junk anyway, take forever," said Gail.

Shelda said, "Going to look around."

Wading through tall grass in thigh-deep water, Shelda

lost a sneaker in the muck on the bottom. Pulled her tied-up shirt overhead, and making sure the car key was secure in the buttoned pocket, handed the shirt to Gail to hold along with their folded-up jeans. Shelda futilely tried to brush aside floating mats of yellow algae, bent into the water, leaned on Gail putting on the shoe. Led up thirty feet of steep, damaged rubble. Concrete steps, some steps entirely missing, the railings just rusted-out sockets or broken away. Gail was scared to death of heights, kept her eyes straight in front of her. Before the top of the suicidal high dive, she laid aside the armful of their clothes, went the rest of the way on all fours. Stood behind her friend, gripping Shelda's upper arms, looking over Shelda's shoulder. They turned around surveying, two small women wearing only farmer's tans and tennis shoes on the massive plinth in the afternoon sun, trying to figure out what in the world to do next.

"That," Gail said, pointing from over her friend's shoulder at a big rectangle of concrete laid into the farmland, "Atlas silo."

"What?"

"Missile installation," said Gail.

Shelda said, "Okay. So?"

"Maybe there's a storage building or something, those flat things sticking up," Gail said, "subterranean garage or—hell I don't know. Wishful thinking."

Shelda said, "Gail wait a minute wait a minute—a guided missile base."

"Took them all away a year ago. Finished up a year ago, I mean. They took away that kind of missile. Fences and all, looks like. It's reverted back to the local school district or God knows, somebody like that, nobody. Derelict as shit."

"Where'd you get all that?" asked Shelda.

"My mom's a peacenik and Daddy works for Lockheed Martin," said Gail, on knees and elbows, head down, hair hanging, "This isn't getting any better."

Shelda turned around, said, "What's not getting better?"

"Don't know how I'm going to get down," said Gail.

·

At the end of the littered corridor, Shelda's flashlight showed a safe-like door to either side and one in the end wall. "Three doors. Huh. Fairy tale, all the ingredients. Us, we're a fairy-tale ingredient," said Gail.

Standing open, lock mechanisms welded and non-functional, any door was heavier than the two of them could move. The flashlight showing them an empty passageway on one side, bottomless stairwell on the other, they squeezed past the middle door. Shone the dimming light around littered battleship linoleum, pale-green brut concrete walls. The tunnel had looked promising, maybe seven feet wide, but there was the claustrophobic likelihood of being unable to get out of the car. Already some graffiti around, including multiple palm-sized black wreath-shaped stencils. They'd seen others of them at the water park.

Shelda tapped the flashlight against her palm, it obediently brightened a little, showed masonry nails driven into the walls. Three or four colors of yarn stretched among them formed a three-dimensional web in the air. The place was way too well visited anyway.

"Striking out," Gail said, "Guess we could look at the silo thing."

Cloudless, not quite sunset, no haze at all, buzzards far up there heading to roost. A shape-shifting black something of indeterminate size and distance tumbled across the sky, sometimes appearing symmetrical, other times not, a sheet of plastic maybe, alien spaceship, prankster hobgoblin. On hands and knees, looking over the rim of the fifty-foot-wide shaft, Shelda tried to see the bottom, lay down, face over the edge. Smelled kerosene. Water down there reflected the sky.

Giant lift machinery and stuff that Gail said would be there was gone; there were tunnel openings, and ladder rungs set into a channel. Graffiti around the rim and along the ladder: hearts with initials, school team names, and the wreaths, cave-painting instinct enabled by spray cans. Shelda zoned out a little, staring into the cavern—the thing was a monster, a straight concrete tube eighteen stories straight down, the water table finding its way in, pooled to an unknown depth. She sat up, looked around again. Blast doors had been retracted; no equipment remnants, nothing remained in place, just a great big hole in a circle of sawhorse-like, red-and-white-striped wooden traffic barricades.

From the low retaining walls on the upslope side, Gail said, "How's it look?"

"Just. I don't know, man. Messes your mind," Shelda said after a pause.

"So yes?" said Gail.

No debris to jam the pedal with, no beer cans evident in the gloom. Gail hesitated, opened the trunk, looked away, got a tasseled loafer, slammed the lid. The Chrysler drove over the retaining wall, hit hard on the concrete, shooting sparks, wrecked its suspension, veered. The machine accelerated, dropped a front wheel over the edge, was guided around the rim of the pit, briefly stuck, laid a foot-long patch of rubber until a rear wheel went over and spun like mad. The big car hung there over the echoing column of air, roaring, just long enough for Gail to begin to turn a palm up, begin a shrug. Shelda had time to begin to wonder how to get at the bumper jack in the trunk. But a little torque did make it to the other back wheel, enough to stutter the car forward a few inches, just enough to lean heavily over into the abyss, roaring engine falling in pitch for its full count of three-second drop down the reverberating hole.

"Well that was . . . quick," Shelda called over her shoulder.

•

"It's men, just axiom." In the dorm room, Gail had uncapped another eight-ounce, taken a sip, passed it to her roommate, continued, "His brain stem's jammed into his brain, pokin' away. I mean how do you deal with that, the guy is trying to steer, leading him a chase. He's a sweetie, gets along with just everybody, but he's hanging on for dear life trying to steer. Chimps! They're chimps. I mean you fuck him, you take care of his head, and, like, he's—just assumes, well, of course, naturally. Like I owe him. Whole goddamn no goddamn fair!"

The roommate, two years older, said, "Gail, you're sixteen."

"So?"

"Un-grow up wouldja? Ook-ook. Mammals I swear to God," said the roommate. She sat down facing Gail on the floor, passed the half-empty Boone's Farm back to her.

"They could kill us," Gail said. Suddenly standing, catching her balance, "Throwing up!"

•

The driver had exited the US highway onto a state two-lane, one of the diagonal roads.

"Whoa whoa where you going," Gail said.

The driver said, "Russell's forty-five minutes, get there

by two latest. Want to show you something up here, you'll love it."

Several minutes later, Shelda said from the back seat, "Bob, get back on 197. That or stop and let us out. Now."

"Hey hey, kay-passa baby, rules of the road," the driver said, turning onto a yet smaller roadway marked by an enamel sign unreadable for all the bullet holes, keeping up a good rate of speed. Slowed beside a pretty creek.

"Look man," said Gail, reaching for the door handle. Shelda let go of her back door handle. Had an odd little smile.

"Oh now, be sweet, you're used to this, I'm being sweet," the driver said congenially to Gail, reaching as if to gather her in to snuggle. Halfway out the door when he managed to grab her arm, "No!" she squeaked; his voice deeper and coarser than it had been, still congenial, "Oh be sweet, you are being such a fussbudget this morning! Careful, careful! You're going to wrench your arm, sweetheart," he said, dragging her in, scrubbing her breast with a hand thicker than the breast. She pushed at his face trying to kiss her mouth,

"Get real you asshole!" Then, "Get out of my clothes!"

He outweighed her by a hundred pounds. Pulled Gail against him, slapped hell out of the back of her head a few times. Gail became uncoordinated. Reaching for the shift lever with his left hand, the driver brushed at something on his cheek, inadvertently dropping it below his chin.

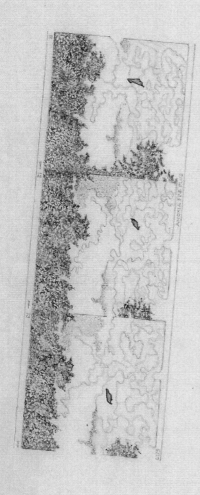

In Which drifts a Sheet of Plastic or something

Shelda was seventeen. It was no trouble at all planting her feet behind the driver's ears. At first clawing at the stout little chain, kicking, heaving his back against the seat, he had quit struggling in seconds. Thinking he was faking, would at any time turn on her, she eased up gradually. Rattling catlike noises lasted another few seconds. The car had drifted off the road. Gail, dazed, managed to stomp on the brake. She jammed the shifter into park, shook her head trying to make her eyesight stay still.

"Jesus Christ," she said. "I . . . No way it's that easy."

·

The twelve-foot moldboard rotated out horizontally, waggled to and fro, lifted one side at a time as the massive front wheels tilted left and right. The blade pitched way down and back up, raised and lowered a couple of times, did all that in jerky hydraulic gyrations, came back to its original travel position. He cut the engine.

"We drank out of one of those tall hydrants, we going to die?"

Startled, he took his foot out of the opened windshield of the road grader, "Hi ma'am, didn't see you. No you ought to be fine right along in here. Sure get your minerals." Young guy in a green work uniform folded his copy of *Mad* around a sandwich, stuffed it with the rest of his lunch into a domed lunch box. "You ladies way out here."

"Yeah, bad boyfriend," said Shelda. "Got pissy and kicked us out."

"That was wrong," he said, and seemed at a loss for words. Leaned way down, put out his hand, and introduced himself.

"Alice," said Shelda—the Allis-Chalmers decal.

"Dorothy," said Gail, "Pleased to meet you." *Mad* magazine, thought Gail, pretty racy for a Mennonite; said, "No, man, finish your lunch, it's only us."

"Oh no, thanks, I'm done," he said. Looked at them expectantly, "Been walking long? You're nowhere."

Gail said, "Just this morning. Camped rough."

Pointing at the machine, Shelda said, "Certifiably cool what you just did."

He adopted a pose, finger in the air, "Every valley shall be filled and every mountain and hill shall be brought low and the crooked shall be made straight and the rough ways shall be made smooth." His expression fell, "Wow, I . . . no. Real wrong to go and kid with that." Resuming his good cheer, "I'm headed back in. Want a ride?"

Hanging in the doors on either side of the operator's seat and its myriad hip-high levers, they shouted to be heard over the engine noise behind them. He was telling Moby Grape jokes, best they could tell. Waited for the longer pause and laughed.

Shelda pulled a souvenir ring with a heart-shaped pink coral off of her little finger, leaned in, said, "Trade ya," indicating the lunch box.

"No ma'am, sorry, should have offered, you got to be

hungry," handing her the black wrinkle-finish box. It looked many years old. "Hope you don't mind eating after me. Tea in the thermos."

Accepting it, Shelda said, "I have to thank your wife for lunch. Please."

The man said, over the engine, "Be not forgetful to entertain strangers for thereby some have entertained angels."

Entirely unaccustomed to choking up, Shelda said stubbornly, "I pay my way. Got to be a verse."

After a moment, the man held out his hand for the chintzy ring. Looked at it, read, "'Galveston Island, Texas.' Never been. Thank you ma'am. For sure she will love it."

Gail, the vegetarian, got the half-banana and most of a wax-papered bundle of pretzels.

The road grader backing away from them, its moldboard performing the half-ton equivalent of a goodbye wave, Gail said to Shelda, "You should not have given him that ring."

Shelda didn't answer. A big front-end loader rolled past others parked in a neat row, dumped and tapped out the last of its four bucketfuls into a truck. No hurry. Everybody took a smoke.

"Hey guys," said Gail. They all straightened up.

"Well hi," said one.

Gail declined a cigarette. Shelda accepted one, said, "What-all you guys do out here—I'm taking mental notes."

A short round man said, "Road sand, miss. Salt and ready to go."

"So where's it go from here?"

"Okay, this time of year they're staging the dumps for winter. All over. County gets beaucoup for it, especially if we use our own trucks."

Shelda said, "Y'all work in winter too?"

"Yes ma'am. Busy time."

Shelda said, "Wow. I cannot imagine. You guys right here keep all the roads drivable."

He said, "Well, best we can. Lots of them, yes we do. Look ma'am, what's up?"

She got to the point. "Do you supply Russell?"

"Yes ma'am, Russell County."

"Staging up there now?"

"Could, yes."

"We'd like a ride."

"Oh! I see. Little slow. Up to him, miss," indicating the feet in the dump truck's window, called, "Hey! Perry!"

Gail got out at US 40, went home to San Francisco.

•

Outside the bunker, he used the satphone to check the weather. Some more coming, looked like. A few hundred yards from where he'd parked it, old Boorham's wadded-up Ram crew cab had no glass; bodywork missing or caved in, blasted thoroughly with wet sand, had rolled, bounced airborne, happened to come to rest on its wheels. Boorham instead walked

102

over to the cleaned carcass of a vintage Chrysler hunkering on what was left of the prairie grass, its rear end crammed under the wheels-up potable water semitrailer.

Hood and trunk lid gone, and two out of four doors, what remained had been pretty well stripped to the bare metal. Hoped he'd get around to checking out an odd stainless-steel cylinder on the floor where the seats used to be. Water still draining from around them, stirred and disassociated, the bones had been hosed down, but many were still in there, the deep trunk offering a container for them to be bounced around in. Tangled with some vertebrae was a slender, round-linked chain, long for a necklace. Boorham fished it out, scrubbed it between his palms. Tumbled to a coarse polish as were the human bones, it was copper, a hefty little thing.

Taking inventory with his rigger and with the crane operator, Boorham noticed first that the office and bunk trailers were simply gone. Then that the site had not after all taken a direct hit. The flatbed semitrailer had been flipped end for end into a drainage channel, upside down but intact, yellow tie-downs hanging off into the water, load of site-specific engineered steel forms no longer around. The crane truck did look promising. Though one side's outrigger pads were skidded off of the concrete apron, the thing was upright.

The crane operator, left arm in a sling made of one of the guys' shirts, climbed up for a look at her machine, kept shaking her head. Came back down, indicated a huge adjacent piece of wreckage with her boot, reported, "Bottom hydraulic pump and line got killed, no fluid, outboard control panel trashed. Truck might start, I don't know. Sand in everything. There's a manual cab-over, off chance there's something to do under there. God knows if it's got brakes. The orange peel is down slack where we can uncouple it, duh, but the goddamn boom pointed way around the side like that—shit. Surprised if the gearmotors work. Sand in everything and, like I say, no hydraulic. Tools and fluid were on the flatbed. Crane might start, winch might work, perfect fucking hog to haul around straight if they don't. At a glance."

Boorham said, "Mm."

The rigger shrugged, "Possible ride."

They skirted the hole, looking for something they could use, didn't see much. Heard exploratory, preliminary cranking sounds from an engine behind them. Diesel tank on the ground, incidentally didn't appear to be leaking, kept by a logjam of skeletal steel and a low retaining wall from rolling uphill to an unfulfilled fate. Batching plant knelt, with large pieces gone, its mangled hopper several yards away, wrapped onto the crane. The carcass of the massive diesel-electric plant remained on its I-beam footprint, stripped to the cast iron.

Boorham felt distracted. Despite her being in many ways Gail's opposite—big, middle-aged, and politically to the right of libertarian—the crane jockey reminded him of Gail, her manner, expressions. He wasn't in the habit of arguing against his crew's loony conspiracies of multinationals and weird cabals, because they made as much sense as anything else, differed only in specifics from the nonsensical crap he and Gail had known to be true. Some of which nonsense had nevertheless proved out, continued to.

The last year or so, Boorham had done work for a company specializing in fortified dwellings, increasingly popular among those who could afford them. He was out here supervising the site prep and initial construction phase of someone's country house in the missile silo. Figured he wouldn't be returning to it after this setback, since the principal of the company, along with her caddy and a couple of others, had been successfully blown up. Boorham doubted, in fact, anybody would get paid.

When Gail crossed his mind, often Shelda would too. Some sense of duty, something absurd but ingrained and difficult to resist, a vestigial notion of rules to be followed, had prompted him to drop the necklace back into the Chrysler's trunk among the bones. Calling himself an idiot, he turned away and went back for Shelda's chain—that had to be her chain. Boorham broke into a shambling trot.

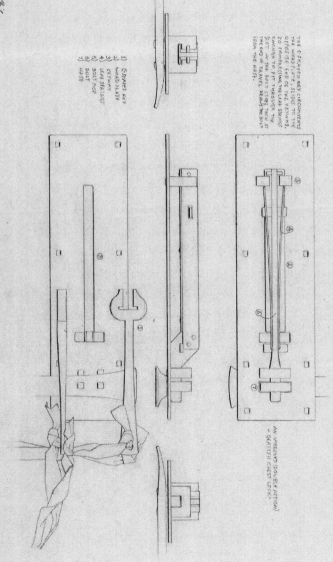

THE C-SHAPED KEY CIRCUMVENTS THE WARD PLATE, SLIDING TO THE OPPOSITE END OF THE KEYWAY, SO COMPRESSING THE LEAF SPRINGS ENOUGH TO FIT THROUGH THE SLOT IN THE BOLT STOP; THEN AT THE END OF TRAVEL DRAWS THE BOLT FROM THE HASP.

1) C-SHAPED KEY
2) WARD PLATE
3) KEYWAY
4) LEAF SPRINGS
5) BOLT STOP
6) BOLT
7) HASP

— AN INTEGRID (DOUBLE ACTION) — GRIFFITH CHEST LOCK

Anders • befallings

Turf overhead slumped between smoke-blackened boards cut from driftwood, and turf underfoot covered everything, piled deeper where people slept near the hearth; the rest of the room, or house, was dedicated to the skinny, shaggy cow grazing the floor. Light and wind came through places in the low dry-stacked fieldstone walls where turf outside had collapsed on itself, and gray light came past a sagging door, the door's iron straps and hinges scavenged to be reworked again and again into ever more essential things, the iron becoming less durable with each reforging.

Feeling around between the irregular roof boards just above the waist-high stone, Edith fished out a C-shaped key from the turf, slid the key into and along a slot in a copper-bound dowry chest, raised its roof-shaped lid shallowly carved with precise, flowing, interlocking patterns colored blue, red, yellow, green. Not much in the box. She stroked a fragmentary shirt of chainmail, myriad small links each closed with a tiny, perfect rivet, the exquisite steel garment the more beautiful for its links being worn nearly through by men she'd loved, or her mother had, or her grandmother, or that one's. Reached to touch a linen mantle's colorful silk embroidery that had become too brittle to touch, instead picked up a penannular brooch made mostly of walrus ivory, and whispering the great-grandmother's name, licked a fingertip, got some ash from the hearth, gently rubbed highlights on worn silver knotwork.

Desiccated straw and husks now, a sachet lay undisturbed in a white silk ribbon. Imagining what spices must smell like, Edith took a long inhalation of the dry dust scent of it, coughed, dropped it onto the turf underfoot, ribbon and all. Stared down at the sachet for a minute. Picked it up along with a little of her mossy bedding, the turf that served as building material and fuel and cattle feed, harvested farther and farther from the house daily; on the barely smoldering hearth, the sachet released the faintest perfume. Her pail's carefully fitted narrow staves had been cut from dwarf trees and shaped with multiply reforged tools that dulled quickly, that bent in use; cords of eelgrass bound the pail since hoops no longer existed—she knew what hoops were, though. Gently blowing a flame alight in the moss and sachet and ribbon on the hearth, she turned her sand-scoured pail over the brief heat to sterilize it somewhat for the next milking, warmed her raw hands on the fragile wooden vessel, felt a sweet unassigned yearning.

•

Aboard her boat, away from her home docks, trespassing for the night in somebody's vacant marina slip, Edith drifted toward being awake, tried to hurry it up, asleep but aware of her dog barking. Still immersed in an intense dream and reluctant to leave it, wasted a couple of seconds remembering, and then another wondering how that dream could possibly feel sweet.

Waking as she went, scooted out from under a thwart and yanked out the hitch she'd tied up with. Left the line to trail in the harbor, pushed her boat *Candyass* out of the slip, hurriedly began to backwater. Free of the dock, hauling on one oar and leaning into the other, spun the stout wooden vessel around in its own length and started making some distance as a man's voice called, "Hey Edie! Gotta run? C'mon, you have to leave?" At dusk, Edith's last fare had left her a half mile from her usual overnight mooring, a houseboat she was reluctant to tie up to anyway, with all the strangers coming and going there now. Unless she'd connected with friends, after some stage of the evening Edith preferred not to walk around town anymore, even to bedsheets and a warm shower in her bedsitter room. The dog left off barking and shook down its hackles and gamely assumed its station in the bow, lay posed like a miniature sphinx with lame hindquarters stretched behind.

•

Because of the men making it plain that they were watching, Edith thought she had somehow gotten crossways with organized crime or the law. There were a lot of possibilities for that, but she'd started noticing the various observers not long after taxiing a passenger to a little floating house that'd newly been towed within her preferred range.

As houseboats go, it was handsome enough, didn't try for idyllic, a marginally well-kept thing that was two or three notches above shanty scow, an actual boat and not an inert platform. Anchored a hundred yards off the pier, having been repeatedly chased away from other free moorage, it was a sound, workmanlike, tiny Depression-era dwelling—low barrel roof, a box squatting in the bleached-out thirty-foot teak deck of a heavily tarred flat hull. A coat of pea-green paint on the cabin maybe the only touch of whimsy besides the boat's name, *Owly Cat*.

Someone she barely knew had introduced the passenger as Anders, then maybe bragging, said that the feds wanted him. Assured Edith that he wasn't much of a desperado, just hard to find for questioning, low priority, not worth much effort on the feds' part. The man merely winced, raised his eyebrows at the woman's breach of etiquette. Edith smiled at her, said conversationally, "Shut the fuck up, you moron."

Rowing him out, by way of conversation, Edith said,

"Where you from?"

"Minneapolis originally. Most recently I am a drifter. Left a teaching job, prefer short-order cook anyway."

"Cool. Enviable?"

"Yes indeed, better than any number of things I guess."

"You don't sound real romanticized," she said, expecting a hint or two at a shadowy past, a hint by which he'd look guarded, possessed of deep ennui rooted in enigmatic experience—she'd invited the guy to sound cool. Took her aback when he just told her yeah, he'd been at loose ends since being ransomed from a Central American jail by friends and family back home. An able short-order cook who could play affable bartender as well, her passenger might find a decent temporary job anywhere, though teaching wasn't any longer an option, schools justifiably scared off by his history.

She'd found him easy to talk to, and he'd without a thought shipped the second pair of oars. Turned out to be ten years older, and that they were related through an uncle or something. Edith nodded amused approval as Anders, possibly wanting to show off for her, grabbed a line from the houseboat's deck and correctly cinched it at his end of her miniature whaleboat. She heaved out his pack and handed up his barracks bag, having been cautioned about a portable typewriter packed in with the laundry. Passed along her calm little gray-muzzled mutt, accepted a hand up for herself, and followed him inside for a cup of tea.

"Okay, so what do they want to talk to you about?" she asked.

Answering that he'd finished college on the GI Bill and taught junior high for a few years, then acting out of conscience, stupidly gone to Guatemala with another social studies teacher who spoke a little high school Spanish. Immediately got in a lot deeper than they'd intended, found themselves among an indigenous band of self-invented Marxist guerrillas carrying vintage rifles, bird guns, and cane knives, along with a few modern Soviet-supplied arms. Husbands and wives in the group, everyone was part-time in the war. Knowing their territory, the group had ambushed the disdainful and unshakably overconfident US-funded goon squads, and by those men's murder armed themselves and other Indians. And after months of intermittent skirmishes, their village having been burned and family members' maimed corpses left lying around, Anders's group had been chased over the border, where that other country's army was waiting for them. At the time still called the British Honduras Volunteer Guard, the troops killed the Maya outright, put him and the other gringo into Hattieville Prison, to be slammed around and interrogated at great length by white guys whose native language was American English. Guys who one day lost all interest in the insurgent schoolteachers and disappeared.

The perfunctory outline left her in appalled silence and sorry she'd asked. As Anders dug things out of the big canvas bag to make tea, he changed the subject to the dog's prosthesis—a well-made, well-conceived contraption something like a big roller skate, upholstered to fit the animal comfortably. Edith stepped on deck into the mist, arranged for the dog to relieve itself over the side. Put up the canvas top on her boat, went back into the cabin, and settled in with Anders for the night.

•

She ran into him renewing the weekly rent on a Sears fiberglass with an outboard, never to be taken out past the buoys.

"Edie!"

"Hiya. You used the flag?"

"Yeah worked great, your boy Neil came out and got me. Couple of hours."

"Good! Hired him because he can work bombed out of his skull. Find two or three more Sasquatch, I'll expand the fleet."

"Where's your dog?"

"Parked her with a friend in the city, go get her tomorrow. I went to America for a week. You get done here, I want to talk, okay?"

Then standing below the quay among the boat rentals and gas pumps and overnight utility hookups, she said,

"What kind of shit are you into, man? Somebody's looking at me. They want me to know it."

Anders shrugged, "Tell them anything you like."

"That's the deal, they never ask. Not like I go up and say excuse me sir what's new."

"Why not?"

"Because they'd just deny it and because I'm not totally

sure it's not my imagination, is why. Who the fuck, Anders! Just . . . all kinds of guys. Suits, some just regular hourly dudes, and one time a city streets crew, Chinese guys."

"Oh. Think so?"

"Okay, sounds a little paranoid. Okay. Maybe not everybody that looks at me and I guess I don't want to know what you're into anyway. So. How's life treatin' you, man? Eating right? Getting in your eight hours?"

Starting to say something, Anders settled for, "I'm nobody, seriously. Marxist guerrilla, but feds would've just picked me up. I think."

"God damn it. Man, do you know where you are? Get serious, people's hero? Hey, prof? Look, man, you're boss. Do some agitprop out here, organize some organizers? Or some really weird shit too, it looks like? I mean you know, God knows who-all's looking at you, and now your cooties rubbed off on me."

Pause. He said, "Lesson taken, but they wouldn't advertise that you were, you know, surveilled. Surely. I think. Funny thing, in this neighborhood I'm a little angel. I like you. Come visit?" Thumped his chest and leapt five feet down into his boat, looked up at her, grinning, to see how that went, pressed the electric starter. From the rental office above, someone bellowed, "Hey! Hey!"

•

Among the things carried around her neck on a soft woven band was a waterproof Timex for keeping any prearrangements. At first, an Ansafone machine had taken a few calls a week, but dockside check-ins were a time- and calorie-expensive nuisance, and ConTel had traced and confiscated the bootleg phone anyway. Some of the walkie-talkies she'd handed out were occasionally used, passed around in the out-anchored community, batteries even replaced. People shouted from piers and boats, hailed her taxi, or passed along messages to her—Edith wasn't so much needed as enjoyed. The most reliable call method was a signal flag system she'd invested in, sewing squares big enough to be obvious within any distance she'd want to row, chartreuse with the black image of a whoopee cap in the middle. The two-part emblem was a pictograph of her uncle's Depression-era grease-monkey's cap, the kind made from an old fedora cut zigzag and turned up, like a beanie with a shabby cartoon king's crown around the bottom. Struck her as right for a heraldic device, right for an ensign, silly enough.

·

Full of fresh coffeehouse chatter and on the way back to his boat pleasantly anticipating writing it up for distribution, her passenger was giving her a taste.

Edith said, "So you're saying it's whoever's stenciling up all those little black deals? I heard about 'black light' acid, you mean it's with that whole thing? Something 'bout weird-ass health problems but anyway of course everybody's looking for it—I got that from the same head that told me about ayahuasca. So the new shit plus the graffiti are a thing. The wholesale people don't put up ads, Albert. Fans do sometimes."

"Gotta mourn the passing of the dealer's traditional customs, but ballyhoo aside, the groundbreaking said-to-be product or service—ain't that a bite? Consensus of rumor says it is nonfiguratively killer shit. Nonfigurative and literal, presumption of mind-expandingness obviously, as well as lethality. And I don't know any of the, like, volunteer subjects to ask, nor do I know any credibles who claim to know firsthand of any such heads, but then you wouldn't know if you did unless they died. So does one ingest, inject, inhale, absorb, get irradiated? No say. 'Intangibles' is the term gaining vogue, as you'd buy a matchbox of intangibles. Absent definitive word on the matter. Edie, love, your flag logo kind of looks like the graffito," said her passenger.

"Yeah I know, all of a sudden and no goddamn fair. Fad, Kilroy Was Here, school kids doing them anymore, means zero now if it ever did mean something. Or nine out of ten little black dealies aren't the one and number ten's it. You know it's just a whoopee cap. My flag."

"Yes! Recognized it. Younger son made one out of my hat, token of his regard. Fads past don't presume the given age's innocence though, for example your Kilroy. Kilroy psycho, nose over your fence, Kilroy's eyes peering over your metaphor, his fingers hanging on your perimeter fence, well-chosen fad, love."

"Albert, have we had this exact same conversation before? I know we have, it's the weirdest feeling."

"Lovely to be remembered but no, sorry, to my knowledge that was another me."

"You never said any of this? But I think I never heard you mention your kid before, your son. Must be, what, forty, forty-something. Where is he?"

"Korea, I'd have to guess."

"Oh God, Albert, I'm sorry."

"Stops with you. Next!"

"Jesus. Wow, sorry," she said.

"Next!" he said.

"Okay uh . . . But so you have the idea it's the juju thing with the bad dope," said Edith.

"That hearsay swirls around the adherent-less stencil cult's proprietary dope or not-dope, yes, but I do not have the idea myself, we gotta take as gospel the word of the drunk that confided it to me. But then it started being one of those with the, like, bidden ones evaporating? Going away. Pfft! You heard that part?"

"No. How do you mean? That's . . . wow, you mean roll the dice then you die or, *or* you get snatched away to uh, to heaven or wherever?"

The passenger nodded, "Except the revolver's mostly

loaded, just one empty chamber when you spin. Or draw lots if that's the game, oh look *you*—no not you, Chuck Fool—*you yes you* behind buster Fool and the rest of those sick people, *you* of the lot get to board the bus! Nirvana-ville! 'Board! Yer on! Arise arise from your wailing heap of fellow culties, many of whom are desperately ill, receive epiphanic enlightenment and float off like a fart on the breeze. Very cool, haute, like, very hip rapture. Ah, here's one pertains to you—Boorham, you met him?"

Edith said, "Albert, we have said this before, this has happened before."

"Love," he said gently, leaned forward as she rowed, "That would come as news to me. I'm just now getting here. Are you alright?"

"Yeah. Sorry, go on."

"Kid came up to me asking about local culture, more specifically the one mystical conman has Neil by the raisins. Young Boorham's not sound. Both hands to keep his lid on."

"He's starving himself, for one thing."

"Oh. Given the choice, the Buddha chucked that in favor of, like, Buddhism . . . So the kid went with your boyfriend Neil and his wife up the coast. Comical, nonplussed the lad so, his running into me—down here we're in context in little buddy's reality, now relocate my context to karmic bedlam! Ha! That confounded planet of mine was here somewhere, he's thinking, left it right here I swear! Finds himself in the Sunday funnies, Little Buddy in Hieronymus Bosch Land."

"Yeah. Well. Hang in there buckaroo, good luck. But hey, Albert, dammit, my boyfriend Neil? Oh right, bullshit! That is such a load of horseshit and I am getting goddamn irritated with it, listen, man, I do not do interspecies sex! Yuck! . . . Wondered why Neil quit showing up for work."

In Which Water Music comes to the Styx

Edie • nondirectional beacons

A child watched her red-and-white bobber make rings in the clear water among the lily pads, watched tadpoles and min-nows appear and disappear among the green marbled shadows below. A sure, gentle elder in the tympani-like aluminum row-boat smiled at her fondly, cast his tiny silver lure into an open place. The smell of a pine forest, the smell of two-cycle gas, noth-ing much in her blissful head but the calls of birds, the warm sun, chilly air. Enormous conifers grew right down to the mirror lake; a kingfisher on a high branch lifted its tail and shot a stream twenty feet, luminous white against the deep shade. "Did you see that?" "Shh," said the other, the husbandman, who ran a long dark bone along her ribs, the familiar touch on her leathery hide soothing her along her daily routine. Running a hand down the coarse hair of her back, the man found a cyst there and squirted out maggots, wiped his hand on her enormous piebald flank. Ambling along her way placidly chewing her cud, and absently stepping great spats of blood into the straw underfoot, the wad of half-digested fodder in her mouth was becoming hard, sharp, extremely heavy.

•

Still imagining the taste of blood, Edith startled awake, tried to get a look through the sun-ruined isinglass. Tossed open a flap of her boat's low canvas top. Still nothing to see but claustrophobic and beautiful and nearly opaque faintly glowing drizzly fog, and a few haloed self-referential lights that lit nothing but the mist around them. Before now it'd been rare that she'd have welcomed some snoring, farting bunkmate. Felt behind her head for the ancient war-club femur, found her paraplegic dog back there as well. Tied up one last time that evening to the houseboat that'd for months been her usual mooring, Edith after a while went back to sleep on her monastic thin futon, on the wooden floor grating of her boat.

•

Coming to the aid of a hapless stranger reacting badly to some psychoactive drug—it was a fairly ordinary good deed of the time, in the same category as pushing someone's stalled car. The tendency is to feel there's a correlation, a transaction, in the amount of trouble gone to and the good-ness of the deed, but she'd never worked for karmic credit, you just do what you're supposed to do until it would be stupid to do more. Having coaxed to safety some fool whose mind was thrashing like a panicked sheep stuck in a fence, and having stashed him out of harm's way, Edith crossed a gangplank back to the dock. Spotted a woman and a big black dog heading away down the pier, trotted to catch up, "Not going to your own party?"

"Where'd you come from, hey girl! In a word, not on your life," Shelda said. "My crazy fuck husband, oh yeah this is one to miss. We got to talk. Someplace."

"I just stuffed brother Boorham in a hidey-hole because some fucker dropped him. Killer shit, to all appearances. Should be okay I guess. He better stay put."

"Thanks. I quit worrying—he's a total train wreck but you see him next time and not a scratch on him. Want to kill whichever asshole friend of Perry's does that, tear him a new one. Seriously doubt it's lysergic they did the boy with either, and I don't rule out it's Perry doing it."

Edith was kneading a deltoid, "I got one more pickup if my arms don't fucking fall off, jeez. Go see Gail tomorrow?" Pointed a thumb over her shoulder in the direction of Shelda's houseboat, "After I help you clean up, assuming it's afloat."

"Yeah how'd that get to be my job anyway, fuck it. No just come find me. I mean, not talking housekeeping here either, talking everything's bad enough just on a regular day—people wandering in and out and back again and they're half of them such douche nozzles. It was art colony stuff at first, whole scene was fun for about a month at first but Jesus. You don't feel like you can just hang out and talk anymore. Like ever. I'll give us a ride in if we locate the god-damn van, he forgets where he leaves it."

A man they hadn't met asked if Gail knew they were com-ing, let them into a clean and sparsely furnished window-lit room, a place of reason, of good order. Edith's gray-muz-zled little dog followed, paddling along on its roller skate. Sepia-color skin and eyes, and loosely convoluted hair the same red-brown, a lanky teenage girl unfolded herself from a Victorian swooning couch and took her quilt away with her. Likely one of the myriad stray children flowing into the city from all over the continent, she must've had something to recommend her. The dog—surprising how few people com-mented about the animal's rig—followed her down the hall-way, where a small child appeared, bent to pet it. The man went to the kitchenette, switched on a grandiose espresso machine, went to answer the telephone in the hall.

Carton of milk in hand, he said, "Gail's doing some SDS stuff, said make yourselves at home but she's still over in Berkeley." Handed out big teacups of the strong coffee, bal-anced two more cups, "Y'all stay as long as you like. Get the door for me?" On the asymmetrical little couch, Shelda took out her Pall Malls, drained her scalding coffee in order to use the cup for an ashtray. Picked up the conversation from the drive over.

"I know, ripped for a week at a time in Dallas fucking Texas, move to counterculture-land and get straight. All the stuff I loved about Perry, shit, it's . . . his lake turned over, 'know? You know? It's like, same guy but cold, lord, it is rotty down under his mind. Ugh. I mean, what happened? His mind fuckin' stinks! The last time Perry and I screwed, penicillin-proof VD. Well what's this, this is interesting, thanks a bunch, lover, but oh lordy what a hog that was. And that antibiotic turns you every way but loose, still got sore tendons. It's like the whole guy is poisonous . . . Hey, he ever quit trying to get into your pants?"

"Matter of fact. Yeah, he stopped acting like that. Wasn't being for real anyway. That's been a little while now," said Edith.

"Oh yeah he was totally serious."

"Glad I didn't know that."

Shelda said, "You picked up on he's putting all kinds of shit into his arm, won't . . . not interested in me either. Thank God. Gave me that parting dose, nice way to end the connubial bliss thing. Then I went out and got my very own case of warts. Can't believe I'm still staying there. Yeah and thanks again for your heroic efforts with that breakfast yesterday, theater of the absurd. So you had warts yet?"

"Not me man, my body's the temple of Hygeia."

"Right, temple to who, you even get it on with Gail or I'm mistaken," said Shelda.

"Went a round or two. She acquired a part-time

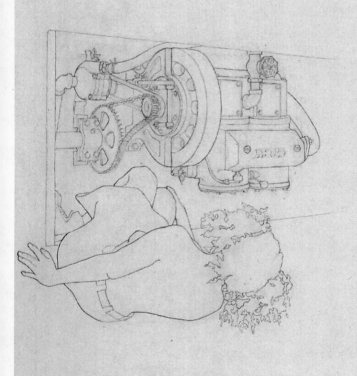

boyfriend, we just met him I guess. No way in hell, who knows where he's been. So Perry's dealing wholesale?"

"Trying to. Trying to break into the market. Looking for a hard-time bust or somebody offs him or just pick the two. Jesus I mean he knows and he's doing it anyway. So I don't trip anymore, like, with that environment over there? Funny! And I am still right there playing houseboat. So romantic. Mostly just too lazy to get the fuck out, 'know? Flashing neon sign out front, bust me first!–flash–bust me first!–flash–you Mafia folks wipe your feet and come on in! Too lazy to get out, that and because you tie up there, I mean your boat kind of lives there, needed to talk to you about it. I go do something else, what's your deal, Edie? Might be time."

"Well, really I got a shitload of other . . . good God! Bail, man, git! Get the fuck out, you need to for chrissakes, don't worry about, oh shit, I had not snapped to that. Thank you, love," jumped up, pinched the sides of her jeans, slid a foot, bobbed her head. Shelda blinked, looked at her for a full second, said,

"What in the flying fuck was that, Edie? Did you just curtsy?"

"Yes. Need help moving out?"

"Nope. Losing the baggage, but thanks."

Edith asked, "People watching you? I mean like being obvious? Like they want you to know."

"Happens. Lordy, if I paid attention to that. You pay

attention to that? They're either checking out your ass or they're checking out your ass *and* they're lining up everybody you know for a bust," Shelda shrugged, "What can you say. What I want to know is, you going to move in with Fidel?"

A person of reflexive checklists, Edith ticked down the identifiers, "Commie revolutionary, Marxist insurgent instigator. Pinko agitprop fugitive from justice. He's a Minneapolis Swede. This place is a goddamn sieve, somebody like notated a one-night stand?"

Shelda said, "Your boat's kind of a giveaway. So you'd know I'm screwing a Green Beret?"

"Sure," said Edith, "You are in bed with the CIA. Seemed a little out of character. A lot. Feel safe with the guy?"

"Yeah no listen! Big, gentle guy. Did super well in basic and they asked him what he wanted to do, he said got any spy stuff. No really! So barely nineteen, all James Bond, tits'n'ass, woohoo, oh yeah that's what I want to do. Anyway, perfect gentleman. Even comes on my tummy, or wherever vicinity we're at. Once in a while I insist and he'll hurry it up and get off like in person—will you inseminate me now please JD, I fear I'm becoming bored. Makes him pop. It's kind of cute, just push the button and yup there it goes."

"He still in the army?"

"Not sure. He says not. Might still have him on the books. Or somebody does, because he picks up a check time to time. They had him up at the Presidio for months, bunch of surgeries, weren't even done fishing stuff out of him, major organs got hit, steel and bone splinters all in there, all this itty-bitty stuff peppered all in there. His front looks like it came out of a wastebasket. Shoulder got it. But everything was working fine after the peritonitis cleared up for good, and he just wandered out and stuck around town."

"He talk about what happened?"

"Answers a direct question. I quit asking after, like, one. Trained some Montagnards 'til the VC buried them alive, couple of kids still sort of alive when he dug them out, accidentally killed a kid he was trying to dig out. On the way back, a Bouncing Betty got him, chopped the guy in front of him in two. A lot of the bone they picked out of JD belonged to the other guy. You know. War."

"Yeah . . . no, I don't. Well. That's pretty horrible. Anders has a story too. And I told you about my cousin."

"I forgot! He make it?"

"Deaf, but last I knew, gets to keep everything." Touching Shelda's five-strand braid bracelet, "Aluminum?"

"Yeah the Montagnards. Just thick electrical wire. The basket weave up the ends, see? Teeny little Buddhist verse supposedly. Didn't do them shitloads of good, or for all I know it did. No, he's just a big gentle guy."

•

The little yellow slip in her post office box instructed Edith to take it to the counter, that she had a package. The postal clerk's expression changed from bored to quizzical as Edith reached under her T-shirt and brought out a Girl Scout knife. Having neatly cut through some paper tape, she pulled a wad of newspaper out of a sawn-off length of heavy cardboard tube, the kind carpet might be rolled on, and withdrew a dark, shiny femur over two feet long.

"Would you mind if I leave this tube and stuff here? Thanks, I really appreciate it," she said, and walked off carrying the club.

Prepared to lease the fields and auction the aged equipment for whatever it might bring, Edith's mom sold the remaining animals and mailed off the bone of contentment. Mailed the family cow prod to Edith as a sentimental gesture of good luck and also a finger-wagging remonstrance— attend to real life, sweetie. Soundly intact—a pronounced ball at one end and big knuckle at the other, the chocolate-color bone's polish the result of decades of daily handling in the dairy barn—it was a femur gracile for its length as in humans, though such a person would be nine feet tall. Most people would think it qualified as a talisman. An uncle known for yarns identified it to small children as the thighbone of an Indian sorcerer who, in the process of making himself enormously tall, couldn't resist a piece of his wife's shortcake, which broke the spell and caused him to fly to pieces. Others said that it came from a Bigfoot, or just as unlikely, some moose with a fatal malformation. Whatever grew it, the femur had very likely been collected fresh as a curiosity and as a war club, then preserved in some way, and then for whatever reason, wrapped up and abandoned by an eighteenth-century Ojibwa who'd obviously valued it. And finally, still wrapped in amazingly supple illustrated animal skin, dug up by Edith's grandfather.

•

Not quite dozing, "Anchor lights. Damn," Anders said.

Peeing into the bay, wondered if he saw objects out there or not, easy to be deceived by drifting fog. Plenty of distant noise, nearby the barely audible gentle bumping of Edith's boat *Candyass* and of his rented outboard skiff against the old tires hung along the sides of the houseboat. Bare-assed and shivering, he climbed onto the roof to strike a waterproof match, light the lamp maritime safety required. A couple of the nearer boats at anchor complied with that one essential etiquette; most didn't and hadn't any means of doing it. Fresnel lenses amplified the tiny flame and the fog reflected it whitely back; it was impossible to see through the light and over the water.

Edith couldn't have been asleep for long, woke when he got back under the blankets and spooned up behind her. She patted his hip, inched away, "Bad dream," she said, staring at the wall. Reconstructing the dream, she made more sense of it than maybe it had had.

•

Superior lay dying, unclean, the last of the immense freshwater seas to succumb, and the vastness of the tragedy almost incapacitated the woman in the dream. The woman, Edith's grandchild, was quite ill. She'd just rolled her mother into a tarpaulin along with some gravel, rolled her off of a decayed wooden dock into what remained of a gracefully shaped wooden boat, the remains of Edith's boat. The woman had yanked out the thwarts, and without them the rickety integrity of the boat was even less sound—no need for it to go far though. She'd been bailing all day, the boat leaked so, bailed to keep it afloat for sunset. Now dropped in chunks of quarry rubble, carefully, afraid of breaking through the hull. And now lay on the dock with a lighter, breathed wearily for a minute, gathering her strength. When the candle in the paper lantern on her mom's shroud was well lighted, the woman eased herself off the dock into the algae, swam the boat several yards away from the dock. "Bye." Illuminated by the tiny lantern, clotted water rose gradually within the boat, took a while to come level with the clotted sea.

•

Clear sky, predawn scraps of fog drifting across the water, Edith's dog had dragged its hind legs up the step onto the deck and begun sniffing around with unusual interest. Seeing that her boat was gone, Edith had climbed onto the houseboat's roof to extinguish the mast light and returned inside to wake her bunkmate for a tour of the marinas and docks in his rented outboard.

Upturned lapstrake hull, graceful, curvy, and faring into a pronounced keel, the boat's thin, broad strakes beat-up but skillfully repaired, thoroughly scraped of old paint and recently recoated, "Okay, shit! There she is." Oars laid neatly underneath, canvas top conscientiously stowed. "What the motherfuck! This a prank? What is this!" Keel-up on dunnage, Edith's boat *Candyass* lay on the concrete pier of a maintenance facility.

"Good morning! What's the deal with my boat?"

"Yeah Edie, your proper old Whitehall. What you want done?"

"Who brought her in?"

"Here when we opened up."

"Oh Chuck, sorry—somebody got their signals crossed or something. I don't know what's going on either. Would you mind putting her back on the water please?" The seventeen-foot boat, now on its side winched halfway upright in the slings, "Hold it there, please," said Edith, leaned in to look at the underside of the board she sat on for a good part of most days, and occasionally slept under. "Chuck, what is that?"

"No idea," he said, poked then tried to peel it off, "No earthly idea." Anders watched with interest from a few feet away. The boatyard man gently pried around the edges with

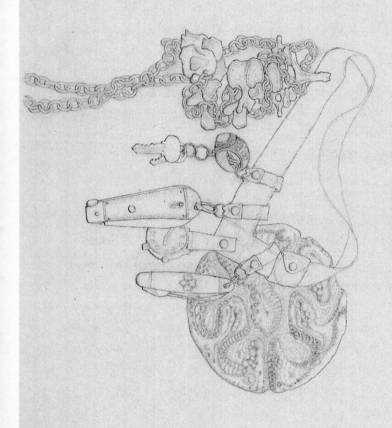

In Which an Oracle's Necklace & that of an Ogress woman are Juxtaposed with an Ominous Object

a dull wood chisel he kept for things like that; the dark lumpy circle fell away from the thwart, taking paint with it. "God it's heavy."

"Wow. Ain't it." Edith pulled a utilitarian barlow knife out of her shirt, clacked the big switchblade open, scraped at the object. Nicked it, drilled at it—moderately hard white metal under the oxide. "You want it?"

"Oh hell no," the man said.

"Maybe it's platinum or something," said Edith, "Lot harder than lead. Heavier too, seems like. Yeah for sure heavier."

"Baby girl let's get you right side up and on your way, and you drop that thing in. You hear? Edie? Nowhere near my dock. You don't want it."

For the first time recalling fragments of a dream, "No I don't do I," she said, remembering an appalling heaviness in her mouth, the taste of blood, an especially bad dream. The oars and tackle were being put back inside, and Edith looked around for the family thighbone. Described it to the boat-yard guys, who hadn't ever seen it.

•

Intending to get back to the clothes tumbling at the laundromat three doors down, she stepped out of the shower, and toweling her hair as she squeezed past the end of the bed, stepped painfully on the bone club that had gone missing.

Wasn't much surprised, just rubbed her foot, tossed the thing on the bed.

It came to mind to pair up more seriously with Anders, since he was a good deal larger than she, and by his own account capable of violence. Felt she might cozy up with the male for the time being—the ancient bargain that carried such cost and risk. "Goodness, girl. Gone primal on us," Edith murmured aloud. For no reason at all remembered leading bullock calves with curly forelocks and big trusting long-lashed eyes, veal calves she'd bottle-fed until legal, out to the trailer to be taken to their slaughter.

•

Anders's was one of few houseboats with propulsion; though people lived on almost anything that floated, most of the house-shaped vessels in the neighborhood were inert floating platforms, passively rising and falling with the tide as extensions of the pontoon docks they were moored to. Edith asked, "You have soap?"

"Lava and Ivory both. And one hundred ten gallons of fresh water, landlord came by today. Cold of course. Got butane—lit the heater for you—never have tried to light the water heater, because I can't find a pilot light on the damn thing."

Sitting on opposite sides of the engine well, Edith studied the engine with a flashlight, Anders looked at her instead.

She said, "Ah, the water heater ritual—light a match and open the gas and blow your eyebrows off, so then all this flaming gas goes up through the coils and out the roof. Step two, run boiling water into the washtub, shut off the butane, then go see what you set fire to up top. Takes about a minute, if you don't have to put any fires out." Indicated the engine, "Did they say if this thing runs?"

"Dead sure they'd kick me out, but wouldn't that be cool? Love to have the option to drive this thing around."

She said, "I know! No idea why either. Take this slab out for a spin."

"They said it's got a high-maintenance raw-water cooling system they don't want to fool with anymore, so they tow it."

She pointed the flashlight at a fuel gauge, "What's that say?"

He tapped the dial, "Not empty." A big dirty two-cylinder engine hunkered at their feet. "Diesel fuel."

"Yeah, about all I know too. And that it would just be a bear to crank the mother," Edith said.

He said, "Want to look at it in the morning?"

Edith glanced up, "Anders keep your pants on, I'll get to you in a minute," pointed, "Lever dealies on the heads. Give us a crank, you see an arrow someplace?"

"Crank only goes one direction looks like. Nothing, won't move."

Clean red shop rag in hand, she leaned over, "Okay try it." The massive flywheel rotated a couple of turns.

"Aha. You did let off pressure, aren't you clever," he said.

"I'll ask around, asshole. Go wash your hands. Lava," she said.

•

Most frequent of Edith's fares among the out-anchored boats was a remnant of a generation of bohemians predating the beatniks, a man whose goatee and short, beat ponytail he'd years before let go natural. His head resembled an eroded pyramid, the yellowed white hair and beard hacked off just below chin level all around. Named Albert and known as Doots—tiny old guy with sun-wrecked skin, what you could see of it, and eyes beginning to turn milky with cataracts, and beard stained orangish around where the mouth should be. Spoke with an accent he'd identify as something different every time he was asked. Albert typed, mimeographed, stapled, and hawked a biweekly six-page newsletter of his opinions, Bay Area music news, street gossip, and to his readers, nearly useless tide tables provided mimeograph-ready at the Golden Gate Coast Guard Station; sold his copies for a dime or half-dollar or a buck or two, depending on what you looked like, sold quite a few locally. Known sometimes to chide people who declined to buy. Since he hitchhiked around town, found himself from time to time in the next state up the coast trying to peddle the local newsletter, what the hell.

It would never have crossed his mind to use the peeling plywood dinghy that lay on the roof, architectural ornament by now, and Edith came three or four times a week to take him to town. He held court or sat in with the inevitable musicians in a couple of bars, or hitched across the bridge to a couple of coffeehouses. He'd make a quarter materialize out of someone's ear, then vanish the coin, pointing smugly at his empty palm. Drew bad caricatures for pretty good tips, regaled friends and fans and anyone who'd put him on their tab—something to eat, a drink, a chai. In mock anger and actual sincerity Doots the performer argued political positions that were concurrently libertarian and socialist. Rumor gathering was better at bars, newsletter sales generally better earlier in the day at the coffeehouses.

"The owner of Anders's pad, not the landlord, but who actually owns it?" the passenger asked. He was sitting behind her this time, speaking to her back as she rowed.

"Nope. Tell me or don't."

"Fu Manchu of the Sutro! Cat that cops that bit, as we say. He who lurk in realms of urban shade," said her passenger.

"Assuming the balding white guy with the long pigtail—right, he bought a houseboat? Bullshit, he's a playactor, Albert, does his creepy shtick with the Fu Manchu hat and pigtail, c'mon where'd he get that kind of coin?

"That he may be a *propertied* street act though, that invites conjecture don't it, love, you'd wonder what other shows he's played in. I'd rate him pretty good. The playact he *does* cop to—in itself a role? Hmm? The part we know is a walk-on in the production that we don't? Hmm? . . . Nah, barbershop mirror is too easy a reach and affords no insight but itself, and does not reflect this, the golden age of cozeners! Everybody and his hat is out on the hustle . . . Oh dear . . . Edith, ah, do you, like, recall this exact scene? This same scene, are we quoting all this verbatim? We've been here."

"Well, you've ridden with me several times of course. Not sure what you're asking. Pretty sure I haven't heard you say any of that stuff before. You okay, Doots?"

"Because I believe you, apparently I ain't okay. Because I can also assure you we are replaying this movie, and this is where we came in. But it's nothing, probably nothing more than a stroke. We press on.

"So. FuDog. Dabbles in loan-sharking but he's nobody. Still he's, you know, deep into his role, brings his lines to life—the cat is serious, with nada does he trifle, but he's nobody. Milks your guy Neil for lunch money kind of loan shark nobody. So ostentatiously over-the-top and unmitigated a nobody that it nags. You know?"

"Could explain some things if he can buy houseboats, but I don't like it. I mean, then I might want to think it's him with some of the other crazy shit too."

An elaborate shrug, "No word, love, a heads-up is all, love. Or heads ahead and let the coruscating rivet bounce off your hardhat, I have made no sense of anything in years."

Seagulls, harbor sounds, Edith rowed. In a few minutes he said, "Here's a lulu—at this end of the bridge, the only one the cat is, like, scooch with is Shelda's. Shelda's clyde, JD, a straight-shootin' manly man shoots the breeze with low FuDog. Misfit buddy movie, Edie love, what could that happen? And too! Lacks corroboration, but it's said as well that our street performer is scooch with the fugacious said-to-be Believers, the Children of the Stencil, adherents of the nonsect that's all the rage only for being totally occluded. A cult of graffiti and rumor and graffiti, what's that? Why it's nothing at all Y'r Honor, I rest my case Y'r Honor but no, look again! There's something there! If only the, like, confluence of so many things. It's a thing of itself, the confluence. Donk! Whose rivet was that coruscating off my hardhat? What, I ain't a rivet catcher, splash fffft! another rivet falls into the confluence. Love, I feel directed, there's a tall canvas chair and a megaphone—a funded production. There is bread-ola falling from the sky. Dr Fu's day job? It just seems, Edie dear, you know? Seems all of a piece."

Occasionally glancing over her shoulder from time to time to check course, after a while slid an oar across the gunnels, turned around, and gently punched the old man's knee, said, "Thank you."

"Var så god," he said.

"Your accent is not Swedish, Albert."

"I'm Welsh actually, ma'am."

"Last time you were Italian Swiss."

"I depend on you to keep score."

"But you're always pulling out the Svenska for me."

"Nod to your forebear, my contemporary, a favorite among the manes with whom I'm scooch."

"Oh."

•

At the top of an outside stairs, through the swinging doors, and through another with a big brass porthole in it, a shotgun barroom hung with cigarette smoke, the place animated and noisy with conversation and clinking glass. She sometimes stopped in at this and the other quayside watering hole, took a stroll through to see if the old guy, or anybody, wanted to hail her for a last ride before she was done for the day, at whatever time of day that happened to be. Often enough she'd be pointed out to a tourist, be engaged for a sight-seeing tour the next day. She let them try rowing the boat if they asked, and half of them did, and tips were good. Edith scanned the room, headed for a two-person booth at the far end, "Thought you'd be slinging hash at Fred's."

"Edie! Wedge in here. No, just now had to quit, Junior's strutting around issuing orders like he's . . ." Anders shrugged, "Anyway I wish 'em well," indicated the big man across from him, "This is JD."

"Yeah hi," she said, "you're a friend of Shelda's. You boys know each other, then."

"Crossed paths," said JD mildly. Pleasant smile.

She said, "Seen Albert?"

"Moved with his entourage to the Deuce up in Mill Valley. That'll be that," said Anders.

"Shelda? How freaked is she? Where is she?"

After a pause, JD said, "Texas. I got her a car or you prob'ly chipped in too, we got her a car so she could take her shepherd. Yeah no she seems totally fine. Doesn't think those guys are coming after her, they just wanted Perry."

"R&R in Texas-land where she can let her hair down and be herself, huh," said Anders.

"No, man, going home. Had enough. Finished her year abroad on the houseboats, child at sea," said JD. Both men were a little drunk and being guys. If JD hadn't known his girlfriend any better than that, Edith wasn't going to edify now.

He said, "Oh yeah Edie, listen, Clovis says he's sorry he spooked you the other night at the marina, he was just stoned and wandering around."

"Clovis?"

JD shrugged, "Doesn't matter. Never mind, you're kind of known."

•

Authoritative hemispherical dent in the middle of the forehead—a remarkably well-placed strike, thought Shelda when she went down to identify Perry. Unsympathetic Marin County cops took her statement on the spot, quizzed her for a while, said she was legally bound not to leave the Bay Area, and advised her for her own good to stay quiet about the murder for the time being.

Settling into the driver's seat, giving the shepherd's ears a rub, "Real tidy job. Kind of thing that'd take you by surprise, looks like. There's that," she said to the dog, "I mean it'd be hard to do such a nice job like that, wouldn't it. We used to be so crazy about each other."

The lightest of baggage already stashed in the car, most of her belongings already abandoned, Shelda took out her keys—one for the ignition and the other an old-style skeleton key—and having no use at all for the scene, left and stayed gone. Briefly showed up again, apparently just to see Gail, who found her newly quiet and older, but warm enough and familiar, and at that point not much changed.

•

In late afternoon, summoned by the chartreuse signal flag with its mock-heraldic device, Edith tied up alongside the old man's boat. Heard his clarinet, found him inside playing swingtime variations on ad jingles, *Rice-a-Roni, the San Francisco treat . . . You'll wonder where the yellow went when you brush your teeth with Pepsodent . . . See the USA in your Chevrolet . . . Light up a light smoke—light up a Lucky . . .*

Halo, everybody, Halo, accompanied by the teenage girl from Gail's apartment—cross-legged on the floor, the girl bowed a viola that she held like a cello, its lower bout resting on her lanky thighs. Plucked the Maxwell House percolator tune pizzicato, in swingtime, bowed it again in a surprisingly deep pitch on the small instrument. A child, maybe four, probably female, clung on to the violist from behind and waggled from side to side. Showed off a recent accomplishment by hopping over to Edith on one foot, then decided to go for it—hanging on to Edith's pockets and stepping onto her sneakers, stared up expectantly with red-brown eyes. Making a surprised face, Edith began dancing the little kid around in a circle, apparently the right thing to do. "I'm gonna get your nose!" The child squeaked and ran, grinned from behind her sister, or aunt, or mother; and to show off another new ability, wiggled a lower incisor. "Your baby tooth," Edith scolded, "is precocious!" The child was delighted but knew when to quit. Began moving her lips, practicing the new word.

On a piece of plywood laid across two file cabinets sat Shelda. In front of a big upright newsroom typewriter and beside an office mimeograph machine, she sat drumming her heels, making the sheet-metal file case boom softly, the oak one thump a dead beat. The two-beat, an incidental rattle tripling the brighter one, a groove the musicians happily messed with. Shiny with sweat, gray calico frock stuck to her in places, Shelda slid to her feet as Edith came closer, their

first encounter in months, as the clarinet and viola continued to converse, to joke in bebop.

Immersed as they were in the insistent music, Edith
took Shelda's hands, kicked a couple of cross steps, drew her
close, flung and retracted her. Shelda passive at first, Edith
felt her friend's nature asserting itself and let her lead; for a
few seconds they slung, stepped through, twirled each other
as if they'd practiced forever.

Shelda abruptly stopped, pressed up; her skin, her
sweat, smelled pleasantly bitter like roasting coffee. Dilated
eyes, rarely blinking wide-open black receptors with tiny
rims of color, suitable for staring into the Abyss, all that kind
of thing. Smashed. Had scissored off most of the sprawl of
hair that Edith'd last seen with owl feathers and junk braided
into it, and now wore a rolled-up black silk scarf as a head-
band. Edith's cheek to Shelda's damp, feverish one, discern-
ibly through the music Shelda breathed a long string of
associations centered around physically revisiting realities
once experienced by oneself and others, murmured about
nonlinear experience, inherited memory, the congruity of a
personality to a previous moment and to a following one, all
that kind of thing. All the kind of thing that had never been
Shelda's deal at all.

Gradually paying more attention to her friend's ramble, Edith sensed it change, to seem to make sense like nurs-
ery rhymes might almost make sense, a narration of sorts
but a nonsense one. Began then to regard it as worthwhile.

Backed Shelda to a partition where, arms flopped around each other, taller Edith leaned onto stoned Shelda for an hour in order to listen, didn't say a word. Things later came to mind as if memory, things that certainly weren't memory.

•

Superior frozen in an onshore gale, the mile-and-a-quarter walk across cresting ice waves had taken more time than she'd allotted, and curtains were already backlit in the narrow windows of a prim little Queen Anne. Someone had put up the storm windows, but not much else had been done to it in years, fanciful trim falling away in sections, the bright colors largely gone from fish-scale siding. Wood smoke from the chimney fell to the ground, hung in motionless air.

Josefina heard a familiar tune being played inside as she twisted the bell, which didn't ring; slapping the thick oak door, "Mailman!" and pulling off a mitten to hurt her cold hand slapping again, she called, "Mailman!" A woman about her age in a high-collared dress and cradling an autoharp opened the door, smiled, turned back in. Used to the courtesy of being invited inside, Josefina followed. Smelled baking rye bread, pipe smoke, the old-book musk of long lived-in wooden buildings, and smelled the damp of a shallow cellar chopped into the rock. The other woman took her place on a worn velvet loveseat, picked up a horn plectrum, resumed chords to accompany a reed organ weaving arabesques around an old hymn tune. On a drying rack beside the cookstove in the middle of the dim parlor were a child's red felt boots and coat.

A kerosene lamp's hemispherical milk-glass shade glowed through the organist's stained white beard and hair. A younger man, unhurriedly buttoning his trousers and slipping back into his suspenders, smiled and nodded greeting, while beside him, head resting on folded arms over the reed organ, a woman stood spraddled with skirts tossed up over her arched back; the round white butt hiked out the flap of her woolies was almost another light source, with an unmistakable likeness to the lamp. Standing gracefully from her raw, embarrassed position with easy poise, and smoothing her long skirt, the woman smiled at Josefina and stepped close to confide something about panicle hydrangeas. Then with a little wave, glided over to ladder-like stairs and up to the sleeping loft, from which presently a sure, contralto yodeling joined the reed organ and autoharp, in open harmony, bizarre and lovely.

Bewildered, Josefina reached past the young man just lighting his pipe, laid her letter on top of the reed organ. The old man looked up at her for the first time, pale eyes opalescent with cataracts. Continuing to play with one hand, he placed a gold piece on the envelope; Josefina hesitated, picked up the heavy coin, "Tack så mycket, Albert. Ett stort tack." The old man apparently smiled somewhere in his beard, "I'm Welsh actually ma'am, and you're quite welcome, välkommen till vårt hem." The theme had come around again and he moved his knee to open the sound shutters, pumped a little harder and played loudly, joining without embellishment the autoharp player's sudden hair-raisingly pure soprano. Josefina wasn't sure she heard him say, "Thank you for coming to see us, Josefina." At last taken aback, she put one booted toe behind her and curtsied, hurried out under the low sky, into the smoke beginning to blow away. Gorgeous music continued as she closed the door, shouldered her pack, began pulling on her mitten.

In the last light during the initial gusts of snow, frequent lightning flashes let her see to backtrack a little ways toward the mainland. In a long trough in the lee of an ice ridge, she scuffed around in the sudden whiteout for a minute before giving up the possibility of digging in. Unslung the tarp and snowshoes from her back board, managed to sit on the oilcloth as it tried to blow away, wrapped up in the tarp and curled into a ball. Found the constant snow-muffled thunder a pleasant sound, felt somehow lulled by it.

The Sepia Girl • a world like any other

A zeitgeist thing, mysticism made its sixty-year cyclic reemergence, this time a doozy; pervasive, inescapable, this go-round proceeding out of seismic cultural reevaluations. That or one of the other categorical fads. Mysticism, both the deeply spiritual and the disingenuous kinds. None of which had anything to do with the rare unsought kind that extremely intuitive people never think of as mystical.

Willing to give nearly anything a brief listen, but by nature not a seeker and not much of a fan of the cryptic or paranormal, she'd explain that superstition is a different deal altogether and that she'd superstitiously decided against changing the boat's name. After the thorough scraping off of a hundred pounds of old paint, and after a spiffy new coat, Edith hired a local pro to repaint the name *Candyass* in hot-pink script across the high and elegantly small wine-glass-shaped transom board.

Rowing for a living in the time and place was something

a character might do, though she wasn't quite old enough to be one. A few of the houseboat people were characters, and most of those living on the anchored-out boats were.

Between one anchored-out boat and the municipal pier two or three times a week, her congenial twenty-minute visits with a kind of freelance culture reporter were something to look forward to, though his news could be disturbing and strike too close to home. Musician too, he performed around town with a young woman, to appearances a teenager, that Edith wanted to know a lot more about.

Chilly midmorning breeze, choppy harbor, Edith's passenger adjusted a little two-wheeler and its fat oilcloth satchel of newsletters more securely between his knees, said that the girl was a convincing fabulist, that he felt she'd make a successful scam artist. The story was that she'd left Madagascar when the Vichy government fled before the Brits, which would make her an unlikely lot older than she looked. That she was one of few survivors of a torpedoing, that she'd been adopted without papers in New Zealand by some US soldier. That the soldier'd gone home, left her behind, and that the girl and an adult male relative had made it to the States looking for him, found him. And that the relative had renamed the eleven-year-old girl Alma, managed to get the completely unrecorded child a French passport before he and the soldier ran away back into the Pacific. If you believed a word she said.

Edith's passenger had lived around the Bay for a long time, seen the Beats come, seen the evolution of their brief hagiocracy, and been around as, with revered exceptions, they mostly exiled themselves again, exile a comfortable condition for them. With irony but mostly because he was a character, the passenger tossed in a little of the dated hep-cat slang and metaphor-burdened speech that the public had somehow confused with Ferlinghetti and Kerouac and all. Not to overplay though, he generally avoided the rhyme and alliteration.

"Just saying, this sheila remains informed, love. No points for saying I sent you, she's got your story in the drawer."

·

"My mom's name is Alma too," said Edith.

"Oh?" said the girl.

"How'd you wind up staying with Gail?"

"Some other time. More to the moment, why I'm still here since she's not," said the girl, Alma.

"Why's that?"

"Utilities still on. Theft of services," lifted the cork from a glass container, "Here, take a good deep sniff of this."

"What is it?"

"Water lily seeds," Alma said, "I grind them for tea. Isn't that lovely?"

"Yeah, nice. So Boorham and Gail paired up? Not a match, doesn't seem like. What's that about anyway?"

"Yeah," said Alma. "But he ain't as dumb as he looks. Nor

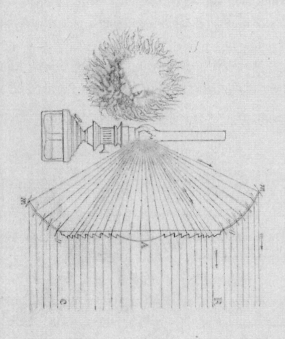

she's as ambitious, so. Here's a water lily crown," she rattled the dark gray disk with its two dozen strange, staring eyes.

"My God, you know what that looks like? Never mind, so where'd Boorham come from anyway? Gail grew up here."

Alma poured tea, "You'd already know that from Shelda."

"All I really know is, he walked into something out here that got way out of hand. And he's related to Shelda," said Edith.

"You have no idea what you're asking me to do."

"I guess not. Wanted your take is all."

After a few seconds, the girl shrugged, said, "They are extremely cousins. Boorham came out to build things for your guy Neil. They're all Texans of some kind. You know all that."

"Neil's not my guy," said Edith.

"So Neil, the man who sometimes works for you, had a sure thing, rich backers, just needed a welder. Here on a welder's holiday is where the boy came from. See, Neil is standing here drooling, with his dick in his ear, just staring into space as usual. One day a random synapse happens to fire and it lights off a brain fart, all that was. The big money was the only fabrication that came to pass."

"But where does Gail come in?"

"Patience," said Alma, "in a minute. You know you postponed the boy's death, right? So. Five kinds of pig meat and eggs. A potato I think. Not a pepper, not an onion.

"When I met Boorham? No, I found an onion at least. But what did you—"

"Shhh. An onion, revised then, thank you. Neil was anesthetized, watched his brother shovel with his fingers, you and Shelda split the piece of French toast, and Boorham swallowed his saliva. He is as dumb as he looks, I got that wrong a minute ago. You let him take *Candyass* for a row and he lost an oar thingie, dropped it in the drink."

"He got a new one over at the—"

"Natch," said Alma, "Whatever they dosed him with at that party—did you know he was the entertainment? Or didn't you know?"

"I—"

"You did good. Real sick little cowboy these days though, I get that from Gail via thirdhand gossip."

"So Gail left with him? He came back? How did she—"

"Fucking minute Edie!" Standing, "I owe you so much less than nothing, where's your manners?"

"Okay, wow, sorry, sorry."

Alma thought for a moment, hunkered again next to Edith on the tuffet of folded-up carpet pad, sipped from her teacup, said, "I apologize, you had the advantage of being raised in a barn. I will try to match your exemplary behavior."

"What? Okay, in a barn, sure. Yeah you could say that," said Edith, "But you kind of lost me back there."

"Yeah that'll happen. To answer your question, Gail was out of the house."

"When?"

"When Boorham came over to say hi to Neil's wife, they were friends back in Texas. Boy came to say hi because his illusion's that the FuDog—you know that guy?"

"Yeah I know who you mean anyway. Why was the wife here at Gail's?"

"Shhh. His illusion's that the FuDog is an underworld villain out to getcha, who wants to tie the wife to the tracks like Gloria Swanson because Neil owes him money. Wife told the boy flat out that that was Neil-babble, exact kind of thing she was taking refuge at Gail's from, total load of horseshit, everybody knows FuMan's the same menace value as a street mime. Bagpiper, mime, FuMan, juggler, Bob Dylan impersonator. And she'd be right except she never actually met him, and the other thing is, the man just can't quit acting, always on, you don't know who he's being, won't turn down a job, so for all you know the role calls for, like, actuality. Prob'ly not but why not murder. Extortion, jaywalking. But so Neil and the boy pretty much frog-marched her out of here and bolted in fucking terror, very un-Neil-like, fleeing in terror."

"Wow. Really?" said Edith, "One, he's fearless, like pathological fearless, and the amazing part's that he followed through on something. Do you mind if I ask—"

"Shhh. In a minute, wrong assortment and Gail's stuff doesn't fit yet. So during the—"

"Could you please stop for a second? I'm feeling real disoriented. We have met before, right? I mean to actually talk."

"Yes."

"Here? This is so funny, I remember we talked about the graffiti."

"It was right here. Do you think you can stand up?"

"Of course I can stand up—I'm not dizzy, I'm just weirded out."

Leisurely circuit around the room that felt to Edith like a set ritual, both stopping to look out onto the street, the tall girl said, "During the trip up 101, Neil developed his habit of picking up and hurling guys face first."

"No, really he was doing that before, too," said Edith.

"Revised then, thanks. He did something brutal to the wife. Something unimaginative probably, and brutal enough for her to seek medical attention after she and Boorham ran away back to Texas."

"Hey Alma."

"Shoot."

"Did you get all that from Boorham?"

"Not directly, doubt he knows my name."

"Where do you, uh, and why are you telling me?"

Ticked a fingernail repeatedly against her teacup, said, "What's your middle name?"

"Lin. Why?" said Edith.

"Short for Linnaeus?"

"What in the hell!"

"Edith Lin?"

"What."

"I like you, I always have."

"What in the hell!"

"This takes a lot out of me and I don't do it for just any-body. I'm happy to do it, but you kind of crowd me some-times, trespass a little bit. Okay?"

"Alright," said Edith, baffled. Strong sense of unreality.

"You, everybody, tells me things. Sort sort sort, tedious. I make up most of it, just fill in the pattern. Doomed to it. I see something of yours, I give it to you, throw it at you, it's what I'm doing—doesn't work but I try to get rid of it this way. Pathetic. We're almost at Boorham and Gail, if you're still interested."

"Josefina, whatcha got?" Edith squatted beside a small child who'd used her forehead to nudge Edith's leg. The kid indicated a re-crayoning of something she'd shown them a few minutes before. Edith nodded approval and asked about the unchildlike volute and whorls, white on blue, on another part of the big shoebox.

Around finger and thumb wiggling a loose tooth, the kid said, "That's the sky. Mama can't see it."

"She says the sky looks like boiling water," Alma said, "I no longer see that. Thanks, baby, we both think highly of the artwork.

"I watched 'em fuse!" Alma said to Edith, pointed at a spot between them, "Right here. Yuck. Appalling. Watched 'em gradually circle in, gravity well or something, came to a proximity threshold or whatever, and all of a sudden just kind of got sucked into one another. Is how Gail-and-Boorham was begat . . . You met Mil."

"Think so, why?" Edith said, "Smallish guy, face looks kind of asymmetrical. That one?"

Alma said, "Five-shot .38 in his pocket, '48 Ford panel truck with a stovepipe out the side like it's signaling a right turn. Out of carny season he's a department-store window dresser. Gail and Shelda—he knows some walled-off history out in Kansas, conspicuous opacity, blind spot I will not visit intentionally. Interesting guy—French Indochina ugly-American deal, did a nickel for smack, oddly light stretch for a scapegoat, considering the volume of heroin. Keeps getting fired from fatherhood—he's Josefina's daddy—I kicked him out too because I was microbiologically incompatible with his boyfriend at the time. I'm tall and Mil isn't, reverse sexual dimorphism, but as it happens we worked in the carnival. Oh Jesus, Edie this is wearing me out, being nice to you."

"Okay, sorry, I'll go. Thanks for everything, you've been—"

"God, I'd give anything to be rid of all this stuff, no, sit, you're not done."

After a minute, confused, Edith said, "Josie's about four, you must've been a child yourself . . . looks so much like you I would've thought virgin birth or spontaneous generation or something."

"Nope. Mil. All his genes are recessive. She's not four yet. Shush please." Deep sigh, "Here you go. You'll need this. Up in Seattle, some dude thought he'd, like, take pro-prietorship of Mil's wife and so the baby's monthly welfare check, since the woman was perfectly fine with that. 'Hey man I just balled your old lady,' and Mil said 'Suits me. This is where I came in.' Dude busted the left zygomatic bone up into his eye socket, so Mil was blind and unconscious and shot the guy dead, femoral artery. Crawled out on the street, hindbrain thinking the dude's still after him, dude's scream-ing, wife's screaming, baby's screaming. Passersby bailed out of a tan '56 Buick, tossed him in, drove off."

"Exactly a Buick, '56, tan, okay. And why'd they do that?" said Edith.

"Shhh. '55, '6, '7, right in there. Tan. With portholes. Why'd they do what? Not the worst circumstances in Mil's career because somebody showed up with red beans and rice or something every few days, and he could've just walked off if he wanted, just an open shed with a water hydrant that only froze a couple of times, but he could not wake up all the way. Kept weaving little holiday wreathes out of bushes and stuff, plastered them with mystery gunk he fingered up out of a can. Fever dream, cycling over and over, frustration dream making these stupid wreaths, couldn't bring himself to do anything else but sleep in the '48 Ford panel truck full of horse blankets."

"Alma?"

"Hm?"

"We did talk before now, didn't we?"

"Yes. We still did talk before now."

"I don't feel right. I remember you got mad at me is all. Hey, did somebody set this up?" asked Edith.

"Dunno. Did somebody send you?" asked the sepia girl.

"Old Doots said I ought to meet you but uh . . ."

Skeptical glance, "Somebody sent you. Who was it?"

Edith said, "I don't know. Did somebody? Never mind."

Alma closed one eye, looked at her with exaggerated skepticism, smiled.

Edith said, "You lost me."

"Nothing to get, really. A dog took up with him . . . or . . . well it did, but, sorry, not your item, forget the dog. After a month or five weeks, Mil could sometimes make both eyes look at the same thing, got the truck running, went to Texas. But there *was* a dog. There's always a dog. There was even a dog with your gramma, dog that ran away up the shingle the last second when that barge rolled over and exploded."

"What! Finish that!" said Edith, not caring if she upset the deranged woman.

Tiredly, "I don't know where that came from either, and it's all I have for you. In there with the rest of your goddamn debris and I don't know anything! Sorting, sorting."

"Wait a minute!" Edith said. Alma's teenage face aged momentarily, flickered scary feral eyes and teeth.

"After he dropped Boorham off here, said hi to his daughter, went God knows. Dressing mannequins and waiting for circus season. Perry had got killed. I think. Don't have that and I should have that, blind spot. Shelda was around somewhere, didn't want company—she was starting into that, you know, that thing. Thing that's got her. All I have, Edie, free to go."

Edith said, "You talk like you're not, uh, younger. Than them. You act a lot older. Like a lot older."

"I'm the same age as your guy Anders, thirty-two, thirty-three."

"Okay. Whatever you say. Seen Anders by the way?"

Pause, then Alma said, "Thought that's why you're here, wanted Gail's take on it, on your current events. He's gone, sweetie, yesterday evening. Sorry, thought you knew."

"Okay, well. Tell me," said Edith.

"Yeah I did talk to Anders. Unmarked Plymouth out front when he got to work, and all these suits waiting, like just ridiculous, and he thinks no, screw it, no, just fade. Got into a Mercedes, some buttoned-down slick in it. Fedora, I'm not kidding. Mirror sunglasses. But the hell with the getup, it would've been easy to recognize him and I didn't. Or her or it. Blind spot."

"JD? You know, the soldier, Shelda's ex-boyfriend?"

"Not him. And smaller. I don't know who it was, Edie."

"Oh shit." Edith put her cup on the floor, closed her eyes. "Not FuMan. Oh seriously now."

"One obvious candidate, sure. No say," enunciating, "I think I may have said that I don't know who it was, Edie," said the sepia girl.

After a moment Edith said, "Anders got my chambray shirt."

Josefina had apparently finished her crayoning, the vivid big shoebox ready to be a prop in a dream. She turned it upside down, lid and all, dumped a wheeled contrivance like an oversize roller skate clattering onto the floor. Josie tossed the labored-over box aside, put her doll in the skate, and butt in the air, began running the skate around the apartment.

•

Once again the business card did its trick—the pay phone connected mid-word to a woman's voice, speaking not the strings of numbers Edith had heard the last time she dialed, but words that seemed at least to link grammatically. Not regionless as before either, a slight East Texas pronunciation, cadence, familiar-sounding manner. "Shelda? Hey Shelda?" The nonsensical ramble went conversationally on and on, sometimes reiterating, all just barely impossible to track, to follow. Interrupted at intervals by the operator requiring more coins. Edith had prepared for that—a protracted long-distance call might cost her an average day's pay. After twenty minutes the voice stopped arbitrarily, as if switched off. After a beat, the coin return clattered. Hair rising on the back of her scalp, Edith began vaguely to remember things she knew hadn't happened to her. Or things of hers that she'd never known belonged to her, some in focus, or nearly so, or fleeting on the periphery of the mind's eye, memory that bore information from the five senses. Queasy, Edith folded back the phone-booth door, absently collected her change, stood hanging by a finger in the coin return. A child's hand held a photograph of her mother's mother, a woman named Josefina who'd gone missing in the early 1920s.

•

Running a fingertip along a seam between smoothly edge-to-edge narrow boards of an upturned hull, she was not idle. Paid close attention to the fingertip and to the freshwater sea in front of her. Carefully watched a pair of ships that were at first on the horizon, now near enough for her to see clearly—the departing one trailing smoke from its stack in the usual way, the approaching one half-lost in smoke venting from places along its length. Seen through the drifting smoke, a lifeboat had been off-and-on visible for a while against a glaring sunrise, as the barge's small crew rowed toward the lake freighter that had cut them loose.

Here at the other end of the day, sun low behind, the land's accelerating shadow progressed over Josefina and down the brief rocky shore, and darkened low onshore swells, and soon reached the two-hundred-foot cigar shape of the derelict vessel. Broadside to her now, enormous now, the hulk groaned piteously.

Smoke jetted steadily, violently, from under enormous steel hatch covers, heat sagging them and warping the air over them, causing a distant flight of geese to ripple, momentarily enlarge or disappear. The smell of the wreck had preceded it by hours, a pinewood fire with the sourness of incomplete combustion, two-and-a-quarter-million pounds of sawdust bound for the paper-mills was smoldering. Josefina observed with perfect attention, noted that her back was chilly, her front was uncomfortably warm, noted that she was coughing, paid exquisite attention to the groaning and whistling of the thing as shadow seeped up it, eclipsed it. Now in shade and quite close as it reached the island's submerged slope and began to roll over, the gigantic iron container glowed dully here and there.

Workaday • on the fly

"You going to bail?" They sat on a bench outside the rental office, late afternoon, starting to get chilly.

He said, "Right this second anyway, not really. Burned through my life savings this afternoon. Tens of dollars up in smoke. That lady over there, surely goodness and mercy shall follow her, she didn't have to give the deposit back," indicated the four twenties on his knee.

"Any other prospects? You get the Trident gig? That was on the list, wasn't it? For last night. And, like, if you want to go a long ways away, where would you go?

"Can't believe that lady, too considerate to chat me up even, you know she had to be curious. So the boat deposit and filling in tending bar tonight buys a change of clothes and stuff. And some distance. No Trident gig," shrugged, "but ask any frog if he needs a Trident gig."

"So besides the one-nighter at the bar, you have some job prospects? I mean here?"

"Get back on at Fred's pretty sure, we parted friends. 'Bout a week, if I'm still unincarcerated, you want to be my fellow traveler? Comrade Edith?"

"Oh uh. Yeah but. I mean dang, Anders. My boat would be okay in lockup for a while but man I don't know—five kinds of cops and the United States Coast Guard, I hear the rustle of good ol' American warrants. Theft Over Shitload Dollars, Felony Mischief, Felony Wanton Dicking Around in Coastal Waters, Felony Public Endangerment in the Commission of Cavorting with Citizens or . . ."

He said, "Piracy! You forgot good ol' piracy."

"Oh jeez, I'm sorry, way not funny."

"Perfectly fine."

"Your house is a submerged navigation hazard," she said, "and . . . oh God, baby, my gut just sank, are you on pretty good terms with your landlord, Anders? Word has it, that's a whole, whole other bunch of trouble. Jesus, I think they're already looking at me too. It's scary, it's that crazy shit, whoever they are, you say you don't know. Almost better the FBI finally bestir themselves. Shine up their shoes. Nope, I'm going to chicken out. Come join you afterwhile, we figure how to do messages."

"So maybe I might, uh, abandon ship. Not wait. Press on to the next debacle."

She said, unable to stop going down the list, "I can swear you had nothing to do with it, but I have been shacking up with you. Guaran-damn-tee you *somebody* will come knocking at my door. I told you who owns your sunk houseboat? FuDog, little joke of a dude, but all that crazy shit, the graffiti thing, he's right in there. Word has it. Might ought to not send stuff to my PO box, it's been deconsecrated for weeks, I get this creepy junk mail anymore and uh and, some real ugly stuff I really wish I had not seen. And it's ridiculous, letters get steamed open and ironed shut, they make it obvious."

"Your boogeymen. Why not, word on the street occasionally has something under it, and you uh, okay it's pretty clear you have a situation. I'm going back and forth, being an indecisive weenie. Don't want to leave a bunch of warrants open. And how serious is it you know? My houseboat burned down, big deal," shrugged, "nobody died. And I should . . . you know, properly stay here and shield you with my manly resolve."

"Could they extradite you? Prosecute, like, here for the overseas stuff?"

"Jesus Christ, Edie. You are a little ray of sunshine," he said, "Don't know. I'm told it's not likely, they just hold it forever, keep me in line. Guatemalan military could give a shit, they already disappeared all those folks, and CIA is way, oh God are they way too busy down there to bother with me. Stray featherweight. I mean, surely. Anyway whatever—you serious about, like, harboring me? Time being?"

"Yeah well the apartment's a broom closet, warning to watch your diet, you start blowing a lot of manly resolve farts in there, you're on the sidewalk, buddy jim."

•

"Git git git! Go to work," groped for the alarm clock. Half-asleep and vaguely amorous, he'd begun to roll on top of her when she heaved him solidly against the wall.

"Jesus! Whoa. Good morning dear," he said. Fairly sturdy guy, he was surprised how easily she did that. Edith wasn't round but she was wide and, unclothed, obviously well muscled under her layer of estrogen-soaked fat. Out of bed to make way for him, she put a kettle on the hotplate, got down some raisin bread,

"Shower, you stink, beg on at Fred's, work a shift, and if you don't mind buy some basics, like your own goddamn toothbrush. I got a chambray shirt you can borrow should fit, spare knapsack if you want it, that's about it I think, pussy maybe, c'mon c'mon I have to shower too, go all over the boat again, I play tour guide at nine."

Standing, half hard, "Wrangling the crew," he said.

Naked, measuring coffee, "Yep, livestock management, basic husbandry, now git, stud!"

"At least we have time for my daily fifty, you go shower first" he said.

"Be the last pushups you do before you have to part your hair to shit! Coffee's ready when you come out. Damn, out of peanut butter. No, there's enough."

•

Walking the neighborhood that evening, whistling for the dog, "So funny it doesn't feel malicious! Roughhousing. Messing with me and they happened to burn you out," called, "Hippolyta! C'mere girl!"

"I don't think you're the, I don't think you're necessarily the designated 'it.' I mean the target, the subject. Things hit close to you and it looks like a pattern but maybe that's just us making sense of chaos."

"I put her out to pee like usual, left the door open. She never took off for more than two minutes before."

"Want to go check the docks?"

"No. She would've just . . . I don't know, let's go home. I'll just keep getting up and looking, see if she came back. So I'm not the designated 'it'? Okay, that kinda ticks me off. No, listen man, you don't get it, they really are persecuting me just because I'm Emperor Napoleon fucking Bonaparte."

"You're the sanest person I know," carefully unhooked her granny glasses, gazed sweetly at her in the gloom, "Stable like a rock in the currents . . . I think you see a swirl, an eddy around you. Not the whole thing."

She said, "Oh my lord, I'm trying not to puke. But okay I think I follow. Nice steady chunk, in your estimation. I am so wonderfully concrete! There you go, I love that, sweetest thing anybody could say about me. We're both seeing a pattern plain as day but yours is much grander, yeah I understand now. 'Scuse me, I'm merely noticing small stuff

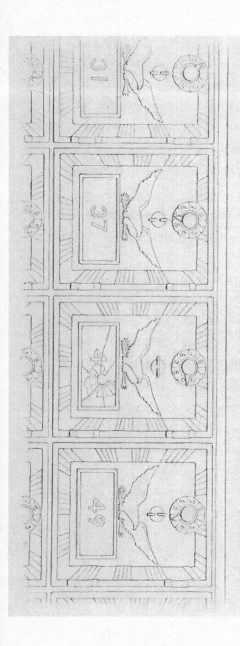

In which an Aegis proves illusory,
really no Aegis at all

172

because it happens to me. So tell me this 'whole thing' you're, like, perceiving."

"Hoo! I said that wrong."

"Seems like," she said. Took back her glasses. "Straight-up hardheaded peasant, yeah man I actually know that, here's a secret, intuition's piss-poor too, but I do get the idea pretty quick. Anders listen, I know sure as anything . . . Listen! Somebody's just jacking with me, but it's, they'd turn right around and murder the shit out of somebody too. I know it! And no ill will! God I hope they don't do something to my dog. Whoever it is, they'd step over your body and go prank somebody else. Anders? My goddamn dog is missing."

Walking in silence for a minute, he said, "It's like I ought to know. I'm lost as you are. You're a name in my file by now, if that has anything to do with anything."

She stopped, put her glasses on, just looked at him.

He asked her, "Who'd that look like? Out there?"

"Wow, on your boat? Bandana guy? Up there at the helm stealing your house. I was thinking that too, you mean JD? The soldier. Maybe, kind of, I don't know him real well. Looked like the Zig-Zag man, can you grow a beard that fast?"

"I sure can't but yeah it could be him."

•

Anders sat up in bed making sounds through clenched teeth, shivering in a ragged palsy. The man's wide-open eyes stared at something that horrified him. Unable to catch a breath, out of his mind as such, out of reach as such. She woke beside him, saw nothing where he was looking, grabbed him hard, wrapped herself around him, pressed her cheek against the side of his head. He couldn't wake up. He said, "I'm sorry," difficult shuddering intake of breath, "I'm sorry," the gasp, again and again.

•

"I have to get rid of these people, 'scuse me I'll be right back. Josie! Hut!"

A small child who'd let Edith in now led her to the other end of the room. Repeatedly picking up crayons as she dropped them, the kid ran back to the door to retrieve a big shoebox she'd been decorating, brought it to show Edith. Around the rim of the lid, a band of lettering in black crayon looked medieval, liturgical—most of the letters in the right direction, BISQUICK OLD STYLE STREUSEL like a dedication or fragment of scripture on a reliquary. The box brought Edith strongly to mind of some sweet forlorn event, something she finally placed as a dream she'd had, about a dowry chest and a bleak room. This current room, remembered as an uncluttered window-lit space whose order had spoken of clarity and reason, was unswept now, its blinds drawn, and empty cardboard boxes lay here and there where an oval hooked rug and an Amish sideboard and a Victorian swooning couch had been.

Talk rose in insistency, running water stopped, the talk continued, sounding belligerent. Edith stepped close to the child, who peered from behind her as a number of young men and women came up the hallway dropping wet towels and fastening their clothes and saying ugly things to the tall fierce teenage girl following close behind, who picked up towels as she went and flailed them against the floor.

"Alright, I'm impressed," said Edith.

"Well. Easy, all these sweet middle-class kids. Somebody's boyfriend kept a key looks like or God knows," the teenager said, "I'm Alma, this is Josefina."

"Hi, I'm Edie," said Edith.

"I know," said Alma, fifteen or sixteen years old, red-brown hair, eyes, and skin, "Whatcha need?"

Edith said, "Josie's a fine one. Little sister?"

"No," said Alma, "Looking for Gail? Or Terrell or what's-her-name?"

Edith said, "Yeah, Gail. She around?"

Alma said, "No. I see the stove's still here, I'll make some tea. Espresso machine took a walk while we were out, all this shit keeps disappearing. Gail went up blissful canyon some-where with Boorham. Terrell's stuff is gone, never have seen the other one."

"Gail left with Boorham?"

"Right."

"Still got a phone?"

"Yes. Disconnected. Josefina! Hut!" The very small girl

reappeared from the landing, closed the door, stretched up and locked it. "Edie, where's your dog?"

"Disappeared, I don't know. Can't find her," said Edith.

"Wow," said Alma.

"You know the old guy from where? Albert."

Alma said, "Doots. Busking coffeehouses. Up here in North Beach peddling his papers. Put out the jar two or three times like commensal feeders, good thing when it happens, he walks up and down and does his bombast shit. I add viola commentary, crescendo as he gets to the point. Or sometimes he does."

"Any particular day? I'd like to see."

"Nope. Unpremeditated."

Edith took a leap, "What, ah, what is the logo on my signal flag? The signal thing people use so I'll row out."

"Where do you get off?"

"Pardon?"

"A little presumptuous, testing my acumen or something, what makes you think that's alright? But your ensign, it's some kind of hat—just flashed on 'Take the "A" Train.' Or 'String of Pearls,' I get them mixed up."

Edith said, "I did do kind of a test thing I guess, wanted to know if you recognized the cap is all, didn't even know I was rude. So now I know. But can I ask a question?" After several seconds without response, "What's the graffiti thing, looks a little bit like my flag? The graffiti you see all over the place all of a sudden, black stencil about this big."

"Just a sec. Hang on. Having to turn off the '40s music, hang on, damn. There!" Speaking gently, "Edie, you have no way of knowing, and it's not your fault really, but you kind of wear me out. Already. But yeah the graffiti is mostly bullshit. It mostly just caught on. Nothing, mostly."

"Okay," said Edith.

"Okay, you need to know. This is yours and I need to get rid of it, what the stencil thing started out as. Ticka ticka . . . Okay I'm going to make this up but it's right . . . or hang on, no. No, what I was going to say is not right, because what I was going to say was, the graffiti started out as advertising come-on. For some, like, mind control shit? You ready for that? What I was going to say was, it's the advertising end of a socio-military R&D job. Picture a roomful of Yalies, there's some acronym on the door and they cook up plots and hijinks and entrapments and intrigues all day. Dulles brothers stop in to shoot the breeze from time to time.

"That's what I was going to say but it's bullshit and it's not even my bullshit, it's a cartoon strip in the rag," rubbed her temples, "I forgot it's not mine. Since that story is bullshit, the only thing for sure is that the graffiti thing, effort, project—it started off organized. That's all. *Now* I will make stuff up. Spray-painting that thing everywhere—it was organized and also half-assed. Inattentive, you know? Somebody hatched all this plot but did not take it seriously. An ad campaign is supposed to catch on, so far so good. So it did catch on and the ad men say okay now what, we only got this vague notion. And there's money to pay for whatever the fuck they come up with. And there's crazy tone deafness about the whole thing. And I have no earthly idea. Cancel and drain everything. The whole deal is nothing, mostly. All you get."

"I saw the comics and I met the guy that draws them, he says he did, I used to see him clipping hedges and mowing those tiny yards with a push mower."

"His old lady did the story and he did the graphics and they split town."

"Where'd they go? I'd like to talk to her, it's like they were reading my mail, 'know? They were so good, the strip was."

"Cuba," said Alma.

"Oh. Why?" Getting no reply, "So what was the advertising selling? What was the, the pitch? You said mind control?"

"After which I said that's all bullshit. That couple made it up. And I'm about done with this, Edie, it was a fucking comic strip! I don't want to get worked up. I saw it in the funnies. I'm getting worked up. Transgressive cartoonists dicking around! I don't know!" An undecipherable, agitated hand gesture, "You want the fucking synopsis of what you already read in the funnies? God you're . . . okay, I am being nice," Alma was taking her own pulse, "Here. This is what they drew. Brain hijacking worked on a random guinea pig one time, some disposable soldier. And it's totally a shot in the dark—kind of like, let's see what happens with this or that disposable boy when we expose him to whatever this stuff is. That's it! Okay?"

"It's what I remember."

"But uh. You've heard those stories though. 'Hey, let's hand out dark glasses and line 'em up outside to watch the mushroom cloud, then monitor their pee for radiation. Hey, next let's see what they do with ten thousand mikes of lysergic.' And you say, 'Whoa, yeah we kind of do know they do that shit, don't we.' And but then you say, 'Oh but seriously c'mon, oh heavens no, *no* rogue agency of *ours* would really do stuff like that for real! We wouldn't let them! I am so very glad it only happens in the funny papers!'" Then Alma said quietly, "And uh. Well, there is a fan club. They are on their own now, doing whatever they do. Autonomous. They pass out the stencils, I don't know why. I am done sorting through this stuff for you, oh Jesus I hate this," fingers on her wrist again, taking her own pulse, "All you get. Back off please."

Edith said, "You, uh. You just . . . answer?"

"What?"

"Who are you?"

"Edie you're . . . Fuck off!" Standing, "It's like you're putting quarters in, go away if you would, please, I'm being nice, go away now before I fucking murder you."

Edith stared up at the sepia girl, thought that it might've been an actual threat, said quickly, "Dark metal, super heavy, kind of flat, and about this big around."

Ready to tear into her, Alma instead paused, "Really. Really. You saw such a thing, then. My my. Guessing it's a dose. The dose. I knew a couple of the, like, converts to the non-movement, or they thought they were. Converts or followers or like that. Not so secretive, or these weren't. Not then, kind of selectively proselytizing in fact. It's called a crown or wreath, don't know anyone who actually handled the thing. You?"

"Yes."

Looked at Edith as if deciding what to say. Finally, "Bye. Oh, I never made tea. Next time. Hope you find your dog."

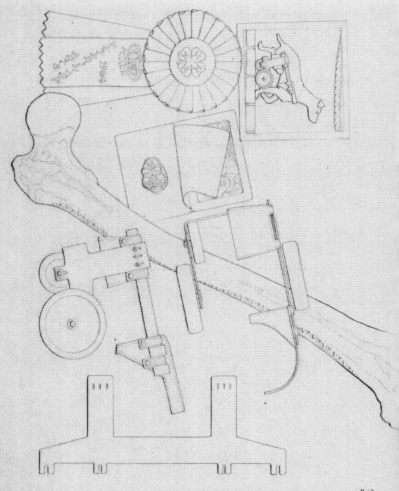

in which Numina Abide

Immersion • the sinking of the *owly cat*

Especially the volatile organic compounds for "citrus" and "floral," synthetic fragrances blended with phosphate detergent's ozone-like sharpness—together a bracing artificial scent advertised as that of springtime; energetic chugging and the start-and-stop torrents of city water rushing in and being impelled out beyond the harbor low-tide mark as an unremediated solution of industrial waste; clothes tumbling in dryers—a tropical percussion of buckles, buttons, and stray pocket change; a gray-haired woman as small as a child, folding warm cottons beside a much younger woman at a long mica-top table, its surface like a pink-tinted photograph of cleft slate polished through in places to the white substrate; and immersed so within the atmosphere of their America, speaking loudly over the racket, the quick and wren-like gray woman reviewed the movie *Blowup* for her younger tablemate.

Behind them at the bank of enormous machines, dressed

in a ratty tank top and her best Wranglers, the ones with paisley gussets she'd sewn in to flair the cuffs, Edith pulled off
her socks and tossed them in, got detergent out of the vend-
ing machine, and started her load. Going through the pockets of her regular jeans earlier, she'd turned up a business
card that represented some things left unresolved, and rather
than use the pay phone on the wall, went a few doors down
the sidewalk to a booth. Keeping the door open—different
kinds of smells in there—by habit checked the coin return,
dialed zero; after a perfunctory exchange with the long-distance operator, Edith fished a handful of laundry-day change
from her pocket, dropped coins rattling through the works.
Without a ring a woman's voice began mid-word, spoke one-
by-one a series of numbers. In American English with no trace
of region, a dozen or two dozen numbers, a pause, another
series or maybe the same series, three minutes' worth. When
the operator required more coins, Edith hung up, smiled.
Amused, uneasy. Innocuous enough prank, except for the fact
it was being played at all. That it took some engineering, that
it may've been intended for her specifically.

•

Designing, building, and washably upholstering a prosthesis for her gimpy pup had been Edith's idea for a 4-H project
one winter, age fifteen. She'd produced with a cousin a slick
little candy-apple-red trailer the year before, took a ribbon

at the state fair. But something unlikely to ribbon, esoteric, kind of urgent had come up this time—the dog's name was Hippolyta, or Hippie, several years before there were hippies. Spine was okay, but the pup's hind legs had been hopelessly crushed by an oblivious three-quarter-ton cow. The dog was adept and agile on the wheeled contrivance Edith had invented that winter, having lived its life on it so far, adjusted as the animal grew. Could wriggle out and get back into it, right it the rare times it tipped over, and on even terrain might glide along head up, chest out like a miniature dog-headed Viking ship, quite a sight to see.

At the moment, a wise dog as dogs go, it kept between Edith's feet to stay out of harm's way in a small crowd on the end of the dock. Edith had run into someone who said there'd be a show of some kind out there—hard to figure how, until it began materializing as she watched, coalesced as the audience repurposed itself as the show, the happening. With her were friends and familiar people, standing around talking, occasionally looking across at an out-anchored houseboat, waiting for whatever was to begin. By twos and fours they ferried over in the houseboat renter's skiff, joined the folk lined facing outward on the small fore- and afterdecks and on perilous foot-wide planking on either side of the cabin, not a completed ring of people yet. Some linked arms, or laid arms across their neighbors' shoulders; small chains of people touched fingertips, swaying in unison. Clear chilly day, the sounds of conversation around her and the skiff's outboard motor and noise of gulls and distant maritime activity outside this alcove, a shallow, relatively calm corner of the Bay. A momentary burst of gray smoke from time to time bubbled from under the back of the houseboat, drifted away on the air.

They'd begun a two-step side to side out there. It became more involved, short kick-steps catching on around the circle, circle now complete, even getting crowded, bunched up fore and aft. As another three people climbed aboard from the skiff and joined the now-united troupe in high spirits, a few began to sing and the rest took it up, well aware they were doing a fine job and celebrating their own spontaneity. They'd invented irony of course, as every generation does, and their plaintive Top 40 love song was rendered hilarious by the chorus line and marijuana. In a while the remaining dozen people around Edith gave up waiting for another run out there, wandered off. She was alone with her dog on the end of the dock, missed the last boat.

A few seconds' gout of smoke enveloped the stern, cleared as irregular popping settled into an even basso rattle, exhaust bubbling steadily. Something happening on the rear deck within the circle of dancers, then someone's head and shoulders came up above the others at the rear of the cabin, a person with a short black beard and red bandana. Ran the throttle slowly up and back down, then turned around to direct some activity behind him; the chorus line at the back of the boat paused to maneuver a concrete anchor onto its perch, and resumed their evolving, mutating song-and-dance routine.

"Where's *Candyass*?"

"Anders what in the hell you aren't out there," said Edith.

"Looks like they're driving off."

"Well shit I guess!"

"Where's your boat, Edie?"

"Tethered to you, man! This is so fucked. God damn it, so neither of us made it back last night." The short rope straightened between her boat and the big one as it turned away under power, abandoning Anders's rental, already drifted a ways off.

He said, "Doubt they make half a mile in an hour."

Looking down this pier, scanning the opposite one, Edith shrugged, "Borrow a canoe, they let us throw all their tent and shit on the dock and they still got paddles, or we could go knocking on doors. I left the walkie-talkie out there. Nothin's all I got within an hour." She turned to go, "Calling Chuck or somebody to take us out there."

"Edie?" He was pointing, "Look where that guy's standing, the bandana guy."

•

The previous evening, ferrying party-goers to and between two houseboats hosting a hundred yards apart, Edith held her boat *Candyass* tightly against a boarding ladder. Because it tracked straight, her boat also rolled if you stood on the rim of it. The first passenger, with ringlets and a handsome strong jaw, steadied himself on her shoulder, then reached inside her vest, momentarily confused by the various pieces of hardware hanging between her breasts on a cotton lanyard. Tweaked a nipple, an inquiring expression on his face, said, "Ooh, uptight," as his hand was yanked by the wrist, flung. She inventoried her hardware—useful items, and also the high school ring of an ex-classmate, a clerk typist so far surviving whole-body blast injury incurred on guard duty. The next passengers, women underdressed for the weather in tiny crushed-velvet skirts and beads mostly, climbed past, the last handing over some bills—tips were good tonight.

"You really don't know who he is?" the woman asked.

"Saw them open for the Yardbirds. Pompous-ass lyrics, the ones he didn't rip off, but he's a pretty good bass player."

"Dear dear dear, he'll be fucking inconsolable, captain."

As the fares debarked into the amplified music and strings of lights, a pair of cops in jodhpurs and splendid high boots, and Sam Browne belts with hogleg revolvers in old-style military holsters, rumbled up the pier and right down the unsound wooden dock. Turned their massive, low-slung, arrogantly slouching Electra Glides back the way they'd come, conferred, parked, pulled citation books from their saddlebags, served notice on the host. Pretended relaxed cool getting back to the bikes. Eyed the dock sitters, assumed the presence of weed among them—a first offense drew one to ten, second offense two to twenty, the third bust five to life—dock sitters who'd already flicked into the harbor their roaches with a few hits left in them, or in one panicky case four film cans of the dry flaky weed of the era and a dozen attractive machine-rolled wheat-paper joints intended for retail, all of which, the kid was appalled to see, floated.

The house party's rock bands had again connected to neighbors' electricity to get enough current, and a landlord had called the cops. Unplugging them hereabouts sometimes caused bottle throwing, and the cops rumbled off, leaving the landlord to his own devices.

Sun going down, preparing to row away from the party for the last fare of the evening, Edith saw a man standing above her among the partiers on the dock, looking right and left, down at his feet to consider, left and right. Saw him compose himself, stand up straight, march off up the ramp toward the pier. Clearly impaired and doing his best.

"Boren! Hey Boren!" He looked around from under the party lights. She said, "Hey man. Down here." He looked into the shadow below the ramp, the water a ways down because the tide was out. "Boren is it?"

"Close enough," he said.

"Stay put, guy. I'll be right there, want to say hi for a sec," Edith shouted over the music. Stood, dropped an oar into a U-shaped brass in the high little transom and sculled in behind the houseboat; whipped a light chain around a piling, caught it on the third try, padlocked the boat to it, hung her chewed-up fender boards over the side. Mindful of barnacle scrapes, sure infection in the septic water and murderous to her wooden boat, Edith walked an encrusted crossbeam and hauled herself up onto a tire, climbed onto the ramp.

Swarming, stomping dancers on the houseboat and on the dock, dancers intent on destruction or not caring if it happened, were abruptly dumped out of their ecstatic microcosm when the music quit, the strobes and strings of lights went dark, and the vibe imploded without a pop.

•

Rising angry objection didn't quite drown out the drummer who, unamplified, had seized a moment, cut loose amid the loud grousing and outraged shouts; then as the voices dwindled into party chatter, the drumming drifted into higher art, varied meditation, drum-tripping as some of the crowd drifted away, some stayed to listen, and some simply milled, waiting for whatever was next, because most were newcomers and this was clearly a scene, and the scene was what they'd come looking for.

Ramp crowded with people leaving, Edith located the kid without difficulty, right where she'd left him.

"Hey man. Boren, right?"

"Uh yeah, Boorham. Neil's chick?"

"Not in this lifetime. But yes you and I met this very morning. I let you take my boat out. How're your travels this evening, brother?"

"Uh well totally fucked, I got dropped, harsh since you ask and rush starting real hard and I don't do this too well since you ask. I lost your oarlock."

"And you very kindly replaced the lost rowlock with a shiny new one, much appreciated, most people just leave it. Let's take a walk. Can you see?"

"Well that's uh, I don't know. Yes I can. Look I don't trust you. I am not radiating," he said.

"Makes sense, but you're in control, just maybe better if you don't talk, okay? We're going right down here," she said, "Don't sweat it, guy, the only sin is frettin'."

Steering him onto a dock down the way and holding his upper arms from behind, guided him across the gangplank and into a shallow onboard gear locker.

"Is that sirens?"

"Shh. Crystal spheres," she whispered, "You ever run your finger around the rim of a water glass? Wow Boorham it's showing you the good stuff, just go with it." Of course it was sirens. He recognized in several of his awarenesses that her patronizing bullshit was said in kindness; too, in that state things were simultaneously true and not. Hoping the kid would remain there for the duration, Edith went up on her toes, kissed him on the mouth, whispered "Déjà vu" into his ear. There, that ought to keep him busy. Clapped the sides of his face soundly, gave him a rough, comradely slap on the shoulder, shut the door, and went on about her duties.

"Bye," he said through the door.

Aboard *Candyass*, commotion on the houseboat deck twenty feet away caught her attention, turned out to be a large hairy man in plaid shirttails, shirt open, uncircumcised and swagging heavily pendulous, pantless, a man named Neil whom she sometimes hired to row passengers. Surrounded by the three women ferried over earlier who were mobbing him like jays mob a nest robber, plucking and beating—Neil had their man by the belt buckle and hair, threw him head-first into the harbor. It was a quirky thing Neil sometimes did, that and going naked in public. Edith extended an oar to the struggling, dog-paddling musician. Neil, slack-faced, turned to go, arms dangling, taking small deliberated steps, Frankenstein's monster.

•

Greasy smoke trickled from under the hatch cover the helmsman stood on; the ring of dancers broke, fanning their faces, coughing, to let the dense foul rivulet fall over the side, as the hatch cover itself began to bloom smoke and Edith took off on the two-hundred-yard run to a pay phone.

The man at the wheel jumped down onto the deck, found the big brass fire extinguisher useless, soda long expired. Handed the sole one-person life ring to a nearby sturdily built woman, laced his fingers for her to step into, flipped her overboard, a few others following her in; the man was calmly gesturing, herding, helping someone out of knee boots.

A yellow flare visible in the cabin windows, somewhere in the smoke the butane tank's regulator had begun to leak and now blew fire that in moments enveloped the interior, broke through glass to the outside. People mostly in their teens and early twenties floundered away from the burning houseboat, formed up again and again to help each other stay afloat. One managed to get out of his own prized shearling-lined denim, another her leaden Davy Crockett buckskins. Mostly, though, people cast off their only set of crummy street clothes, got naked in the fifty-five-degree seawater as part of a splendid irrationality beyond any possible expectation.

Anders panted, "Can . . . so diesel just lit off like that?"

Edith, out of breath and excited,

"Red-hot engine, just kept going, I was scared the prop'd get somebody. Lord that didn't take long, did it—we thought about doing that too, joyride."

"Can't do a damn thing can we," he said.

Shook her head, watching, fascinated, "Try to keep track of the people."

Multiple sirens in the distance, a small explosion popped away what was left of the hatch cover as fire blew out of the ruptured rear deck, and in places the hull began to burn to the waterline, the whole cabin burning inside-out. Two dozen kids treading water, the chorus line of a few minutes before only a few yards away from the fiery hulk, many ducking under as the heat got intense; the stern sank lower and suddenly-quenched parts detonated like fireworks, louder still under the surface. Coming up for air, some found dense spent steam and smoke evil to breathe. One later explained his shaved head as the result of surfacing under a floating mat of fuel and oil mixed with tar that had melted off of the hull. After several minutes of drama the old house only just floated, the last two feet of bow pointed straight up. Edith's rowboat had been dragged far enough down to swamp before the burning tether separated; awash but on the surface, possibly still sound, adrift, all four oars were being used for their slight buoyancy as people made for the houseboat's square prow standing unmoving in the low swells. Some reached *Candyass*'s nearly submerged gunnels, where a guy began bailing with a cowboy hat he somehow retained, being funny, the party wasn't over.

Half a mile out, a seventy-foot dhow's diagonal boom rose smoothly, unhurried, carrying up the broad, low triangular mainsail as anchor cable was hauled in hand over hand. The elegantly formed flexible shell of its hull was stitched together with thousands of neat lacings, perfect. All weathered gray African mahogany and neat white antifouling paint, finely joined and copper-roofed, it was a deep-water engineless sailing vessel just ornate enough, strikingly beautiful, eminent, seaworthy, and possibly silly. The steersman hung a big brown relaxed arm along his tiller, made a couple of hand signals to the crew, turned toward the shipwreck, noblesse oblige. From the metal-clad roof, crew set the launch upright onto the deck, prepared to put the miniature version of the dhow onto the water.

A little farther still, a sleek white twin-hull with a yard-high outboard snarled, rose mostly out of the water, bounced away barely under control from its two-masted yacht toward duty. People on unlicensed, dismasted, cat-infested fiberglass carcasses, and on a flatboat with oleander bushes growing all over it, on dead cabin cruisers tied rafted together three or four to an anchor, looked on. Some stood in small boats yanking on starter cords. A person in hair curlers rowed to the rescue in a tiny dented aluminum marsh scow.

•

When none among the two dozen rescued could think of anyone who might be missing, Edith called her mainte-nance-dock buddy Chuck, a homely man of shoulder slaps and side hugs, mustard-smelling beard stubble momentar-ily placed against her hair whenever they met. Fine with her because he was an okay guy, and she was pretty free with shoulder slaps herself. The amount Chuck asked for pump-ing out and towing must've been his cost and not much more, Edith figured, so she tipped well, cleaned out her cash.

Though in an unlikely scrap of good news, Anders had been given his boat deposit back.

Outside the boat rental, holding out something in his closed hand,

"Here you go."

"What," said Edith.

Anders dropped a chintzy souvenir ring into her palm, "It's nothing, really."

"Right," she said. "And?"

"Uh well it's all I own besides the very clothes on my back. I already offered you the boat deposit. For some reason."

"Yeah that was stupid," she said. "Why are you giving me the ring?"

"Try for gracious?"

"Oh. Sure, okay, thanks, this is real sweet of you, Anders, it's very nice."

"You're welcome. Glad you like it." He waited.

"What . . ." said Edith. After a second, not knowing what to make of this little exchange, gave an uncertain shrug. Lifted her glasses, examined the heart-shaped pink coral set in thin stamped silver, "'Galveston Island, Texas,'" she said, "Thank you, it's lovely. I must see this place. Okay, your turn."

"Dunno, never been there," he said.

"Look, I'm kind of tired."

"I was supposed to give it to Shelda. Not likely to see her at this point, since neither one of us lives here anymore."

"Okay. Who gave it to you that knew her," Edith said.

"Mennonite couple in Marquette, Kansas. I was flipping burgers behind the counter and they just walked in, with about four kids in tow, lady took it off her finger and handed it to her husband. He said if I should run across Shelda."

"Shelda by name? What!"

"Yeah! I have no idea, none whatsoever. They were real relaxed and friendly, but kind of distant in that way they have, and I asked what was going on, and he shook my hand and said a King James verse," turned his palms up, "then I landed here and met the person Shelda."

"Oh God. You are weirding me out brother. Okay why didn't you give it to her? Just tell me what you're doing, I don't like this!"

"Met her briefly once, before she left town, didn't have it with me. The silly ring. Didn't know JD 'til after she'd split. Whole story."

"Just tell me what you're doing. I don't like this. Everything. Do not."

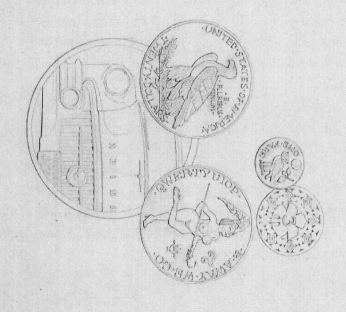

The Carny, the Columnist,
and the Obol • riding the rides

A car made a lazy U-turn in the boulevard in front of her. Alma looked back, saw it stop for the old man and Edith fifty yards away.

"Hey! Hey!" Kept staring up the busy street, the car no longer in sight. Traffic passed, a driver on the far side of the street demanded she put her foot back on the curb.

"Mama," reminded the child; after a second, Alma went back to her.

"Doots afraided you, Mama." Didn't seem to need reassurance or comforting, just confirmation. Given her difficult circumstances and temperament, Alma had mothered well.

"Yeah. Yeah. It's fine, baby. They're either okay or they're not, we can't do anything about it. Doots was just telling us 'bye anyway and he won't hurt," staring up the street, "He had a nice time with us today, we all had a nice time. Pretty good day so far don't you think? Remember how to cross yourself, baby?"

•

"What's the black stuff on your hair? Trying to look younger?"

"Hm? Who knows. Ah, typewriter ribbon. Have to get like one inch from the keys."

Albert normally tipped his ferryman with a fresh mimeograph copy of his newsletter, and it was barely three pages this time.

"What are you going to do for . . . you know, money. And, well, you know," asked Edith.

"Asking the wrong person, love," he said.

"Buy you a beer?"

"It'd be rude to say no," he said, "No thank you."

"What's the schedule?"

"City. See if I can find Alma, strut-n-fret-n-tweedle me hour 'pon the stage and hope for a real lot of coin in the clarinet case." Shrugged. "Has happened," he said.

"Hitch over with you."

In position as if waiting for them, the sepia girl sat cross-legged on a fringed cushion like a skinny Buddha, tuning her viola. Tuning an octave low, bridge and nut grooves expertly shaved to accommodate oversize Perlon strings, her bow a burly student model. Ear to the back of the instrument, the violist was unperturbed by the small child hanging on to her and wagging from side to side.

"I'll watch her, Alma," said Edith, by way of saying hello.

Over her shoulder, Alma said, "You can ask them for a chocolate chai, baby, careful don't burn your mouth okay?"

Her daughter looked doubtful, all those grownups at the counter. Went off to give it a try, Edith trailing unobtrusively.

"Hey, love," Albert said, laid out his clarinet case, dropped in the few coins and bills he had in his pocket. Assembled his instrument, tested the keys. The viola case was a satchel, awkward for donations, and Alma dumped the pump-priming coins and dollar bills from her child-decorated #10 tomato can into the case.

Too early yet for regulars, the coffeehouse was filling with late-morning tourists—business looked promising as they shut up the crowd with a straight *gymnopédie*, deftly traded it into the Old Spice theme. A little laughter and applause led by Edith from the side, and Albert seized the room without a pause and orated the hell out of it after being unable to get much of his stuff typed up the previous night. Alma accompanied, melodramatic highs and lows on the cello-like fiddle, the bard sometimes joining in on clarinet, punctuating his narrative—in those intervals of playing together, the ephemeral knotwork of music they built in the air would've been a diabolically complex but elegantly symmetrical mathematical expression had a physicist managed to deconstruct it.

•

"Your dog ever come home?"

"Not in this lifetime," said Edith. "Not when her skate turned up in Gail's place. Your place. Still don't know how it got there?"

"No. Hear from Anders? I get nothing on the street. Some bullshit maybe."

"Yeah. No. Be a shock if I ever hear from the man."

Alma said, "They ever, like, quiz you about him? All those different cops."

"No, huh-uh. Crazy, right? Total silence. Almost wish they would," said Edith, "I think my . . . it's got me seeing stuff in the shadows, that they never came around, creeps me out, that all by itself. Just as soon *not* meet my guardian angels, or whatever's holding all those guys back. You keep expecting somebody to jump out and yell boo, you know, like you're waiting for a loud pop and you jump out of your skin."

The legendary Highway 1 was a city boulevard much like any other; as the four walked toward it, Alma changed her mind about hitchhiking over the bridge, thought she might do some tarot reading here in the city, auspicious day for carny work—several ones and fives among the coins divvied up from the clarinet case. Sitting in a swing set in a park on an iconic street, they passed around a box of Triscuits and some grapes, and peeled off slices of American cheese. Handed bottles of Squirt to Edith to uncap—she could be relied on to pull something serviceable out of her shirt. The little kid was teaching herself to pump a swing, hadn't yet asked to be flung skyward.

Edith said, "How'd you come to stay at Gail's place? Said you'd tell sometime."

"If ever," said Alma, "I don't think so. Let's leave it like this, feels pretty good."

"But we'll leave it nonetheless and for now we are on a roll. So?" said the old man.

Alma sighed, "Yeah well I'm a citizen of a country that doesn't exist, where they have like twenty surnames of which mine's the most common. I have a French passport that's not in that name that expired ten years ago. Kind of have to work off the books. But Josefina's an actual person. Even knows who to ask for vaccination records." If she answered at all, Alma often answered to a broader point, was annoyed when pressed for precisely what was asked.

"So why'd you go to Gail's? Like from where," Edith pressed.

The old clarinetist said, "What's your story this time?"

Alma poked his shoulder, knocked him sprawling out of his swing. "Oh shit man, you okay?"

Dusting his trousers, "That would be your carnival up in Calistoga this week?"

"Yessir," Alma said, "We're packed. Just need to line up a ride. Can't hitchhike because we look like runaways."

The old man, Albert, Doots, said, "Polka-dot hankie bindles over your adorable shoulders, the tall one and the little bitty one, 'Calistoga or bust' written on your little red wagon full of dollies."

"Dicey riding the 'hound. Everybody decides they're the authorities. Gets for real for real and especially we're not correctly white. Jesus Christ, heat-wise, you wouldn't believe how quick normal people turn into assholes when just one of 'em starts, they gang up, 'maybe we should notify the police.' God damn! One starts and they all pile on and ask their fucking questions pick pick pick like it's a sacred fucking obligation!" The other three waited for her to go on, "We will ride the show. Get Midwest eventually. Kindergarten with the Lutheran ladies. She's already reading! Fair chance I achieve existence this time, I called them up, got a new angle. I will hang on to my kid and it's easier if I exist."

"You were with a carnival?"

A snort, "Oh yeah here we go. Vicarious," said Alma.

Edith, who'd contributed lunch, "My high school band competed at the . . . competed in this local fair, I played glockenspiel, ought to sit in with you guys."

"Do."

"Glockenspiel! Why didn't you say?"

"Right," said Edith, "Anyway, and a carnival came to that town and everybody was already in the mood and it was great, I stayed all one day until it closed. The carnival people were like they were always on duty and they wouldn't really talk to you. So I'm curious is all."

More attentive than most people, actually hearing the lulling surf-like hiss of the traffic, savoring the gentle kinesthetic mobility of her swing, Alma crunched a Triscuit, shrugged.

•

The traveling show she described was normal in that time, conventional, American—top-hatted ringmaster, the trained elephant, a lion tamer, duo of horseback acrobats, dogs doing backflips through hoops, and combinations of those things. A middle-aged couple on the flying trapeze. In fright wig and gray body paint, the Borneo Wild Man with a bone in his nose, a ruff and tutu of long spiky bristles, who'd escape his cage and threaten the audience in the bleachers until recaptured by his whip-cracking keeper three shows a day. A clown pulling tiredly frenetic terriers and strings of sausages out of his pants. A one-ring circus.

That was the draw, but the big top barely covered expenses; carnies had much better ways to take in money, half of which went to the management in the office trailer. In a loud garish disorientingly chaotic narrow street of temporary structures beside the main tent, smart and skilled talkers entrained daddies and swains into tests of manly prowess—by artful insinuation and personable joshing and optimistic promises in front of wives, offspring, dates, and buddies, got some to try over and over, "No sir you just threw the ball too hard—you got an arm on you." Amid plush toys and mylar-spangled prizes and wooden milk bottles and rings on strings and wobbly basketballs, the habit-forming plinking away at moving targets in the shooting gallery, kiddy games and games of skill that employed deceit and games that were straighter, the talkers and noise and commotion induced a kind of fugue in midway-goers—to achieve a state of fugue was why everyone came, what they were looking for, women, men, and little kids, and big kids on dates, if she with an oversized blue teddy bear and demure smile and sleepy-eyed glow, then he a cat with canary feathers all over its face, and they'd be steadies by the time they found their way out of the Hall of Mirrors.

Luridly illustrated banners lured crowds down the way, promising unlikely things inside curtain-fronted twenty-by-twenty-foot stages the show folks called joints, where a juggler on stilts or a barely costumed Girl blowing fire would draw people out of the eddying crowd long enough for a talker's pitch to bunch enough of them together to jam into a tent, where the inside talker would, in spellbinding hyperbole, present the Turtle Boy and the Fat Lady, or the Tattooed Lady or shrunken heads—quite likely actual ones, a kind of intermediate between living human beings on display and the carboys of pickled devil babies and the mummified mermaid twins embracing in their exotic sarcophagus. That is, a single talker equipped with a persona and an endless patter and a slender cane would expertly maneuver a bolus of the public through a chute and have it file past the live attraction, the wonder, the living person whose deformity had become a job title; or rather than a live human on the other side of the rope, the public might be presented artfully fraudulent taxidermy and cunningly believable gruesome things in jars. Or another of the indistinguishable talkers might introduce the blade box show, for which the Girl must remove her costume behind a screen because it is too confining for the contortions involved in dodging all those blades. The Rubber Man who appeared to swallow his forearm to retrieve a shill's diamond ring, the two-headed something or someone, the nudie cuties dancing backlit behind scrim, the fire-eating, torch-juggling triplets in aluminum body paint, and for only three dollars more, a peek behind the curtain for a look at something truly horrifying or miraculous or titillating. A pair of burly bare-chested roadies wearing satin turbans and vests and pantaloons and curly-toed shoes stood cross-armed outside a fortune-teller's dim brocade caravansary tent within the larger tent. Enormous box fans everywhere ventilated the joints and blew the crowd's paper trash around the midway, kind of interesting in itself, abstruse science demonstration.

Diesel fumes, pink molten candy floss spinning out onto the expertly manipulated paper cones, the mesmerizing taffy-pulling machine, a variety of things to eat brought up out of vats of hot lard; the six-car Tilt-a-Whirl, the carousel, and a forty-foot Ferris wheel on whose guy wires people continually clotheslined themselves despite festoons of sequined pennants, and under which among the other concessions and rides was the small but essential dunk tank. A Giant Hammer, the nut or bolt it occasionally flung picked up by a passerby and returned to the ticket-taker—"I think you dropped something," the townie would say—though the machine appeared to work fine without it. Dueling calliope and up-tempo out-of-date popular tunes over loudspeakers, music enhanced by the roar of the generators; and suspendered stripe-shirted men talking, talking, never less than exuberant, never going hoarse, gesturing with slender canes that no one else had gestured with for a very long time—a one-week stand in a field behind a car dealership, 10 a.m. to midnight, local curfew permitting, children under seven free.

"You ran away with the circus! So cool, every kid's dream," said Edith.

"Some Lutheran ladies kind of sponsored me growing up. Couldn't bring me into official existence. So yeah I ran off with the carnival. As assistant bookkeeper. Excellent option for a non-person, ideal résumé."

"So wait a minute, how'd . . . sorry," said Edith, canceling a question when Alma's face almost subliminally flickered a snarl.

"Picked up jobs around the lot for shits and grins and whatever they'd pay for green help. Sweet old lady elephant flattened some jerk the act picked up to do the stable. Jerk liked using the cattle prod. Piece of shit human was replace-able, elephant wasn't. Guess the flat guy died, I never heard. Everybody but me and the trainer were scared of that sweet old girl, office wanted me to keep the leg irons on her, but fuck 'em. Big animal. Major shit-shoveling. So I got the job. You know they have binocular vision if they want to? Put her head down like about to charge, scared the pee out of me the first time but she's just looking with both eyes. High point of her week I'd depilate her with a gasoline blowtorch. Scrub her all over with a hose and push broom. Beauty par-lor. She'd shiver that ton of elephant hide, brush me with her trunk like reciprocating. Looked at me one eye at a time like conspiratorial, 'know? Mil's the show's gaffer and sign painter. I got pregnant, I kicked him out, and Jesus! Why anybody would want to hear this!" said Alma.

Standing in the sandy rut behind the kid's swing, push-ing her, "Come on spill it," the old musician said to Alma, who after a minute said,

"I'd bally for the dunk tank. Get a crowd up, get 'em to compete against each other. If we couldn't hire three or four shifts of local Black kids, then I'd go sit the tank. When I was in there I'd taunt the shit out of passing guys. It's over the loudspeaker, and the guys take it seriously, taunted in pub-lic. They just jammed up for tickets. 'Hey look she's a girl in there!' Can't you see the boys hurl that ball, lot of wild throws but I got dunked a lot and pretty fucking often they'd throw right at my face, at the shatterproof glass, bam. Bam!

I'd flinch but I wouldn't quit talking unless I got dropped in the water. If you sold a lot of tickets you got a bonus. I wasn't thinking about that, just got into the tease."

The Tilt-a-Whirl braked rapidly, the ride's music stopped, the operator drawled into his mike—"Hey rube, hey rube," a lackadaisical all-hands announcement over the speakers. Riders began to rattle their restraining bars, make querulous objections as the operator walked off the ride, told the ticket guy to let 'em loose, give back tickets. At change of shifts at the dunk tank, Alma had climbed out—soaking wet, she was showing—and her replacement had climbed in. Five or six young men she'd earlier pissed off had approached her with no idea what to do next except be intimidating. Harm was possible, manhandling likely. The Tilt-a-Whirl jockey patted the sepia girl's shoulder, stepped in front as some popcorn vendor joined him. A talker strolled up from a show next door, another ride cut the music, slowed. The pair of big roadies from the fortune-teller's tent, somehow more convincing for their curly-toe shoes and turbans, hadn't quite gotten there, a few fair-goers turned to look. Now clear on what to do next, the aggrieved guys moseyed backward.

"Mine. They would hurt themselves for you. I mean, not that particular night, but always. Wanted me to see they were mine. Or I was theirs or like that. Miss that. One was the first Vietnam vet I ever knew. Rig driver. Demonstrably not white, only other one on the lot but me and the local kid in the dunk tank."

"You're African? Like from Africa," said Edith.

"Uh yeah, been African for a while. Pliocene kind of deal. L'continent aîné, mais non?"

Edith risked specifics, "What country?"

To deflect Alma's certain sharp response, "She's wanting to locate you, love, think of the broader sense," he said.

Alma, mildly, "Madagascar people are like, like, the same kind as Filipino sort of. Then with Somali and Indian and Bantu and everybody. Papa was a . . . Papa was French. That'll have to do."

"Ur-red," said Albert, "You are the same color as your viola, whose sound is also that color. It is a sound that smells like you've got dessert baking in the oven." The little kid in her swing turned around to look at him.

"Think you scored with that one," said Edith.

Alma said, "Yeah she says stuff like that."

The old man said to Alma, "The fortune-teller? A story eh? You? Eh? Nudge nudge."

•

Alma said, "Sure. I'll recite the fortune-teller because you kind of could use it. Yeah you could use it but it won't be the nice one you heard before, Doots. Your circumstances anymore," shook her head vigorously, "Okay separated yours out. Nope! Oh for God sakes. Cancel. Not telling that because right now is good and this other thing is bad so we keep the good one,

In Which Abrogation came Abruptly

see." Standing, "Pasteurized processed cheese, Edie, must've pained you to get it, my daughter thanks you. Doots, good incarnation, brother. See you next time around."

"A given! One of the welcome givens, given it necessitates meeting up, but why is it I'm always so old every time. And hey kid, by way of cajoling, this here, our golden idyll is already in the drawer, hm? It is. Out of harm's way," he said.

"Ain't telling, Doots," she said.

"Lay it on me. Ego te absolvo, kid. You in, Edie?"

"What? Yeah I want to know, is that what you mean?" And to Alma, "Josefina doesn't get bad dreams or anything? I mean, you can be pretty heavy."

"God damn it Edie! Who gave you . . . No, you're fine, I get asked that question, see." Alma and the child simultaneously reaching to brush hands as the swing passed, "The stuff you hear, baby," Alma said to the child, "You can pitch a good fit but you never go dark, I know what that's like and you never do. Way too late to start protecting your little ears at this point. You wake up with a bad dream, we cuddle for a minute and you go back to sleep." To Edith, "Knows when I'm about to say something that would upset her. 'Two jumps ahead of the smoke,' the way her occasionally outlaw daddy describes her." Brushed fingers with her daughter as she swung past. "I'm more likely to get upset than she is. Preschool informal thing at the SFPL two days a week. Daycare a couple of mornings at the Y so she plays fine with other kids. She's okay, alright?

"But I don't know, here's your stuff. Gypsy is the job description not the ethnicity. Looks and sounds kind of German. Granny lady, superstitious as hell. The kind that gets stuck in the house because they keep going back to the stove to make sure it's off. In her case some weird thing about the arrangement of her skirt and all these just crazy-ass rules. Like for what position she has to assume relative to an adult male, alright? But what a pro at her game. Upstanding local citizens get hooked hard, can't turn loose, skulk in on their lunch hour. Crystal ball, tarot, buy another ticket and slip her a tip to see if she had doubled their money again, sworn to secrecy lest break the charm, invoke the Gypsy's curse.

"See, show people never think of themselves as having, you know, powers. Skilled artisans, no hoodoo. But there's a, an unexplainable, the whole carny thing, not just this lady's kind, but also the talkers' way-delicate feel for the crowd mood, the individual mark, the 'how'd he make me do that' kind of hoodoo. Crystal ball bullshit but at the same time . . . a good showman does mess with reality. For real. They do. This lady did. And they snap-to so quick, they're ahead of you, already a second in the future. It's kind of real. So alright well . . . I don't know, somebody got to the Gypsy."

Edith said, "Wait, is this going to be the graffiti thing?"

Albert said, "Taste of the fruit of the tree of knowledge and ain't that a bite. Manzanilla de la muerte wouldn't you know."

"These suits had a word with the ticket booth, like the

ticket guy's her secretary or something, and all these carnies are watching. Tickets at eye level or above, left over
from shortchanging townies outside the city gates a thousand years ago, so here's the dudes on tiptoes craning up,
can't do that with subterfuge. Took the old lady to her trailer,
roommates are gone to work on the midway. Making this
up now. They'd deport her and the grandkids would go
hungry, uh they'd arrest her son-in-law and he'd never get
out. She agreed to something. Folks wanted to help her but
she wouldn't spill. Tape recorder during her act and for a
whole goddamn week this just insane big TV camera looking through a hole in the curtain and bright fucking lights
in the Gypsy tent! Swear! I know, what idiots would think
like that! And uh. They must've dosed her, that had to be the
point, before-and-after experiment. She um . . . Anyway the
monitors followed us to the next run and then we didn't see
them anymore."

"Oh my lord that's horrible. So what happened to her?"
Edith said.

Albert pushing Josie's swing, "Enhance a fortune-teller's
insight, no."

"I mean, a clusterfuck like that, who could possibly tell
anything because everything is everything! . . . I'm getting
upset, I don't want to be upset," said Alma, head bowed, eyes
closed, taking her own pulse. "That's the deal—the whole
enterprise is random. I mean, but I collected it. The graffiti and the tales of wondrous powers and the people that

nobody's ever seen and all this elaborate shit. Or I made it up that it goes together and it really is just random. You know I make things up. So the monitors stopped coming back. The fortune-teller got sick and went away. Trying to remember where you heard this all before, Edie?"

"I remember almost everything all the time and it doesn't make any difference. I never heard the story but it's almost like I had."

"Being afraid all the time just stinks don't it, brave girl. I believe I am in love."

The old man mused, "Edith blushes. Hadn't known that."

Eyes on her fingers on her own wrist, Alma said, "I don't think I'm making this part up. Romeo and Juliet plus drunk Uncle work for the carnival. They keep hearing a nice story about the . . . this club, circle, convergence. Ascendant congregation. They hear that this family has come into being. Carny Romeo and Carny Juliet want to belong to it. Now I'm making this up. Belong so they'd acquire the power of flight or eternal life or whatever they're supposed to get, or a giant cosmic goddamned hug, whatever. Or maybe to join up for a war because the whole thing smells like a crusade." Eyes suddenly angry, "Hurry up, urgent! Chase the rumors, you fuckheads, get religion, there's no one to follow, there's no prophet, no der führer, no face. No other followers either.

"Doots, I don't know whose shit this is! I mean, it's in with your stuff and Edie's. The wad I'm looking at, there's no straight, no three of a kind, no two pair, no pattern to fill in, Jesus, why did I tell this one, I see exactly no pattern. Could be armies of converts and I wouldn't know. Because listen, you got to know *somebody* would materialize and seize control! Of like jizzed-up throngs and *somebody* would've flashed on that right from the fuckin' get-go! But, uh. If for some reason I have it right, it's just Romeo and Juliet and Uncle Thud and if you dream up your own marching orders you don't even count. And the word on the street is so uniform. And the metal hoodoo deal that Edie pried off her boat, you want to think it's, like, germane."

"As one does," said the old man in a W. C. Fields voice. Struck a W. C. Fields pose, flicked ash from an imaginary cigar, swung the child on her swing.

"Tend to blame somebody proximate for something irrelevant when I'm pissed off. Stock warning. Getting tired of this junk. I don't see anybody I want to hit," Alma was a little agitated, "File and ignore, fine, I just don't want to be preoccupied, pisses me off to be preoccupied. I am taking it personally." Quiet for a minute. "If it's some evil genius, okay, fine," her voice harsher, "Or if it's cooked up in the break room over KitKats and decaf, cool, a sardonic origin story," voice rising, "Wherever this came from, who cares, outer fucking space, it's messianic as hell and everywhere you look you start looking some more and bending all this other garbage to fit! Manipulative assholes! Let me alone! Stage the Second Coming, tell us we gotta get some! And you know what, they totally lost control! True–not true, gimme a break, it's vampire UFOs and they showing us the *Path*, c'mon!" voice rising, "Messiah is somebody's total load of shit, yuh! What makes it believable, yuh! I believe I believe! Here come our master gotta obsess allegiance, man, and you know what else they lit off? It's fealty! *Bam!* It's fuckin' f-e-e-e-e-lty!" baring her teeth, stretching the word, tiny droplets of spit sparkling in the sunshine, "Have us craving to anoint our new savior with it," shouting, eyes wild, "or just get it out, secrete it or discharge it or ejaculate it out of us like some kind of body fluid! God damn! When they—"

"Mama," little girl's voice.

Instantly, "Oh," Alma said, lowering her arms. Composed her face, went to her daughter. Finding Mama's mental state acceptable, the child returned to the swing.

"Applause, love, however inappropriate," Doots said to Alma.

"So but uh . . . just pulling this out of the air, but I'm thinking it *is* a thing. And there have to be a bunch of people. At it, in it. And it kind of looks like it happened once. The third-eye thing, the transcendent thing. Can't see a plan. Doesn't mean there isn't one. Wasn't one. But sure as hell nobody planned Shelda. I don't want this. I want to get shed of this." A bewildered look passed across the sepia girl, distress showed her age for only a moment, once again the flicker of bared teeth, the feral. Shook her head, "Okay so when the Gypsy left I got promoted. All I have for you."

"Jesus, Alma," said Edith.

Old Albert's hand on the little girl's head, little girl hanging on to his fingers, "So Yahweh, Allen Dulles, Lucifer, and Coyote walk into a bar . . . it was just a coincidence."
Edith said, "You did the Gypsy booth?"

"Briefly. The Gypsy is called a 'show,' and where the show happens is a 'joint.' I'm Mademoiselle L'Gitan. My own show, my own joint, my own banner. I was pretty good. Didn't have the chops for, you know, larceny. So many ways to blow that and then you're so screwed. Tax evasion, now, mon métier, still did the books for 'em. Got no sleep. Left to go produce Josefina, got no sleep. Went back for a season, baby on hip, towel down my shirt, they tolerated, it was fucking hopeless. Stopped in a couple of months ago to say hi. And to answer your earlier question, Mil was back, drove us down here, it's like he ran a shuttle to Gail's, is how I came to stay there. She isn't doing too good. Her one true Boorham's about a deadster at this point. According to rumor."

•

Turning Albert's clarinet case vertical to put it into its stash in the bulkhead, Edith heard something rattle down inside it. In the poor light it looked like a brass carnival token, over an inch in diameter. Substantial little thing. Edith pocketed it as a tip.

Boorham • in the event of a breakdown

Passenger window rolled down, the driver of an SUV leaned over, peered at him—the cloth hat and aluminum cane, the obsolete brick-shaped backpack. On the shoulder ahead of him, the driver got out, "Is that your old car back there?" Tattoo-covered plump dark brown arms, a 9 mm, probably, strapped over her fatigue pants. There was a similar one weighing down the man's backpack—guns were presupposed, though many conventions were no longer observed. Trudging up to the matronly driver, he took off his sunglasses, waiting for more.

"Dude, get in. You can't do this kind of shit . . . hey can you hear me?"

"Yes ma'am. Thanks," the old guy answered, "I could use a lift." Tired and sore, he hadn't walked more than two miles. The driver, snort and headshake of mock wonder, opened the back.

Relieved to unhook the stiff padded belt, he slid out of

the shoulder straps, found a space to shove the pack on top of stacked shrink-wrapped cases of canned and dried food, tampons, detergent, various ammo, first-aid supplies, a broken carton crammed with random bottles of vitamins.

"You got to hurry it up."

Pulling shut the passenger door, "Thanks a lot."

"Yeah any time, where you going?" Get to the point then.

Boorham said, "I need like bolts. Nuts and bolts, like a salvage yard? Mechanic?"

Unclipping the twelve-gauge from the side of his seat and jamming it beside her door, the driver said,

"Don't know. We pass one, sure. Take you as far as I'm going, got to get off the main road up here though. Roadblock."

"Just saw a Guard patrol. Maybe they cleared it," he said.

Another mocking snort, "Man, you are . . . It's a Guard roadblock. Confiscate your shit quick as anybody else. Quicker."

"Let me out when you get to your turnoff? If you would, please," said Boorham.

"Dude," said the driver, "No, look at me. Are you fucking senile? You cannot. Hitchhike anymore." Looking at her as he was told, Boorham nodded acquiescence, smiled, settled back. So many decent people, even now. Kept coming across them, surprised him every time.

He'd heard the diminishing pling. Two seconds passed

before the Peugeot's rear wheels locked and he found he'd made it off the road. Still breathing hard, flopped on his back, Boorham saw the transmission housing pulled away from the engine. Pretty much left it to the hand-brake cable to hold on to the back end of the car. Hiking back a ways he finally found the part, had to be the one, rendered useless under three successive wheels of a passing MRAP. He looked at the mangled bolt—the French had turned a few threads onto the end of an eight-inch bolt and this was the last of four to back out. Replacing them was unlikely. The next thing should've been to get some long skinny SAE bolts, grease 'em up, carefully cross-thread them into the soft aluminum of the engine, drive away.

After a few trips, the toolbox, spare tire, and other things carried in a car for the car's sake had been toted downslope to some abandoned roadwork, stashed in the sunflowers and knotweed; and there among the now-permanent stacks of concrete traffic barriers, Boorham threw in nearly all his other stuff. Kept the canteen bag, some socks and a sweater, the rain poncho. Then decided on a few small things from shelves and drawers back home, the half-full liner out of a box of granola. The pitiful hoard to be left behind he wrapped in a green tarp, tossed some rubble onto it.

Chewing the last apple, Boorham hefted the big superannuated rucksack, knowing before he shouldered it that, two-thirds empty, it would be more than he wanted to carry. Left the car unlocked.

•

The almost-new crew cab he'd used in business was lost in one or another thousand-year weather event, shortly before car insurance became as good as unavailable in Texas. One sunny afternoon he parked his new used Outback and unlocked his front door, heard something behind him. Shoved through and stumbling forward, on hands and knees he twisted around to see a couple of scrubbed young women in girls' school uniform blouses and culottes, the larger like a heartland farm girl, the smaller East Asian, who handed off her short military rifle to the other, the weapon so tricked out with shooter's accessories that it looked like caricature. Staying beside the line of fire, she took Boorham's phone out of his hand, pupils tiny dots invisible in her dark eyes. Retrieving the keys from the front door lock, the two drove off in the Subaru, no word spoken.

After plugging in an old notebook to charge sufficiently to call the cops, he stared into space for a minute, absently wondering if the Canadians would let him in since his estranged daughter was a citizen. Probably not. Only a year ago they would've considered it, likely letting him over the border while they did so. Three-fifths of the world on the move so far, that border had gradually hardened, and had now become tighter still with the resurrection of smallpox in the vast Mediterranean migrant camps. Yet to be fully verified was the horrifying discovery that the live-virus vaccine, the one that had eradicated the ancient scourge, now somehow caused acute illness—that news leaching away much residual public faith in science.

At the top of the pull-down stairs, he located the camping gear half on, half off a sheet of plywood, behind Christmas decorations and two or three Halloween costumes he'd been particularly proud of making, junk not visited in years. Might ought to inventory the outdoorsy stuff just for fun. How about that—there's Gail's old cane. She'd never gotten well enough for hiking, and he'd found it kind of depressing without her. Folding away the attic stairs, Boorham reconsidered, thought better of calling the police, then did so anyway; hard to accept that calling the cops now carried risk of its own, for an older middle-class white man such an odd thing, at least a long-forgotten thing. Wiping dust off a framed piece of Gail's calligraphy, he propped it in a chair. Picked up a Polaroid snapshot he'd run across—his dark ponytail, Gail's ruffled Carmen Miranda tube top. Grinning, hugging alongside a blue-and-white VW van. Laying the picture aside, "I just fucking want to go home," he said flatly, aloud.

One cop dutifully repeated Boorham's answers, translated into report-speech, into his tablet; the other officer said,

"Hoo what we got here," indicating a plump snack-sized baggie printed with large asterisks. It had appeared on the side table, on top of the photograph.

Sighing, Boorham just looked at him, waiting.

The cop taking notes said, "Sir, you might as well be my own dad—maybe we can work something out."

The first officer said, "Class A misdemeanor or felony possession, depending on the prosecutor, either way jail time and a humongous fine, you got a criminal attorney? But first you'll be in County 'til they get around to you, arraignment, bail, and whatnot."

"Sir, let's just take care of this. We'll handle it," the first one said. And in a few minutes at the ATM,

"Sir, they don't like federal scrip downtown, so let's do Citibank, Amazon—spends a lot better for debts public and private." They looked at his meager cashable savings, charitably left a little bit.

Gail had made merciless fun of his intermittent Peugeot restoration during their last four years together, her last four years, decades ago. He imagined her coming across the crappy old car in its own little carport, the ghost of her whipping back the car's silvery, fitted protective shroud, laughing merrily. He'd had a whole life since Gail, married for years, raised two kids. His boy survived multiple deployments, had become an entrepreneur, had become a schizophrenic, had dissolved into LA. And Boorham had tried to keep in touch with his daughter through his ex-wife—both women thought well enough of him, neither wanted to have much to do with him.

More than ready to cut his losses, chuck the house

right this red-hot minute, he'd try to sell it online. Go see his daughter. She taught college in Victoria, a remote quaint never-never land of British architecture and cherry trees on Puget Sound, a polite someplace to drive toward, a rumored lost civilization to go exploring for. Wished he'd been able to find someone to go along. Aging faster than he, his wife and once-close friends had mostly drifted away.

Degradation had been incremental—slow enough that few felt spurred to abandon jobs or real estate, universal enough that most hadn't any place better to go, and Boorham hoped he'd be the exception.

·

High-altitude dust and smoke made for a colorful sunrise, and with the dirty-pink stripe of predawn in his rearview mirror, his empty gas tank inspired a fresh round of second thoughts about the sanity of relocation on impulse. "Goodness gracious, lookee there," said Boorham—a big truck plaza calling itself Tradin Post, apparently thriving, catering to trucks with drivers. And . . . Yes! Cars as well . . . Blast of a baritone airhorn reminded him he'd slowed too much. Yanked into the exit lane as a four-truck convoy of Idaho Guard rolled past, their white cross insignia a lot like that of the Wehrmacht.

Waiting for his breakfast order, he asked the tall kid behind the counter, "Okay to take a nap in the car?"

"Everybody does. Anywhere away from the pumps and plugs, up by the building."

Boorham thought of it as an overtly gay manner of speaking—kid must be tough as a boot. The TV on the wall was repeating aerial footage of European landmarks amid frantic looting, men and women flailing, shoving in front of smashed storefronts, the screen labeled US Navy Reconnaissance. Low-light, grainy images in grayscale looking like archival images, something from a safely historical catastrophe.

The voiceover was put together from dispatches the BBC had managed to send out over analog equipment—essentially A. G. Bell's telephone—that had gone out across the few still-viable transatlantic cables. Transmitted across museum-piece equipment, business-as-usual BBC voices sounded like artifacts of an older war as they enunciated chaotic dissolution, city blocks burning in otherwise starlit darkness; it had been some time since the BBC had been so free of political oversight; what they described was a civilization in the democratic part of Europe that was over for the time being. There were a handful capable of causing it, including commands of the US military that had taken themselves freelance. Whoever it was, they'd clearly felt impeded or affronted by the last beleaguered centers of liberal democratic governing, and they'd beaten down half of them in one stuttering pop.

"Surreal. This isn't happening," said the kid.

Boorham said, "But uh, you remember when it was, you know? Nicer. I mean I guess it's been a little while, is why I ask, I don't know how old you are. I mean, plus the epidemics and the crazy weather, jeez."

"Nicer," said the tall kid, "Oh my yes, yours was l'âge d'or for sure. Do I hear a wee smidge of condescension? I'll make an assumption here, friend. Your ship crash-landed and you are just pining away for Planet Deep State." Not rankled, just an assessment, "You tried to take our liberty away," set down a plate of waffles, scrambled eggs, surprisingly some sliced tomato.

"Looks great. Got any Tabasco?" said Boorham.

•

The GPS said tersely, "No Sat."

"God damn it," said the driver.

"I think I know where we are, sort of," said Boorham, "There should be a right-hand split in, I don't know, not five miles. Parallels the interstate more or less. How far up was the roadblock?"

The driver looked doubtful, didn't say anything, after a while took the right-hand fork.

"What next?" she asked.

"I don't remember the number of the road. Might not even be one anymore, the interstate wasn't finished yet. It'll be a left then a quick right anyway, if it still goes through. I think."

"Interstate wasn't finished. You shitting me!" she said. The pavement they were on hadn't been maintained in many years. Swerving to avoid a tilted slab of roadway,

"God damn it! Rip a fucking sidewall down here!"

"Somebody's got drones up," he said.

"When'd you snap to that?"

Passing a familiar-looking crossroads, "This is good here, here's good," Boorham said.

The driver checked her mirrors, momentary "whatever" glance in his direction. The hatch closing behind him, he went toward the passenger-side window to thank her, wish her luck. A small flat can of King Oscar smoked herring sailed out the window, clattered to the broken pavement in front of him as she drove off.

·

What was new about the place was the security bars and the shrine to Santa Muerte in a big black fiberglass niche by the door—the rest much as he'd remembered, a cinder-block cabin built into the hillside. Behind the low, upslope back of the house, surrounded by big floppy yellow blossoms, a woman stood up amid staked-out strings of squash vines. Fastening her trousers she said,

"Help you?" Catching himself about to answer with some irrelevant scrap of yore, he said,

"Used to know people who lived here."

"You don't now." The sound of a motorcycle was getting louder.

"There used to be a mechanic down at the 425 junction. Not still there, are they?" Her face remained expressionless, sort of an answer.

Turning to go, he looked over at the neighboring lot—house apparently occupied, new razor-wire-topped chain-link fence, new outbuilding, the wooden barn out back partially collapsed. Halfway down to the road he stepped off into the brush to get out of the way of a bike bumping up the rocky drive—a tall Yamaha with two teenage boys, faces impassive, one of whom kept a rifle pointed at him as they passed. Humor, conceivably.

Great disheveled raven in a dead cottonwood practicing something it'd heard, from its murderous beak the musical burbling and muttering of a pair of women in conversation. "Gail?" Boorham said, "Glad you could make it, and who you do have with you? Shelda! What joy, lovely of y'all to stop by." As if by correction, the creature grated its primeval shriek at him, flapped twice, caught a draft, and sailed over the opposite rock face.

Finished taping up blisters, Boorham drained the last of a two-liter water bag into his mouth, hoping he could make his way around the next-door house without being challenged. Didn't hold out much hope the stream still flowed behind that collapsing barn, his best possibility was all it was; still, there were recent-looking washouts and things looked surprisingly green. Much of the area had been built on since he'd left, but these two lots, backed up to federal land, were still the only driveways on this stretch of drilled and blasted-out granite palisades to either side and across the road. Skirting the house, happy to note the electric co-op still lit things, he busted brush thinking about tick-borne diseases, wary of some big dogs' barking. Head down and bent low and stopping for deep gasps every few steps, Boorham made his way up the hillside and gratefully shed his pack beside the rivulet. About to splash his face, instead locked eyes with a dead coyote in the weeds, its head and forequarters in the water.

Off and on during her last little while, Gail made her truelove a birthday present. She'd taken up calligraphy, and one particular piece was her best—on heavy vellum in her gracefully austere script, a small block of text in the center of an otherwise blank page. The initial letters of three sentences were illuminated on gold leaf, illustrated minutely, highly personally. In her omnivorous reading she'd run across a story by someone named Lafferty that contained a love poem. She'd written a passage for Boorham,

> You are the water in rock cisterns and the secret spiders in
> > that water.
> You are the dead coyote lying half in the stream, and you are
> the old entrapped dreams of the coyote's brains
> oozing liquid through the broken eye socket.
> You are the happy ravening flies about that broken socket.

232

Whispering to the dead animal, he recited his beloved fragment, crouched there for a minute, gathering his own dissipating thoughts. Walked upstream, picked his way across using the cane in lieu of a sense of balance; water bag filled, Boorham dropped his pack over a barbed wire fence, ducked through onto the empty national forest land beyond, where he planned to spend the night on ground once beloved. Back home in America. Deep breath.

Snapped awake from reverie or sleep when two or more bikes snarled across the slope above him, followed by a few quick full-auto bursts. Jesus Christ. He'd left behind the yellow tent of course, but had indulged in a ground cloth and foam pad. Grabbing those and one-shouldering the pack, Boorham shambled, bent over, downhill straight into the barbed wire.

Opening his eyes to full dawn light coming through missing siding, feeling cheated by the dumbness of the last dream, stiff and sore, he registered the ground cloth on the damp dirt under his butt and legs, noted the backpack lying beside him with miscellaneous contents and the military surplus Beretta lying on it. Registered hunger, the desire to brush his teeth, registered the crust of blood on his face. Slumped over beside a ruined wall inside the barn, dirt stuck to his cheek, he'd tried to sleep sitting up in hopes of the ridiculous wound clotting solidly. It had taken some tries to unstick his fingers without restarting the bleeding, holding the wound closed and applying superglue, squinting cross-eyed against the fumes as the acrylate catalyzed in his skin. A two-inch barbwire cut, even a deep one, used to be trivial. This one would certainly get infected before he found a clinic still in business. And for heaven sakes, fool, he'd bisected his nose top to bottom. Pretty damned succinct, the old man smiled, a First World internally displaced person with a truly ridiculous wound in the middle of his face.

Finally noticed the guy. Hand resting on a holstered weapon, the man said,

"Hey. How we doing?"

Slowly putting his hands on his head and leaning away from his own gun, Boorham said,

"Fine, sir. You?"

The man said, "Walked here from where?"

"I was on the Land Management side, kind of got run off by gunfire," Boorham said.

The guy nodded, "Yeah. Boy used to be a pretty good little old hay hauler. His daddy disappeared, one of those sweeps they kept having. Hand me that, butt first. And before your campout?"

"Car broke down," Boorham said, "ride let me off a couple three miles south." He had taken off the car cover, folded it neatly, and left town in the Peugeot the day before yesterday.

"I'd get that looked at," the man said, touching his own nose. "Bring your stuff."

The man put two big, well-trained dogs into another

part of the fenced compound, beckoned him toward the house.

"You eat eggs?"

Ducking through a children's swing set, Boorham raised his eyebrows, "Yeah," he said.

The man went in, "Cecelia," he called as he shut the door. Boorham sat on the steps, Oh? Suits me, I'll take it, he thought. Soon got lost, mulling next moves—he'd never been quick. Then, "Hell's this though," spotting a sau- cer-sized black lumpy object lying on the porch behind him, under a child's bicycle.

"Thank you sir, ma'am," standing to accept from the man a large just-made flour tortilla full of hard-fried eggs with chorizo, onions, peppers, beans, salsa. Cecelia handed him a mug of coffee, surely an expensive courtesy. Went back inside. Boorham was at a loss. In jobsite pidgin Spanish for some reason, he said,

"No es lo que uh esperar. Por favor Señor, mi, uh, traba- jando?" (This is not uh expect. Please sir, my, uh, working?)

The guy refrained from rolling his eyes, but did flick a tiny dismissive gesture. Boorham ate, sucking back snot, eyes wet, plainly emotional. In order to preserve the hapless old fool's dignity, the man said,

"Little hot?"

Clearing his throat, Boorham answered, "No, love it. Compliments to the chef."

Wiping his hands on his pants, clearing his throat again,

"Hey what's this dealie here?" Toeing the flat dark circular object. "Used to have one just like it."

Skeptical, the man said, "Yeah? No idea. Found a bunch of them," pointing down over the edge of the porch at a two-foot-long metal cylinder on the ground.

"Can I look?"

Guy shrugged.

Neat bands fastened handles onto the mud-smeared stainless-steel cylinder, the thing so heavy Boorham had to put a knee on the ground to prop it upright. Unsnapping the couple of draw-latches that weren't already loose, he lifted a convex cap off its stiff, cracked gasket, and winced. "Yeah, kinda ripe," said his host. The top one or two of the lumpy objects had been partially unwrapped from thick orange foam-paper packing, stuffed back into the canister. It was a stack of maybe a dozen, with room for a few more. Boorham redid all the latches.

The man said, "Found it when the back wall of the barn washed out."

"If it was me," Boorham said, "I'd put that one back in, ditch the whole thing where nobody'd find it."

"Why?"

"Mine, ah . . . the one I had was real major bad luck," Boorham said, "You know those things have some kind of gunk inside?"

•

The man ejected the magazine, "You won't find 10 mm." Racked the gun, snapped it, "Grit in the slide." He reached up, shoved the weapon accessibly into the backpack, then slipped in the newly charged laptop. Said, "Go left at the highway. Two miles, that might get you long skinny bolts, maybe-maybe. No medic, you out of luck there." Shifting in the packframe to try to ease his soreness, looking really old with the sun in his face, Boorham was in fact a great deal older than he looked. Never so much as a cold, and abnormally slow to age after nearly dying from an inconclusively identified virulence that had come over him right here a long time ago.

Putting on sunglasses and cloth hat, he made a quick V-sign and started walking. "Yeah. Peace. Right, okay," said the man. Called after him, "You don't want to be somebody's evening entertainment, you hear."

Formerly belonging to the Bureau of Land Management and still painted light green, an older SUV with a Valley County Sheriff badge decal on the door stopped on the shoulder in front of him. Boorham trudged up to the big-bellied uniformed man, took off his sunglasses, waited. The sheriff opened the back of the truck, said, "Drop your gear in there sir." The cop was inclined to just dump the crime-bait over the county line, out of his fiefdom, go on about business; Boorham just assumed he was being extorted. Instead they went down to the county building, where a uniformed young guy and a poker-faced older lady looked up from their PCs. "Hat off," the sheriff said to the younger man. The woman stood, stretched; the sheriff took her seat. The woman motioned Boorham down a hallway, opened a cell door, took off the cuffs. She returned in an hour or two to pass a Styrofoam plate and a spork through the slot in the bars. Microwaved Spam, a canned beet plopped onto a scoop of instant grits. All actually warm. "Hey, thanks," he said. Pretty sure it was the woman from the squash patch the evening before. Thought that he'd been pretty lucky with the road food.

Sheriff was scrolling down reports from the last several days.

"Hey Connie, look at this—home invasion no, carjacking no, break-in? Took some guns and tools?"

"No sir. Too recent anyway. She thinks it's the same people took her bullion."

"Anything else on that?"

"No sir, nothing you don't already have."

"Somebody ambushed Amy. Caliber come back yet?"

"No sir. It was Gilbert," she said.

"How's she doing?"

"Might lose that arm. Lung's messed up."

"Cattle rustling. And this one . . . That old bird's in his floppy hat and he's in a dog pack of real ugly hard-ass pistoleros, just a-shittin' and a-flyin' down the road on a chopper, yessir. Connie, the thing with those kids over in Gooding last week, that took some luring. Maybe a grandpa? The chupacabra one. Jesus. Love to get ahold of that one for about a minute."

Connie shrugged, "No sir. Wouldn't be this old boy."

The sheriff ruled his thinly populated swath of the West as he saw fit. Thought he might offer the quaint pinball a ride. Smiled, might join him.

•

The Peugeot hadn't quite made the border. Its timing chain suddenly just too worn out, the quaint memento began to blow black smoke from the middle of a tight procession of vehicles driving too fast. There were no barricades, and no gunfire or thrown rocks—only feebly beseeching crowd noise reached Boorham as his impromptu convoy forced a way through a large group of homeless attempting to block the road, the second such he'd encountered that day, a skinny, despairing battalion who'd recently been actual people, and who remained stunned to find themselves like this. As the cars ran away leaving behind them only the greasy smoke, hungry men and women continued to call out and gesture weakly after, marginally hopeful faces resuming expressions of angry bewilderment. Boorham now carried the jarring image of a pair of little kids, one in a fairy-tale princess's blue frilly dress and glittery tiara, the two holding hands as if about to jump into the air and fly, both of them watching him expressionlessly as he passed, staring like ghosts of children with eyes he remembered as having no irises.

•

Washington State's ferry schedules still listed British Columbia destinations—after a long side trip Boorham was told at the terminal that those destinations weren't for him. The foul, shuddering Peugeot had banged out flames for miles by the time he bumped it over a curb and coasted down an embankment, dead car coming to rest in the ditch on the wrong side of the interstate. Shambling his backpack across the southbound lanes and into the broad forested median, and out the other side of the parched and heat-stressed scenic enhancement, he stood and watched for a break in the insanely speeding cars. Made it over to the northbound shoulder. Stuck out his thumb and started walking, sticky with fragrant resin that had bled from the beetle-eaten conifers.

Occasionally touching his hot and swollen nose, now greasy with antibiotic goo, Boorham stood patiently in a different line of cars, these admitted four at a time through the first gate. Less reluctant than others of his fellow citizens who hadn't managed to store their firearms on the US side, he chucked the Beretta down a chute provided for the purpose. The gun confiscation and threat of disarmed repatriation was meant to discourage the Americans, keep

the crowds down some. Inside the second bollard fence, armored and helmeted and particle-masked Canadians searched him, watched over by other alert, bored professionals stretching open the wrists of their nitrile gloves from time to time to dribble sweat out. Permitted to drag his strewn gear to the side for a hasty repacking, Boorham hauled his few remaining belongings to the portable toilets, took a drink from the water he'd been given, dropped the pack and sat on it. Slumped against a bollard and watched the cars being sent back in the return lanes. Figured the processing was going amazingly fast, fifteen or twenty people rejected in an hour.

Middle-aged daughter's birth defect had her bedridden for the first time, according to the son-in-law, and she didn't feel like talking. Boorham had no idea of her inclinations, whether or when she would go through the effort of contacting immigration, and even less idea if anything might come of it if she did. Limbo was okay though; he daydreamed, reshuffling uncertain, unresolved perceptions, arbitrary realities.

Whenever he came back from the toilets, at first infrequently, the reverie resumed; mulling now on the heavy little misshapen disk on that porch, how he'd picked it up and handled and sniffed it, almost against his will. And Jesus! That military-spec canister full of them. Eroding out of the barn next door to where he and Gail had gotten sick. Sweating, head in sharp pain, Boorham jumped up and ran

242

for the toilets, this time not dragging along the pack, vomiting along the way, thinking this wouldn't help his immigration chances one little bit.

Less than three days since he'd run into the barbed wire; gash really didn't look or feel all that bad—systemic nastiness couldn't be from that, not yet surely; maybe drinking from the stream behind the barn? Lordy, ton of bricks, he thought, slipping horizontal. Remembered Gail smacking him hard on the forehead from time to time as sarcastic congratulation for understanding the obvious. Smiled for a second. Loved that woman. Smiled again—some things, too, she would just not talk about, a couple of which he'd just pieced together recently.

"I do I do I do believe in spooks," he said, now crouching, hangdog sphinx, couchant cowardly lion on the pavement, feeling a little better at the moment. Watched the cars creep past on the other side of the bollard wall.

Gail had thought their next-door neighbor up on the mountain was a huckster of little consequence on the streets in San Francisco, definitely not a guy for sophisticated machinations despite his shtick playing a man of mystery. He'd struck Boorham as more sinister than that, a good deal more able. Maybe not. Whole lot of episodes along about then hadn't ever settled into nice comfortable rote. Feeling lucid whether he was or not, shivering, arms and legs jerking a bit, Boorham revisited things. Kept finding nothing useful under there when he'd winnowed everything he knew.

Over and over. Lay on his side hugging his pack, trying to get comfortable.

•

Tried once more to send a text message by rotary-dial telephone. Keyed the cradle buttons by hand, rather than using the automatic counter of the dial—a quicker or firmer touch, an angled fingertip, might suggest to the telephone which of the triplet letters he meant to say. Two clicks, wishing abC. Eight nuanced taps, tUv. Shivering, lying in soaked clothes, he kept losing his place in the message, starting over. At some point he was aware of a voice coming from the black Bakelite receiver. He'd lost track of where the receiver was.

"Honey you smell awful."

"I had something I wanted to show you. Here somewhere, can't . . ."

"That guy sent up a flare you know, the one Shel killed, I always got a smirk out of the spiritual incest you and Shel had going. Seen her lately?"

"I guess I don't, uh, understand. Any of that."

She gave him a near-miss congratulatory pop on the forehead, "See? There you go, you get it after all!"

Background voices then, talk of transoms and borrowing a single skeleton key from each other to lock and unlock rooms. Saying Boorham had stolen a ladder someplace, gotten the attic fan working.

He smelled hot, dusty wooden rooms, dirty sheets, desiccated wallpaper, lay on his side facing the faint warm steady air current coming through the window. Smelled honeysuckle vines in his fingers, and the pervasive jammy scent of a fig tree, leaves sprawled on straw-dry August thatch, inhaled the straw scent too. Felt in the dimness for the rudimentary brown iron key, closed his hand around a terrible pang of love for her, or a seizure,

"Gail? The place in the boonies, up in the rocks, we'll circle back soon. Get your stuff out then, head on out. Stay, yeah you wanted to stay. Absolutely that would be a good place."

"Thanks, lover. Is that all?"

(noise and voices, including hers; temblor rattling walls and windows, a shuddering rumble ending in a clap of backfire; banter of three or four young adults)

"fucking Matchless, second fucking floor"

"right, y'all take 'em to task, I'll hie me tender pink ass to the sanctuary"

(minutes of seismic thumping, three guys guiding a four-hundred-pound bike down the stairs of a stick-built house)

"back there . . . no thank you man, pass, sinking into the yurk and sepsis of collapsed drains"

(sound of a joint being carbureted; someone speaking through held breath)

"little incense covers a multitude of sins"

"but for the termite holes, blow up from the fucking gas leaks, them acid-head candles" "you know she rips those off from that church, votive candles"

"sending heavenward petitions made of entropy how far you figure, one foot, two"

"cycle-o-life . . . hey you leaving comrade"

"ayep, off in the service o' Br'er Rabbit"

"oh louche . . . y'all mind the tar-baby now y'hear"

"apostate . . . you err, uh, br'er"

"great Lugus your righteous prankmaster and besides a spiff laurel wreath"

"mistaking Pan"

"mistletoe or something wreath"

Breeze from the window getting a little chilly, Boorham curled up, breathed it in. Breathed out, pronounced the exhalation, "Gail?"

"Ooo, uh-oh look out—Lord Coyote just pricked up His ears, lookin' your way," said Gail, but not to him, had forgotten the old fellow was still around.

Intelligent canid eyes, not so unknowable, incompletely alien, profound native understanding having displaced exquisite wordless cunning. Unambiguously menacing yet somehow a little sad, distracted from the business at hand, Coyote felt the dulling loss of its cunning—determined not to let that get the better of it, but forlorn, bereft. The Low-Dog bore up with good cheer as befitted its station. Still looked the agile, mangy dun-color beast of prey it had ever been, Varmint of perfect self-esteem and estimable if not grand teeth; it could slink and dance and make *ferality look effortless, although it was not, could unerringly feint, seize, shake a rip in its neck-snapped quarry, so change from dun to red. Yip out a prey-freezing chuckle and dance away on hind legs. Play-nip as it lolled near a pulsing artery, abruptly sit up on haunches, cover eyes with paws and not be there anymore. Implacable humor in its glance, intractable love in its harrowing lingering regard, a fine radium green glowed in enormous nocturnal predator retinas.*

Light softened, eased along with the stare of perfect attention and the taut, crouched, flat-eared creep of a canid nearing the kill. Slaughter began to feel to Boorham and to the beast itself not so much a compulsory as a voluntary thing. Coyote's thin black lip drew back benignly; with regal affability the Cur relaxed, panted recognition and greeting. "Hey Shelda, how you been, love," Boorham breathed. A perceptible dial tone had come gradually forward, the old American dial tone, electromechanical hum an F and an A, he hadn't heard it in years, the signal that all's well and you are connected, a two-note hum immaculate in its neutrality, the notes' small interval neatly unitary now with all of everything in an extended, faintly glowing green Om, endless, oh yeah that'll get it, I love this, keep it up, he thought, thank you, he thought.

•

A strong yellow with true black, the aposematic colors nature so often selects to signal "I will poison you." Figures completely covered in those colors—hard to know their age and gender and all the rest—but at a guess, they were young male soldiers that plopped Boorham, still in fetal position, onto a bare steel gurney.

Moving Day • flatlined

She in pale pink lipstick, legs shaved, he pressed and bar-
bered to look credibly wholesome, sweet newlyweds stood
in a courtroom talking to their lawyer. Bail had just been
lowered to something their combined families could mort-
gage their houses to achieve, but disbelief, denial, was the
prevailing mood because the boy had drawn Judge Lou.

Dyspeptic and angry with a political opponent that
afternoon, Judge Lou had previously, famously, sentenced
another first offender to life for agreeing to sell a reefer to
a convincingly smelly guy who'd joined him on the way to
the park. Sunday in the park, people throwing for their dogs,
sharing french fries at municipal picnic tables, smoking cigarettes and socializing on the lower plinth of Robert E. Lee's
pedestal. Narc hadn't handed over the three dollars before
an unmarked Plymouth rolled up, doors opening before it'd
come to a stop. Though the maniacal sentence itself couldn't
be appealed, a Texas criminal appeals judge on a whim

reduced the time to something a lot less. Still plenty enough to do the trick.

·

"Yeah it's a neon, takes almost no juice. And this is a transistor of some kind that makes it blink, so actually it's off more than it's on. So it lasts forever, shelf life of the battery almost. Radio Shack man had everything, way simpler than I thought."

"You're going to seal it in there? Can't replace the battery?"

"Yeah, won't need to, I'll be out by then."

"Wouldn't be that hard for me to unsolder the glass, replace the battery."

"No. Please. It quits, it quits. This is for you in place of me. Hard to explain. You can't really . . . seems like . . . you know, do anything if this is me. Me here at home."

·

Skillern's had apologetically fired her, "let her go" was the phrase, when she came in for that evening's shift, because her enormous belly at kids' eye level had caused a customer to complain. Lying in bed in her second-floor duplex, she was watching an old elm sparkle in the streetlight as the rain let up. It was cooler now, a fall shower after such a long summer. From within the stained glass hanging in the window, a fraction of a second's wink—don't be stupid, just a droplet on a leaf, the light's been gone for two weeks and more. There, again! She sat up, put her feet on the floor, rubbed one eye at a time, intent. The rice-grain-sized lamp remained lit for a full second, part of another second before going dark. Keeping her eyes on where it would appear, holding up her belly, crossed to an upholstered chair to wait for the next glimmer of heartbeat. In a few minutes put her feet up; stayed there until she couldn't any longer. Lying on her side in bed, snapping awake frequently, she kept vigil.

·

"This is pretty," holding a stained-glass panel, handing it across.

"Lowell made it for her. Used to have a little light in there he put in there, inside that heart."

"Awful it didn't work out. She had such high hopes for when he came home."

"Yes." The panel went into a box with some colorful yarn god's eyes and wind chimes and junk.

Gail • towing by example

At Boorham's hands-up in her side mirror, Gail stopped backing and set the brake. Bright midmorning by the time the vans were positioned and the makeshift hardware laid out, and snow was already melting in the yard as he first squatted, finally rolled on his back to link the two minibuses in tandem.

His tenth-grade metal-shop teacher had pointed out the design flaws of the tow bar, an eight-foot steel pipe with loosely jointed ends, though it had been used several times since then. Because towing was often called for, a VW's front axle had a factory-installed towing hook intended for a length of rope, and rope worked okay if there was a driver back there being towed, someone with quick reflexes, but a tow-bar arrangement needed only one driver. This version's vacillating mechanics invited catastrophe when the front car braked, one of several things the shop teacher had explained. "Toss me that poncho to lie on? Thanks."

"Going to get the rest of the stuff. So, looks like we're actually doing this."

"Sure."

His rear bumper needed bolstering if it were going to pull anything, survive a best-case outcome, and Boorham was under there with wrenches and U-bolts and wooden spacers, fastening on a stout piece of channel iron, the only sturdy part on either vehicle. The iron was attached to a bumper attached to a van largely made of rust.

Both buses drivable, the rear one, the gray, had its cardboard heater hoses gone from the engine, obviating any windshield defrosting—with everything intact and working, it wasn't possible to warm the cabin with the waste heat from an air-cooled engine whose displacement was that of a mayonnaise jar. But sometimes, not dependably, piped the whole uninsulated way from the motor in back, enough warmth made it to the windshield to keep it clear. Rust under the paint of the front van, the blue-and-white, rumpled it in contiguous patches, and much of the rusted-out floor had been replaced with aluminum roofing panels held in place with tar and dozens of pop rivets. "Safe" wasn't a factor given undue weight, safe was just another element in the intuition as to whether you'd get where you're going or not.

The engine was still warm enough not to put out visible smoke when Boorham brushed the wet grass off his pantlegs and climbed into the cab of the front van, pulled the skinny door shut, then carefully closed it more firmly. Having walked over from their place two hundred yards away, Gail tossed in sleeping bags, got into the passenger seat, and wedged an overstuffed daypack between them.

"Grave concerns, lover," she said.

"Okay! Wish us luck."

"Geronimo," she shrugged. The vans crept off across dead grass and gravel and mud and rutted snow in the yard, dropped off down the steep drive. Skittering a bit on the long slick rocky curve, the vans picked up momentum and, with a hail of gravel rattling under the floor, straightened out onto a two-lane blacktop, still accelerating but now going uphill, the towed one briefly slung and fishtailing, dragging the front van fishtailing with it on asphalt wet with snowmelt.

"Yee-ha!"

Before slowing, losing traction on a stretch that was in shadow most of the day. It wouldn't've occurred to anyone out west to sand a tertiary road, and snow compacted, partly thawed, compacted, refrozen, was nearly frictionless now with whatever it is that turns road ice black. Boorham began the constantly recorrecting work of trailer-backing the other vehicle—the towing bar's double-jointed ends made it mechanically impossible, though he wasn't aware of that and managed it well enough.

"Alright! Take another run at it."

"Honey, that has to be twenty yards of ice," Gail said, "No way in hell."

He said, "I put the new tires on the rear." She glanced over at him.

They backed past the bottom of the hill, up the opposite slope for an eighth of a mile past their own driveway. Accelerated for all the satchel-sized engine was worth. Together, the two linked box-kite vans had enough mass to carry them well into the icy shade, get them good and stuck, and now ninety degrees to each other.

He climbed into the other bus to steer it; she, with an infinitely subtle feel for clutch-work, eventually got them maneuvered around straight, if on the wrong side of the road. Never crossed their minds that the feat was remarkable. That they could do things like that, that such lore just came to them, or that they had worked together not only sure of what they were doing, but sure of what the other intended at a given moment.

Gail put her legs over the gearshift and scooted over the little backpack onto the passenger seat again. Boorham got in as a big, dumb, heavy tan Buick with chrome-outlined holes in its front fenders ground past.

"Should've got those tire chains when we had the chance I guess."

"Had no money, honey," she said, "just get us alongside the driveway—weather stays like this, that stuff will melt and we can go tomorrow."

"Well but that'd be too late though," he said. His stammer was giving him some trouble.

She said, "Right, I know. We should not do this. Let's stop doing this now."

"But no really. I mean like, at this point? Now?"

"Okay then, if this is God's plan for us, we need some chains," she said.

"Sure as shit not going to ask next door."

Far enough off the road, he cut the engine and said that he wanted to change his sneakers for hiking boots, didn't know what he was thinking with that.

"You were thinking that the tread peeled off your boots," she said, "So you really don't suppose this is Perry's van back there?"

Locating the boots, he examined and tested the messily reglued soles and ruminated, considered that the vans might in fact get across the icy patch individually. Weighed that against the other factor, that he really didn't want to lie on his back in the slush getting the tow bar off, and then to get under there again to rerig things for towing.

"Yeah or . . . oh hell I don't know. Could be Perry's. How many gray '62s in California is all. This whole deal we're doing now, this whole thing's what people do all the time, and the guy said it is not Perry's, so."

Gail dug into the daypack and passed him a handful of Cheerios with a few peanuts, raisins, M&Ms. She talked, mostly not on the business at hand. It was her usual way of getting past his reflex obstinacy—if they were going to do this thing anyway, they'd function better as a unit, a factor in favor of towing, both of them in one van where she'd be able to talk to him. After a while, condensation running down the windows, Gail said,

"Let's see if Lowell has something. Chains or something."

"Last night the asshole all of a sudden decided he hated the sight of us," Boorham stammered out, "something was sure eating him."

"Who knows. Maybe he had an attack of mixed feelings about giving us the van," said Gail. Started walking up the drive, "Not too sure it's his to give either."

"Okay. We go ask the asshole for a favor."

Lowell brought along a fat ivory-color remote control with four or five unlabeled buttons.

"Alright, if we can get the persnickety bastard started, I have the plan, kids," he said, "I so do want to see this bad juju out of here."

Pressed a button—the headlights flashed, horn beeped. Pressed another button and held it down, with no apparent reaction from the bus; another then spun the starter. The battery sounded okay, good surprise.

"Just showing off. See if we can start it for real," he said.

"Guy was paranoid," said Boorham.

"Somebody did fucking kill him," said Gail.

"Clearly felt he rated a classy murder. His clippers, as I understand it," said Lowell, opening the engine flap, "they favored blunt instruments. So I'm told. Pull out the choke all the way, and when I crank, count one and punch it closed. Easier from back here. It'll take a few tries. I'll do the pedal."

Boorham said, "Right, we know the drill, she and I'll start it."

Lowell gave him a little smile of toleration, stepped up into the driver seat, Gail and Boorham exchanging a look.

Both buses idling, "What's this, Goddess of Mercy or something?" Gail touched a blobby, saucer-sized dark plaque on the compact dash.

"Oh I so hope not. Squashed forensic doodoo more like, to me. Ishy. Okay here's what you do," Lowell said.

Having gained all the speed they could, Gail gunned it at the bottom of the hill, and with the tow bar kept straight by her frantic steering, the push-pull got the front van just past the ice, where Boorham's tires caught and hauled the skidding gray van along with him onto dry pavement. Where, heart vibrating, she continued to stomp on the gas as he tried to brake to a stop. Bolts ripped out of rust, the tow bar shoved his back bumper onto the pavement, jacked his back wheels up off the road as the tow bar with its attached bumper rammed forward. Gail blinked. The parking permits on his rear window were inches from her face. He got out to look—her bumper was pushed down a little on one side, its quaint overrider rail bent, otherwise no dents on the gray one. Her front axle looked okay, his engine was still running but loud now, the muffler having taken the brunt of the rogue tow bar's violent wedgie.

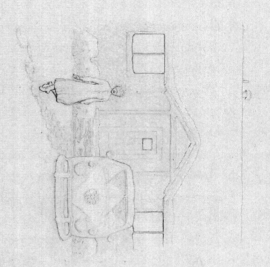

In Which her Curtsy looks almost Weightless

260

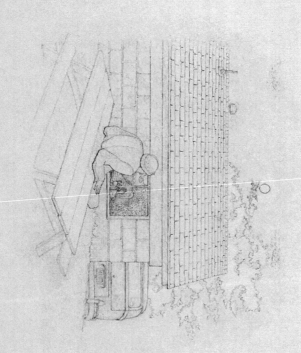

In Which an Actor disinhabits his Character

"Well dang," he said, reached in and cut the noisy engine.

Still panting, she asked, "Baby, we got the two, sure we want to sell the good one?"

"Yeah," he said, "Ridiculous amount, we get there on time."

She took a deep breath, "True. One, no title, and two, can't very well take it back to the house. I like that house." Then, more of a sigh, "Long cold haul with no relief driver, no company. And I got that job, shit, I can't no-show for the interview."

"It'll be fine," Boorham said, already on his back under the van in the middle of the road.

"Parallel play," she said to herself, then loudly, "Fuck are we doing, Boorham?"

•

Standing back from his window, he'd watched the new ten-ants arrive in the afternoon, start unloading things from a microbus the same model year as the one in his own yard. And now, the overcast evening barely below freezing, Lowell wandered over to the neighboring backyard in the fading light. Can't stay out here long, going to be a very dark night before you know it. His neighbors' rented three-room cin-der-block cabin was built into a hillside, two horizontal slider windows on the back, one lit. Sitting at an A-frame picnic table, Lowell looked down at the couple arranged on an oval hooked rug very much involved with each other. It apparently wasn't urgent down there—over and over she took him out of her mouth in order to say something. Had a lot to say apparently. They realigned on the hooked rug and the girl without preamble straddled the boy, allowing her free verbal expression, her friend no longer a speech imped-iment to her. Lowell on the other hand had no use at all for best buddies. Soon enough found the show boring, briefly picked his nose, and headed back, absently whistling "The Snake Charmer Song," Little Egypt's hoochie-coochie tune, he happened to know, from the Chicago World's Columbian Exposition of 1893.

The next afternoon's scattered sleet had turned to fine, light snow flurries that would last all night. In the early eve-ning, seeing that the blue-and-white van had made it back from wherever they'd gone, Lowell knocked on his neigh-bors' door, bottle of respectable wine and corkscrew in hand. Conversation before long turned to the similar vehi-cle at his place—leaning forward confidingly, told them that he'd been given it by a friend who felt the machine had absorbed the negative chi of a previous owner, a person involved in shady business that had led to his death. Lowell at that point still had the notion that he could cash out the van, began grooming these two lambs to carry out a bait-and-switch for him.

•

On the weeks when he took the Mercedes out of the barn, made the trek down to the coast to conduct business, Lowell suited up in a convincing persona he'd perfected over the course of several months. It was that of a mystic gangster—it allowed him to loan-shark a certain kind of individual, and to do it single-handed. This persona was his best effort so far, had even been accorded a comic book–style street name, keyed to the market. Couldn't've done better had he planned it himself. The persona was said, of course, to be a dangerous and crazily unpredictable genius, and also said to have a growing following of devotees. Lowell had taken some pains to encourage that crap, tie it into the existing subculture rumor mill.

He'd recently made a bad investment by loaning money to a man trying to set up an independent heroin distributorship. A number of other things in the man's life may've contributed to his murder, but in any case Lowell was out his money; settled by having the guy's VW van ripped off. The money involved was pocket change, but Lowell did after all work at the retail level, and as a point of pride hated to be stiffed. As well as stiffed on the loan though, he'd gotten word that he was now badly outgunned too. Gotten word that senior players felt entitled to the collateral, chickenshit as it was.

Aware he already had too many games running—worked

as freelance liaison and courier and expeditor for mid-level criminals, and lately, though he wasn't sure how, seemed to've signed on with a different kind of agency, corporate or something else with a bigger mandate, a potential gold-mine and a way to streamline his business. Or maybe it was an opportunity he should stay clear of for now, because at the moment Lowell found himself in inadvertent conflict already, with whom he wasn't sure. Wasn't able to say exactly what the problematic new game was. He hoped that either a competitor wanted to establish pecking order, or that the dead man had an unsettled account with a wholesaler— good chance of surviving those. But Lowell's persona had a pretty narrow purview, and he thought he may've walked into some other enterprise, something else entirely.

Tense and distracted, Lowell paced, "three-card monte outside the big convention," playing with the safety on his collectable little .32 automatic, thumbed it on and off and on. Paced, "low-grade rackets, chaotic little eddies, minor incidental friction in the prop wash of the RMS *Titanic*," the safety's precise oily snick, felt rather than heard, "tolerable chatter in the gears, in the machinations," snick, snick, "that it slides when slid, not a matter of volition," click, metallic susurration, eject the magazine, clack clack snick, rack the slide, snap.

Some potentially exploitable trust already gained with the little lambs next door, a bowel-loosening phone call told him where and when to deliver the silly damn Volkswagen.

So that was that. Change of plans. No money to be recouped. He could avoid showing up for his own murder though, avoid being further extorted, exposed to immediate harm, he'd just send the lambs.

•

Steering column between her knees, butt perched on the uncontoured seat, armpits sweating in the chill, and fog-wiping towel wet on her lap, she followed Boorham onto the shoulder of the four-lane. They'd been leapfrogging with the tan Buick for two hundred miles, the old car on the shoulder with the hood up, or refueling, two men and a woman milling around it. And the car again passing the vans, whose top speed was fifty-some-odd at best. Behind them now, the Buick was doubling back on an oiled one-lane parallel to the highway, toward a brick ranch-style set well away from the main road, now disappeared behind the house. No lights on over there. Gail got out and stretched, took off her mittens, tapped her nails on his driver-side window. Still craned around looking out the back, he rolled down his window,

"What," she said.

"I don't know man, I nodded off about four times in the last ten minutes."

"Saw you nearly ditch," she said, "And you were going about thirty a minute ago. You wondering about stopping here?"

"That tan car doesn't live here either, I bet anything. Highway patrol hassles and tickets the shit out of you, they see you sleeping in the car," he said.

Gail said, "Right, what a break this is, man! Lucked right into getting rousted for trespassing."

He said, "With expired out-of-state tags. Registered to a dead fucking dope dealer."

"Honey baby, maybe we ought to think this through before we start," she said, sweet smile, reaching up to smack at his forehead, which he leaned forward to receive, a thing they did.

Boorham quietly mouth-breathing nearby, she woke briefly in her sleeping bag on the linoleum. The couple a few feet away getting it on politely, hushed but demonstrably soggy, oh great, Gail thought, really don't need to catch her period right now . . . and Gail thought, drifting off again . . . not much highway noise, is it Sunday? . . . here's somebody limping along on a flat tire, sounds just like the lovers over there . . . a Sunday? . . .

Behind the house, sun not quite up, "Let's us, let's blow off the car deal bullshit, just keep going in the gray one," he said, "Seattle."

"God damn it, my stuff! No! And I like that house, found a goddamn job too," she said.

"We'll circle on back pretty soon. Get your stuff out then."

The couple from the Buick were two more white nineteen-, twenty-one-year-olds of the time's ubiquitous drifters, the older guy with them given no deference. Friendly enough, blank, distant, the three said very little even when spoken to. Obviously knew the larger area pretty well, the minimally vandalized house for sleep, and yes, they knew the rendezvous for the extralegal car sale,

"We're going past there. It's a ways," the younger man said. "First we're meeting somebody at the roadside park up here."

"Guys, come here," the older one said. He was looking at the gray VW's dashboard, "Wow, so just like that! There it—" and the couple from the Buick interrupted simultaneously.

"Okay well, y'all about ready to roll?" the woman said.

In caravan, massive squatting tan '56 Buick Special, its absurd row of three vestigial exhaust ports along each front fender indicating an inline six; blue-and-white 1962 Type 2 VW Transporter, rust tentatively held together by the paint, containing happiness and truelove, a toolbox, camping gear, car parts, the usual; and the gray bus—an otherwise empty shoebox of truelove, bad juju, and the ishy object.

After an hour at the roadside park, the Buick people politely turning away attempts at conversation, Gail said to Boorham,

"Let's just go on, need to start watching the time."

"Yeah."

"I don't think we need to say goodbye."

"No."

The gray one wouldn't start. Gail in the driver's seat, briefly grinding the starter when asked, the Buick people came to watch, the older man kibitzing a little. Boorham, on his knees at the open engine compartment, narrowed the problem to coil or condenser, and having a replacement for neither, took diagnosis no further. Did have a polypropylene water-ski rope though. Tied it to Gail's front axle, and the other van now lacking a back bumper, ran the other end through a pair of ripped-out bolt holes. And rather than tie the two vans tightly together, jeopardizing his engine and wrecking the gray's front, Gail would pilot the gray at the end of the rope. Felt kind of proud to do so.

"Person ya'll were going to meet—they ever show?" he asked, mild stammer.

"Looks like you're all set back here, then. Ready to roll?" said the young man.

The caravan moved on, until torn sheet metal sawed through the stiff plastic rope. Rope reattached, the caravan moved on, at about thirty-five miles an hour because Boorham wouldn't tow his beloved any faster than that. They did not, however, get pulled over by the police.

Coming to a gap in the windbreak of volunteer trees enveloping road-front fence, they followed the tan car off the road to a sagged tubular steel gate and watched the older guy get out, unwrap an unlocked chain, pick up the gate and walk it inward over a cattle guard. In the driveway beyond, the deepest ruts in the parallel tracks had been filled with caliche, though high weeds hissed under the vans' floors as they were led to an empty, open three-bay wooden shed, where they pulled up beside the Buick; no one in a hurry to get out, Gail said to the older guy walking back to the sedan, "No way we'd found it. You sure this is it?"

"Yes," said the woman in the car. And rolled up her back-seat window.

Having turned the big car around, the younger man made a momentary goodbye gesture without looking at them, and the Buick slouched back down the drive. Boorham cut his engine. Multiple dogs wouldn't stop barking somewhere.

•

Lowell lit a cigarette, paced the floor tapping his chin, aware he was doing an impression of a worried man. Idiot. Did so merely wish. Did so let all out of reach. Out of sight. Idiot. Like it'd just evaporate somewhere out there. Mercedes idling in the yard, he re-padlocked the barn. Consulted a map, steered for the delivery point he'd been given.

A metal building just off the highway on a compacted gravel private road. Barbed wire fence, farm gate, well maintained, normal. He drove a half mile up the highway, parked on the shoulder, cut the engine, and waited, smoking, watching the building and the analog clock set into the burl veneer. At around one o'clock he gave up. The gray bus hadn't shown, no one had. Lowell had already decided on the next thing; took a pill, chewed it, another one, drained his cold gas-station coffee, tossed out the cup. Made a U-turn toward the Bay and hauled ass. He would put out feelers, clean this up, get back to business.

A box truck backed up to Lowell's barn, followed by a nondescript new Plymouth. The two drivers went to the back of the truck, one carrying a pry bar, continuing an earlier conversation,

"No, he don't like this clown. Clown's smart, he will take this gentle reminder that he is pissing in the tall grass with the big dogs."

"That other one never got it, would he."

"Oh yeah he got it!"

"No, I mean he never got the message. Know what's weird, fucker kept claiming he was under somebody's protection."

"I know! Oh yeah sure, like 'Must be some misunderstanding, boys! Oh see, it's just a jurisdiction thing!' Crazy fuck. Wonder who did off him."

"Shit, there was a line around the block. Crazy fuck."

They released the J-latch, rolled up the door, pulled out and secured the ramps. One took his pry bar over to the barn. One went to the front end of the cargo area, grabbed a tow hook, began unreeling the winch cable, preparing to take Lowell's Mercedes.

"Oh boy look at that. Oh shit."

Hasp and lock dangling from the open door, they were looking into the empty barn.

"You get to tell him."

·

"What time?"

"Got here a little after noon," looking at her watch, "Three fifteen."

"Right day and all," he said. Gail said, "According to Lowell. Or they left at twelve on the dot."

The radio still worked in the gray bus. It was easy to drain a six-volt battery with a vacuum tube radio, and Top 40 didn't much appeal to him, but he clicked it on again anyway and tuned around through staticky livestock reports, said,

"You know all those little wreath dealies on the wall over the workbench?"

"Gunked-over seedpods or something, yeah," she said.

Boorham said, "Know what, that thing on the dashboard looks like that."

"So much does."

Then after a while he said, "Besides those license plates in there, we got no clue, right?"

"They expire New Year's anyway," she said. One-shoulder shrug, "They seemed positive this is the place."

After a while he said, "Sunset's an hour I guess, days are

so short." And in another while the Buick nosed far enough up the drive to see they were still there, backed out again.

"Let's bail," she said, "Just leave the key in it. This is fucked."

"Uh yeah, really. I can't top that."

"Getting cold," she said.

Boorham said, "Hey, want a souvenir, that thing?"

"Sure. No. I don't know."

With the blue-and-white bus idling and them waiting for the smoke to stop, he said over the broken muffler,

"See if I can find the slim jim. Comes off of there we get a souvenir out of all this bullshit."

Gail, very unhappy to see the gate had been closed and re-chained, looked up and down the darkening windbreak.

"Honey, careful," she said, imagining ambush as he made his way over the cattle guard. The chain turned out to be unlocked. On the other side of the gate, "Hold on," she said, and went back to secure it.

Crossing a bar ditch and beginning to turn onto the highway, he braked abruptly to avoid being fatally clipped by a Mercedes, forewarned by its searchlight headlamp beams in the air as it topped the hill. Brake lights already lit as it passed, it came to a stop six hundred feet down the black-top from them, paused for a contemplative ten-count, laid a short patch of rubber, and the taillights winked out over the next rise. The dark lumpy object—heavy, too heavy for lead and too hard to scratch, slightly cracked now—lay nestled among the maps and other debris on the under-dash shelf. Gail kept leaning forward to check the side mirror, seeing if she could identify cars behind their headlights.

•

Beyond the glaring apron it was first light; Boorham was paying the attendant as Gail came out of the ladies' room at the side of the gas station, handed the restroom key with its attached stick to the yawning pump jockey. "Guy says cut over on 205, miss the construction," said Boorham. Some clear, waxy liquid had leaked onto the map—Gail sniffed it; lord only knows. Reached under the dash, found the dip-stick rag, put it back and found the clean one. It had the unidentified viscous yuck on it too, and she dropped it in the trash on her way back to the restrooms. Map wiped off and hands washed, she climbed into the cab, where they leaned together over the daypack, searched for 205.

Snowing again, not deep enough yet to make it tricky getting up to the house. They'd taken turns driving straight through. Woolly from lack of sleep in the freezing bus, ears ringing from the busted muffler, snow really coming down, their only thought was to be indoors. Boorham glanced toward Lowell's place, but the figure pulling the barn door shut didn't register on him, nor did movement within his own house. At the window, a woman watched as they gathered a couple of things from the van, clumped toward the house.

•

Gail hadn't been confident she'd spot the place, the gap in the windbreak, much aware of her unreliable memory, her chronic inattention. Maybe getting better longer term but not this week. At the moment she couldn't be more clearheaded, a little euphoric even, until she got out of breath undoing the gate chain. Guessing nobody had a key and that it was nobody's job to put on another padlock, undeniably those people'd had the knack for finding accommodations, backing into someone else's shell like a hermit crab. Keeping at it, bracing against the overgrowth, pausing to rest, reaching and tugging at the gate, she was surprised to find it could be pulled open, eventually shrieking outward and allowing her to drive over the otherwise impassable cattle guard, didn't have to entertain crawling the gate inward.

But for being empty, the yard was as she and Boorham had left it. Not a surprise, God, just half a year. Placing the cane carefully, Gail undertook to heave herself out of the Peugeot—Boorham had junked the bus for something more reliable, easier, about the last thing done before he cratered. The hospital he'd eventually gotten to in Texas wouldn't tell her anything, she had no legal status to ask, and his kin wouldn't even talk to her, suspiciously close as she was to their lost girl Shelda's perverted, alien culture out there, too close to Shelda's disappearance and now to Boorham's medically bewildering set of sicknesses. But he was probably not dead.

Dogs still barked, the license plates still lay there on the bench. Hanging on to the workbench at first, she slid down the cane, crouched. Weepy lately, wiped her face with the back of a hand, picked up one of the saucer-sized things that had fallen off the wall, got herself standing again. The object was the worse for a little aging—shiny, dark, smeared-on coating had dulled, come off in places, woven structure of pods and stems now visible, now brittle. Day-camp nature project. Why so heavy? She dug around in it—oh for chrissakes, lead tire-balance weights. Tossed it away. Looking capable of sailing, instead it dropped upside down straight to the hard dirt floor.

Crossing the bar ditch in the Peugeot, Gail banged on the steering wheel repeatedly, shouting, wronged and angry, casting around for a proximate source, some antagonist to rip the shit out of. Paused at the highway, bemused for several minutes by the open gate in the rearview mirror, hadn't she just done this same thing a minute ago? Tried to gather dissipating thoughts, dissipating anger. Found she was unable to remember which way to go.

•

The woman waiting inside had said,

"Hey guys. Knew y'all wouldn't mind." Held up an old-fashioned skeleton key, brown iron, a kind that still fit a great many household door locks in that time, "It's from your mama's house, Boorham."

Three-way hug, a sweet thing of significant shared history, Shelda's cheeks damp and hot against their chilled faces, her eyes dilated.

Gail said, "Girl! Where you been?"

"You guys are completely trashed. I'm out of here before long, came by to tell you a couple of things."

"Back here," said Gail, led into one of the cabin's three rooms.

Built into the hillside, the upslope rooms stayed a little warmer. Snow was drifted most of the way up the small horizontal window at the top of the wall, allowed in only dim light.

"Just leave it off, would you mind," Shelda said as Gail reached under a fringed lampshade. "So nice in here, kind of Alice in Wonderland."

Boorham lit the ornate little butane heater, Gail broke a couple of sassafras twigs into a teakettle, stepped over Shelda's outstretched lace-up knee boots, settled in with her on a floor cushion, leaned back with her against the little Victorian couch.

Shelda had already begun talking, quietly, matter-of-factly describing occurrences and impressions in the first person, disarranged things that didn't even correlate, shuffled with plausible things that almost certainly hadn't happened, or might be imagined to happen in the future. An undramatic, conversational-sounding ramble that brought no sense at all but that of foretelling, foreboding.

"Wait a sec Shel, are you telling our fortune?"

She found that enormously funny—her laugh had always been a big, free thing, in a register below her speaking voice,

"Yeah okay Boorham, I'm telling your fortune," cracked up, got hold of herself, wiped an eye, resumed what she'd been saying. Repeated a little, it seemed like, before moving on. Eventually just stopped, a word then no more words; Shelda stood, stretched, walked out of the room. Ten minutes later Gail couldn't find her. Boorham was flopped across a couple of tasseled cushions, asleep by the time Gail lay down on the little couch.

•

They'd fallen asleep not much caring what else might be expected of them. Boorham woke to a provisional-feeling, tenebrous kind of daylight in the room that misdirected attention more than it disclosed things; snow had continued to fall, now covered the window to some depth.

As he watched, a hand cleared off part of the window and Shelda looked back at him, snow in her hair, crouched out there in the drift and still dressed only in a coarse cotton frock, a black silk tied over her eyes as if for blind justice, or for a firing squad. Boorham felt her lock eyes with him through the silk. Her open hand pressed against the storm window, a foggy aura formed around it between the panes of glass, and as he put fingertips to her dimly haloed hand, Shelda stood and waded off through the drift.

"Bye," he said aloud.

"Boorham? Honey?" said Gail.

Postcard • commencement exercise

When squatters caught her attention she'd go have a chat with them, unnecessary so far to call in help for the evictions. Checking on his boat in any case every few days, Edith hadn't given up on old Albert. Two mementos neatly sewn into a disk of chartreuse cloth—the rabies tag of her missing dog and a gold coin she'd found in Albert's clarinet case; not conscious of the prayerful gesture, Edith touched the keepsake through her shirt. Stepped into the cabin. Smelled men. Uneasy that she was backlit in the doorway, she spotted them in the dim interior.

"Hi, Edie, been a while," JD said. Clean-shaven, hair just long enough to part, seated behind the typewriter where Albert had composed his newsletters.

JD indicated another large man relaxed against a partition, "Clovis."

"Pleased to finally meet you face to face," said Clovis. He held the long bone she'd daily reassured a dairy herd with, the bone of contentment, a fond thing from earliest childhood. Obviously a war club in this guy's hand, nothing pastoral about it. Pissed her off—mostly that he'd arrogated such familiarity, carried the bone so negligently, as if it were his. As if she were too, somehow.

Edith said, "You put out the signal flag. Need a ride somewhere?"

"C'mon, no, just wanted to say hi," said JD.

"Seems like a good time to ask why. Like for a year? That you've been messing with me."

JD said, "Well yeah, seen you around for a year but not in a little while really. Not clear on what's 'messing.' Yeah, so, been a little while, how you been? But you are asking why. Why what? Never thought about it, kind of never got the hang of thinking about that. A huss over here, Clovis? Got a 'why' here right off the bat and I never got the hang of it, if you would, sir."

"Don't know if I can field that one either, but your question is 'why' and not an 'if' somebody's yanking your strings, and at this point, I bet what you mean by 'why' is because you're tolerable to look at and everybody and his dog knows you, and because you live in a seething hotbed of cultural upheaval. Is why. But see, if there's any scrutiny or messing with of you beyond that, it would have to be . . . or any fiddling with young Edie's placid existence, such as anything strikes you as odd, sweetie, I mean *here*? Strikes you as odd? Now don't quote me on this but it'd have to be somebody's professional curiosity. And 'if' that is what it boils down to, they would just be watching the test do what it is going to do at this point, until it runs down of its own accord, I mean, can't turn it off and why try to anyway, and I bet a hat you wanted me to say that, didn't you?" said Clovis. A few seconds, the gentle sound of the water outside the hull.

"What on earth does that mean?" said Edith.

Clovis said, "Uh, well, it is open season on you? Trying things out here, JD has a point, I never thought about 'why' either. And not really on the subject of 'why,' but an 'if,' if you are some specific somebody's hobby too? Don't want to stray too far afield of your question or use any crude expressions, so for the sake of argument I venture that you have got a secret admirer? Just seems reasonable. I know you wanted me to say some such darn thing so there you go, but if I knew anything for a fact, sweetheart, I would tell you."

"So what's *your* deal? What exactly do you have to do with all that, whatever that was, and what about all the rest of it!"

JD said, "Uh well I'm not sure I follow, but yeah what he said. That sounds about right. I'd go so far as to say, wouldn't be surprised if there's a little money riding on you, Edie, if any of what he said's right. But see, there's so many independent actors in your case wouldn't you think. Self-motivated. Seems like everybody and his dog is in on the act and sometimes a dog will just get the idea to hump your leg is all. And I guess that's messing with you," he shrugged.

"I mean, you're talking about a total train wreck," said Clovis, "not the kind of thing you can straighten out. You'd have two dozen logbooks because you would be logging different entire sets of metrics, I mean, goodness, even the bookkeeper would throw in the towel. Throw in the pencil. Throw in her number two-and-a-half red lead and run away with the circus."

Edith blinked. "Holy shit. Wait, what, who were . . ."

Clovis talked over her, "If there is any common factor, which I doubt, it's you. You little law of physics you," and abruptly cut a fully asserted backhand with the ball-ended club, struck with great authority at the other man, who managed to intercept the hit aimed at his forehead, lunge over the typewriter, and wrench the weapon away. Flicked Clovis across the mouth with the knobby handle end, the whole exchange in just over a second.

"That's the thing anymore, Edie, you're kind of fun, you know that? Since you bring it up," Clovis said, wiped his mouth, looked at the blood on his hand. The other laid aside the club and rubbed his badly contused palm. Squeezed his genitals, unhurried, looking at her.

"Mind if I go first?"

"Be my guest," Clovis said, and pressed a palm to his bleeding lip.

"Okay with you if I take care of the other thing too?"

"You mean simultaneous? Do the deed, man. If I'm going seconds, makes very little difference anyway. To me."

Edith said, "Wait, what? I don't . . . you don't have to, uh . . . What do you mean? For God's sake, why?"

"Well and there's 'why' again," said JD, mildly exasperated.

JD picked up his overturned office chair, sat. Quiet sound of the water, a seabird, faint harbor noise. Edith assumed her heart was audible; beyond that her mind had nothing to say to her for an unknown stretch of time, small cornered mammal watching with perfect awareness for its very last instant to dodge the predator.

JD drummed his fingers on the chair arm, "Don't mean to be rude, hadn't you better run on now, sweetie? You don't like to be out after dark. And we have to vanish into thin air, or whatever it is you think we're supposed to do."

Clovis said, "Oh here, Anders sent this." Extended a glossy photograph that had been torn in two. Edith didn't immediately take it, remained frozen, body acting without her mind's being aware of it.

"Better scoot now."

In the cold shock of the bay, knew that she'd run straight over the side, now swam with difficulty toward her boat, its line cast off or cut. Ducked under to get out of high-top sneakers and carried them in an awkward sidestroke.

•

"Honey, I think your clothes are done," said the lady a couple of chairs over. A rude buzzer had sounded, the shoes had stopped thunking around in the dryer.

"Thanks, yeah, I'll get it. Don't think anyone's waiting. Thanks," said Edith, resumed her study of the photograph, still damp and the worse for experience.

In the foreground a man's bare feet, khaki trousers rolled up mid-calf. Retreating out of sharp focus underfoot, uneven smooth brown stone sloped into water with foam as from low waves. It was barely possible that an unresolved object near the water was the head and robust forequarters of her dog, withered back legs dragging behind it invisible from that angle. Just had your eighth birthday, puppadoodle, she thought, turned the picture over one more time, "c/o gen. delivery Red Cliff Res, Wis" in blue ballpoint. Tell you what, Anders, I hate the shit out of your courier service. Tell you what else, everybody's gone and keeping my own counsel gets old. She flapped the photograph, "What in the hell am I supposed to do with this?"

"Beg pardon, honey?" said the lady a couple of chairs over.

•

"Ma'am, the call did go through."

"Can you wait a minute please operator."

"One dollar thirty cents, please," said the operator.

Rattle of coins through the pay phone and change being shunted noisily into the coin return, Edith heard voices on the line. Occasionally made out scraps:

".．. the place in the boonies, up in the rocks, we'll circle back soon, get your stuff out then. Head on out. Stay, you wanted to stay. Absolutely that would be a good place. Forever."

Shuddering rumble ending in a sharp clap, minutes of thumping sounds and indistinct voices.

"One dollar thirty cents, please," said the operator.

".．. from the fucking gas leaks, them acid-head candles..."

".．. you know she rips those off from that church ..."

".．. hey you leaving comrade?"

".．. off in the service o' Br'er Rabbit ..."

".．. you err! ... righteous prankmaster and besides a righteous laurel wreath ..."

A minute more of young adult banter. Someone's breath right into the receiver, much clearer than the other voices, the wrenched exhalation formed a word, "Gail ..."

"One dollar thirty cents, please. You have no idea."

"Operator?" Coins rattled through the pay phone.

An extended dial tone, songlike in its way, for the time left on the call. It was oddly satisfactory.

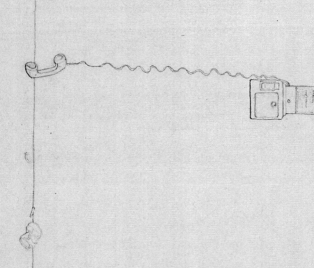

In Which the endless Om is Cut to nineteen seconds

acknowledgments

Thank you Carol Polk— the world is so full of a number of things. More specifically, this book exploits the lore of a slew of people including, say, Mark Sauer on the 1965 dairy barn and Gerald Burns on the noble carny. And I'm much diminished without the accumulated insight of my literary betters, none of whom is likely to read this book, their interest in it having been squandered on early drafts.

Thank you all
for your support.
We do this for you,
and could not do
it without you.

PARTNERS

FIRST EDITION MEMBERSHIP
Anonymous (9)
Donna Wilhelm

TRANSLATOR'S CIRCLE
Ben & Sharon Fountain
Meriwether Evans

PRINTER'S PRESS MEMBERSHIP
Allred Capital Management
Charles Dee Mitchell
Cullen Schaar
David Tomlinson & Kathryn Berry
Jeff Leuschel
Judy Pollock
Loretta Siciliano
Lori Feathers
Mary Ann Thompson-Frenk & Joshua Frenk
Matthew Rittmayer
Nick Storch
Pixel and Texel
Robert Appel
Social Venture Partners Dallas
Stephen Bullock

AUTHOR'S LEAGUE
Christie Tull
Farley Houston
Jacob Seifring
Lissa Dunlay
Steven Kornajcik
Thomas DiPiero

PUBLISHER'S LEAGUE
Adam Rekerdres
Justin Childress
Kay Cattarulla
KMGMT
Olga Kislova

EDITOR'S LEAGUE
Amrit Dhir
Brandon Kennedy
Dallas Sonnier
Garth Hallberg
Greg McConeghy
Linda Nell Evans
Mary Moore Grimaldi
Mike Kaminsky
Patricia Storace
Ryan Todd
Steven Harding
Suejean Kim
Symphonic Source
Wendy Belcher

READER'S LEAGUE
Caitlin Baker
Caroline Casey
Carolyn Mulligan
Chilton Thomson
Cody Cosmic & Jeremy Hays
Jeff Waxman
Joseph Milazzo
Kayla Finstein
Kelly Britson
Kelly & Corby Baxter
Marian Schwartz & Reid Minot

Marlo D. Cruz Pagan
Maryam Baig
Peggy Carr
Susan Ernst

ADDITIONAL DONORS
Alan Shockley
Amanda & Bjorn Beer
Andrew Yorke
Anonymous (10)
Ashley Milne Shadoin
Bob & Katherine Penn
Brandon Childress
Charley Mitcherson
Charley Rejsek
Cheryl Thompson
Chloe Pak
Cone Johnson
CS Maynard
Daniel J. Hale
Daniela Hurezanu
Danielle Dubrow
Denae Richards
Dori Boone-Costantino
Ed Nawotka
Elizabeth Gillette
Elizabeth Van Vleck
Erin Kubatzky
Ester & Matt Harrison
Grace Kenney
Hillary Richards
JJ Italiano
Jeremy Hughes
John Darnielle
Jonathan Legg
Julie Janicke Muhsmann

Walmart   pixel ||| texel   ALLRED CAPITAL MANAGEMENT   RAYMOND JAMES®

LIFE IN DEEP ELLUM

EMBREY FAMILY FOUNDATION

COMMON DESK

ADDITIONAL DONORS, CONT'D

Kelly Falconer	Mary Cline	Patrick Kukucka	Stephen Harding
Kevin Richardson	Max Richie	Patrick Kutcher	Stephen Williamson
Laura Thomson	Maynard Thomson	Rev. Elizabeth & Neil Moseley	Susan Carp
Lea Courington	Michael Reklis	Richard Meyer	Theater Jones
Lee Haber	Mike Soto	Sam Simon	Tim Perttula
Leigh Ann Pike	Mokhtar Ramadan	Sherry Perry	Tony Thomson
Lowell Frye	Nikki & Dennis Gibson	Skander Halim	
Maaza Mengiste		Sydneyann Binion	
Mark Haber			

SUBSCRIBERS

Joseph Rebella	Ned Russin	Nicole Yurcaba
Michael Lighty	Laura Gee	Sam Soule
Shelby Vincent	Valerie Boyd	Jennifer Owen
Margaret Terwey	Brian Bell	Melanie Nicholls
Ben Fountain	Charles Dee Mitchell	Alan Glazer
Ryan Todd	Cullen Schaar	Michael Doss
Gina Rios	Harvey Hix	Matt Bucher
Elena Rush	Jeff Lierly	Katarzyna Bartoszynska
Courtney Sheedy	Elizabeth Simpson	Anthony Brown
Caroline West	Michael Schneiderman	Elif Ağanoğlu

AVAILABLE NOW FROM DEEP VELLUM

FORTHCOMING FROM DEEP VELLUM

MARIO BELLATIN • *Etchapare* • translated by Shook • MEXICO

CAYLIN CARPA-THOMAS • *Iguana Iguana* • USA

MIRCEA CĂRTĂRESCU • *Solenoid* • translated by Sean Cotter · ROMANIA

ANANDA DEVI • *When the Night Agrees to Speak to Me* •
translated by Kazim Ali • MAURITIUS

DHUMKETU • *The Shehnai Virtuoso* • translated by Jenny Bhatt • INDIA

LEYLÂ ERBIL • *A Strange Woman* •
translated by Nermin Menemenciöglu & Amy Marie Spangler· TURKEY

ALLA GORBUNOVA • *It's the End of the World, My Love* •
translated by Elina Alter • RUSSIA

NIVEN GOVINDEN • *Diary of a Film* • GREAT BRITAIN

GYULA JENEI · *Always Different* • translated by Diana Senechal · HUNGARY

DIA JUBAILI • *No Windmills in Basra* • translated by Chip Rosetti • IRAQ

ELENI KEFALA • *Time Stitches* • translated by Peter Constantine • CYPRUS

UZMA ASLAM KHAN • *The Miraculous True History of Nomi Ali* • PAKISTAN

ANDREY KURKOV • *Grey Bees* • translated by Boris Dralyuk • UKRAINE

JORGE ENRIQUE LAGE • *Freeway La Movie* • translated by Lourdes Molina • CUBA

TEDI LÓPEZ MILLS • *The Book of Explanations* •
translated by Robin Myers • MEXICO

ANTONIO MORESCO • *Clandestinity* • translated by Richard Dixon • ITALY

FISTON MWANZA MUJILA • *The Villain's Dance,* translated by Roland Glasser •
DEMOCRATIC REPUBLIC OF CONGO

N. PRABHAKARAN • *Diary of a Malayali Madman* •
translated by Jayasree Kalathil • INDIA

THOMAS ROSS • *Miss Abracadabra* • USA

IGNACIO RUIZ-PÉREZ • *Isles of Firm Ground* • translated by Mike Soto • MEXICO

LUDMILLA PETRUSHEVSKAYA • *Kidnapped: A Crime Story* •
translated by Marian Schwartz • RUSSIA

NOAH SIMBLIST, ed. • *Tania Bruguera: The Francis Effect* • CUBA

S. YARBERRY • *A Boy in the City* • USA